desecrated
FLESH

Paperback ISBN: **978-1-990675-28-7**

Hardcover ISBN: 978-1-990675-30-0

Proofread by: Kim Bookjunkie

ALSO BY C.A. RENE

The Whitsborough Chronicles

Through the Pain

Into Darkness

Finding the Light

To Redemption

The Whitsborough Progenies

Ivy's Venom

Carmelo's Malice

Saxon's Distortion

Gabriel's Deception

Desecrated Duet

Desecrated Flesh

Desecrated Essence

The Reaped Series

The Reaper Incarnate

Hunting the Reaper

Claiming the Reaper

Hail Mary Duet

Blue 42

Red Zone

Sacrificial Lambs

Sing Me a Song

Song of Tenebrae

A Verse for Caelum

PLAYLIST

Praying – Kesha

Thank U - Alanis Morrissette

Beautiful Goodbye – Amanda Marshall

Rise – Katy Perry

Not Ready to Make Nice – The Chicks

Strawberry Wine – Deana Carter

Jesus, Take the Wheel – Carrie Underwood

I'll Stand by You – Carrie Underwood

Remember When – Alan Jackson

Amazed – Lonestar

Like I'm Gonna Lose You – Meghan Trainor, John Legend

Undo It – Carrie Underwood

Body Like a Back Road – Sam Hunt

Fight Song – Rachel Platten

Breathe – Faith Hill

DEDICATION

Life's path isn't a smooth paved one, it's rough with gravel, and full of bumps. When your feet become weary of the difficult travel, remember this: Stop and enjoy the view around you. Watch the sunset, feel the breeze through your hair, and find the intersections of people worth traveling with.

Kailey-Himari

PROLOGUE

"You know you want it." His hot breath hits the back of my neck. I shake my head, but it's sluggish, and the movement makes the surrounding forest spin. "Yes, you do. I've seen you watching me."

I never watch him. I'm too busy watching his younger brother.

"No..." I moan, but it comes out weak because I can barely form words.

I drank way too much. I tried to drown my sorrows, but instead, I got myself in to more trouble. My papa is probably looking for me, I can bet Brody is too. Why did I come down here? Why did I follow him? Because I trusted him... I've known him since I was in diapers.

The grass I'm lying on is tickling the exposed skin on my legs and cheek. I wish I could get up, but my body is like lead. I feel his fingers reach into the waistband of my shorts as he pulls them down to my knees.

"Please..." I try to shake my head again.

"Fuck, I love it when they beg." I hear someone else chuckle, and my stomach sinks. Who else is here? I didn't see anyone else. I only followed him.

"No." I try to sound stronger, but I'm so drunk, it's hard to speak.

"Shh," he says as he props my waist up in the air. "Check out this fresh pussy."

I try to move my head to see who he's talking to, but the world turns, and I close my eyes to make it stop. Suddenly, a ripping pain tears through me, and I open my mouth in a soundless scream.

The onslaught doesn't stop, and I feel tears coursing down my cheeks and dripping onto the earth they press my face into. The rough movement makes my cheek scrape along the ground as the pain I'm feeling all over collides inside me.

Mama was right. Boys can never be trusted.

DESECRATED FLESH

Kailey-Himari

ONE

Senior year starts today, and I am that much closer to being done with J.F. Kennedy Prep and every person in it. Well, not every person. My best friend, Kimmy, will always be in my life, but the rest can fucking burn. To say my high school life is torture would be an understatement.

"Kailey-Himari Richard!" my papa calls out from the bottom of the stairs. "You will not be late on your first day, young lady."

With a groan, I roll out of bed. Fuck my life. My hair is sticking at odd angles on my head as I swipe at my eyes, dislodging the crust nestled in the corners. I should shower, I should also care about my appearance, but I can't seem to muster up one fuck to give. My phone chimes from my bedside. so I grab it to swipe open my messages.

Kimmy: Girl, try to look at least presentable today. No more sweats and hats. Wear something hot, and for fuck's sake, SHOWER!

I don't even know how she does that. Knowing my moves better than I do. I quickly tap out a reply.

Me: I will shower, but fuck looking hot.

Kimmy: Go for a shock effect this year. Take your no fucks given attitude up a notch. Show 'em what you got packing, bitch.

I stare at her message far longer than I should. Should I? Should I send every brain-dead kid into that school on a tailspin? I won't lie… it sounds tempting. During the previous three years in this school, I've tried to stay under the radar, not attracting too much attention because none of it has been good, but it's gotten me nowhere. I'm still bullied. I still have shit written on my locker weekly, rotting food stuffed through the grate, food thrown at me in the cafeteria, and the best: my clothes stolen from my gym locker. You try wearing sweaty gym clothes after you ran two miles in the Louisiana heat. Maybe Kimmy is right... maybe it is time to take back my last year of high school.

Shower it is.

Don't get me wrong, I don't take the bullying lying down. I'm mouthy as fuck and tell just about anyone off. It hasn't gotten physical yet, but if it did, I would have no problem throwing down. My bullying isn't typical, I'm not the meek little girl or the nerd who stands out, I'm bullied because my ex-best friend thought he could ruin my life in some kind of revenge ploy. He has yet to succeed because I still get up every morning and bring my ass to school, just so I can smile into his pitiful face. I do this because I have already been through the worst, and high school bullies don't scare me.

I get into my bathroom and start the shower. With a single look at myself in the mirror, I cringe. I look a mess. My light brown hair is in waves and sticking out all over my head, my olive skin is flushed and still has sleep lines embedded into my cheeks. My light hazel eyes reflect at me, looking tired and swollen. These features are unique because my mama was Japanese. My eyes are almond-shaped and slightly slanted upward, and my pert button nose comes from her. Papa is Cajun through and through; that's where my hair and eye color come from.

Once the shower is steaming, I get in. I know I don't have long to get ready today, so I have to cut it short. I wash my hair and condition the knots, and then I scrub myself down with my coconut shower gel. It'll have to do. I jump out and wrap myself up in a towel. Usually, I would take my long, thick hair and twist it up into a messy bun, but today I decide to blow dry it and set it with some mousse, letting my natural waves set in. I don't know if listening to Kimmy is such a good idea, but I have to admit, I've hidden myself for far too long. It's time I take back my body and reclaim my femininity.

With that being said, I head into my closet and push aside all the oversized hoodies and baggy jeans. Can't wear that and reclaim shit. I pull out clothes I've bought but never had the nerve to put on. A black pair of high-waisted skinny jeans and a white lace crop top. Underneath, I pull on a white spaghetti strapped sports bra. I haven't worn a pair of heels in over three years, but looking at them, I can't deny I want to.

Standing at 5'5", I'm not too short by any means, so I've never felt the need to wear them until today. Slipping on a strappy pair of sandals, I exit my closet to sit at my vanity. A lot of this makeup is old—again, not something I cared about—but fuck it.

Today, I'm tempting the devil.

I pull into the parking lot and rest my head against the steering wheel. Maybe this was a bad idea. Students laughing and greeting each other sets my heart pounding, reverberating through my eardrums. I breathe in deep and exhale slowly. I can do this. I have been through much, much worse. A knock comes to my window, and I sit up straight with a scream on the tip of my tongue. I look and see Kimmy standing near my car. Her eyes widen when she sees me then does a slow clap, backing away so I can get out.

"Girl!" she squeals. "I really didn't think you'd do it."

"I'm regretting it." I let my head fall back on a groan.

"You look gorgeous." She wraps her arm around mine and forces me to stand in front of my car window.

Kimmy is beautiful. She's a natural blonde with big bouncing curls to her waist. Her big blue eyes shine clear against her white porcelain skin. I used to envy her looks, still do if I'm being honest. Being called multiple derogatory terms based on my race for years will do that. We're the same height, but where I am athletic and toned, she's curvy and sexy.

"Look at you," she breathes. "Beautiful. Is that lip gloss?"

"Mm-hmm."

"And mascara!"

"Let's get this over with," I whine. "Allons." Let's go.

She nods and turns me back in the school's direction. We walk by different groups, and most of them set to whispering as I walk by. I don't care, I don't care. I repeat the mantra in my head.

Then, straight ahead, is the group I want to avoid. The four guys who started my misery here.

"Keep your damn head up," Kimmy growls at me as we near them.

I don't look in their direction, and, for once, the four of them are silent as I walk by. Not one sneer, not a single word spat at me. It's weird, and to be honest, a little nerve-wracking.

"Wow," Kimmy chuckles. "They were speechless."

"Shut up," I grit out.

She looks over her shoulder then quickly whips her head back around. "They are staring at you."

"I knew I shouldn't have done this," I whisper.

"Own it, boo. You can do this." She's right, I know she is. I just have to continuously remind myself I have been through worse.

Up next, I face the bitch crew of JFK Prep. The four guys may have started my misery, but these four girls are the ones who enact it, like a pack of dogs.

"What do we have here?" Georgina cackles. Her highlighted auburn hair shining and full. Her big blue eyes narrow and fill with hate. Georgina is really tall for a girl, hitting 6', and her curves are full and lush. Every guy wants her, and all girls want to be her.

"A human," I snarl. "Might be a good idea for you to actually learn this year. You'll need college to amount to anything."

"Do you have lip gloss on?" Casey snickers. Georgina's right-hand bitch. She has blonde, curly hair like Kimmy's, only hers comes from a box. She's a lot shorter than Georgina, maybe hitting 5'1", but she's as mean as they come. Her green eyes shine out of a face full of freckles I would find adorable on anyone else but her.

"And mascara too!" Connie joins in. Bitch number three. Black curly hair and brown eyes, showing her Creole roots. She is easily the most gorgeous in the group, but her ugly insides leak out through her very pores.

That leaves Faith. She's the quiet one, but don't think she's not as bad as the rest, she is. Her dark brown hair, always styled into perfect waves, flows down and over her shoulders. Her dark blue eyes give her an innocent look until she opens her mouth.

"Fuck them," Kimmy declares and pulls me around them.

"He'll never want you," Georgina calls after me. "You can put a dress on a dog, but it still barks."

"You can take your herpes medication, but you'll always have it," I counter.

Kimmy chokes on a laugh, and a few students near me snicker and give me appreciative looks. That's new. Maybe they don't recognize me. I really hope I'm not making my last year here the worst by doing this.

"Where's your locker?" Kimmy asks.

"First floor next to study hall. You?"

"Second floor, science wing." Fuck, that's far.

"We don't have a single class together either," I moan.

"We have lunch, though," she grins.

Thank God because last year we didn't, and I spent most of them in the library or in my car. At least I will have someone to sit with this year.

"I gotta get to my locker," she says, releasing her hold on me. "Remember, head up. I'll see you at lunch." I watch as she hurries away, her yellow sundress flowing around her knees.

I swallow down my trepidation and head towards my locker. Georgina, Casey, Connie, and Faith. The four fucking hound dogs that have stalked my entire high school career. Georgina is their leader and is Brody Landry's—my ex-best friend's—girlfriend. Then her little band of whores latched onto the other three. Casey with Cooper, the all-American blond headed quarterback, Connie with Caine, the scary steroid wrestler, and Faith with Zeke, the swim team captain. My tormentors.

I huff out a breath and open my locker. I stare into its clean interior, knowing it won't stay this way for long.

"Hey Kailey." I look around and see a senior guy named Andrew. He's never spoken a word to me before.

"Hi?" I say back, sounding more like a question.

"You look good." He gives me a once-over. I take a deep breath and calm the jittery feeling that begins in my stomach.

"Thanks," I mutter and turn my head back into my locker.

I'm not used to male attention, and I would rather it stayed that way. I have never dated, and I really don't plan on it soon. That's why I found it so fucking hilarious when the pack of hounds spread the rumor about me being a whore.

"Look what we have here, y'all." Fuck. "Miss KH herself, looking fucking fine."

I look up from my locker and into eyes so dark I can't tell the irises from the pupils.

"Cooper," I grit out. He whistles and fingers my lacy crop top. I twist out of his hold and glower at him. "What do you want?"

"I'm not fucking sure, to be honest," he chuckles while backing up. "But I will let you know soon, mon sha." My sweetheart. He winks and disappears into the crowd of students.

Cooper Fontenot, most popular jock at JFK. Constantly smiling and joking around, even while tormenting the lesser folks. I bet I could sink my forefinger into the first knuckle in his dimples, they're that deep. His skin is a deep, golden tan because of shirtless football practices in the blaring sun. Then that bright blond hair, naturally highlighted by the same sun, sits like a mop on top of his head, constantly getting into his eyes. Not that I ever pay much attention. We used to be friends in primary school. He even came to my house a couple of times. But he's part of the group who's headed my bullying.

Without too much thought on them, I whip my locker door shut and head off to start my day. One day in, and a fuck ton more to go until I am free.

By lunch, I'm an irritated ball of energy. I want to lash out and slap a couple of people who stared at me all day. Fuck! What is it? Didn't they realize I was a girl underneath the hoodies and baggy clothes? Probably not.

Nerves hit my stomach hard as I watch students enter the cafeteria. Since freshman year, I have developed a fear of large gatherings. It's hard to determine who threw food on you when they crowd all around you. It's a legitimate problem.

"Mon sha." Cooper's voice sounds behind me. My eyes roll so hard into the back of my head, I fear they may be stuck for a second.

"Ech! Cooper, will you fuck…" I turn around and instead of seeing just Cooper, I meet the four sets of eyes I never want to face alone, effectively shutting me up.

His ice-blue eyes cut directly through mine and into my very soul. So much like his brother's, it makes me feel sick. I used to look into those eyes and swoon. Not anymore. I inhale slowly and try to calm my galloping heart. It's too much. I don't know why I thought changing my appearance would go unnoticed.

His dark brown hair—still messy—is tousled on top of his head and cut shorter on the sides. The ends still curl a bit in towards his face, giving him a sweet, innocent look. It's a farce because Brody Landry is not any of that. He's the complete opposite. He's tall now; I have to crank my neck to look up at his face, and his body is lean with a hint of the muscles he's packing showing through his t-shirt. All these things contribute to him being one of the best point guards JFK has ever had. He has a straight roman nose that doesn't dominate his face. But that mouth? Like plush pillows, pink and fleshy, they fight for the first impression with his eyes.

"Kailey! There ya are!" Kimmy's high-pitch voice instantly calms me down. "I'm starving something fierce. Let's see if they have seafood gumbo today." She grabs my arm and steers me away.

"Kails." His deep voice saying my old nickname stops me in my tracks. I turn around and look at Brody, raising my eyebrow. He looks at me from head to toe. "Watch yourself."

I don't reply. It wouldn't matter anyway. He's just trying to intimidate me.

"Allons," Kimmy says loudly as she drags me into the cafeteria.

Watch myself? What does that even mean? Is he warning me before he makes my life a living hell? Can it actually get any worse than it already is? Than I've already had? The answer is no. A hell no. I've survived the worst, and now I am about to show them just how much of a survivor I am.

The cafeteria is boisterous today. There are students standing on tables filming TikToks and others running between tables catching footballs. This school has never been good at the discipline aspect, I should know. During my sophomore year, I broke down. Two years of bullying, and I could barely make it through the day. I went to the dean and begged him to rein it in. I was told it wasn't as bad as it seemed, and I just needed to stop being so emotional.

Why? Because I was reporting on the Golden Four. Yes, that's what everyone calls them here. Their fathers donate millions a year to this school. They have infiltrated every sport, and they've crowned themselves the leaders. The Golden Four. Brody, Cooper, Caine, and Zeke.

"Why did he tell you to watch yourself?" Kimmy breaks through my thoughts.

"I don't know," I answer honestly.

"Ignore them. They're clearly trying to intimidate you. They see you looking like this and know they didn't succeed." She's right. They didn't succeed in breaking me.

We sit at our regular table in the back corner and try to block out the surrounding noise. Kimmy pulls out her phone and starts texting her boyfriend. Henry used to be a senior here last year. Now he's at Tulane University playing for the Green Wave football team.

The Golden Four will attend the same school next year. That's why I applied to the University of New Orleans for sports medicine. Far away from them so after this year, I will never have to set eyes on them again.

"Henry says hi." Kimmy looks up from her phone and smiles.

"Tell him I say to kick ass this Sunday."

"You should come to the game with me." Her eyes go wide with excitement.

"Nope," I shake my head. "They will be there."

"The stadium is huge, boo. They would never see you," she whines.

"I'll think about it," I concede. He also goes there, so I don't want to go.

Kimmy rolls her eyes, knowing that means no.

"Those four have been shooting you looks nonstop." Kimmy looks up discreetly from her phone. "Shit. Looks like Cooper is on his way over here."

Nope, fuck that. They will not corner me into any type of altercation with them. I hurriedly get up out of my seat and push my way out of the exit leading to the football field. I continue to walk around the side of the school, back towards the front entrance, when I hear voices around the corner.

"I don't know what he meant," I hear Casey whine.

"Tell me again what he said." Georgina speaks slowly like she's talking to a two-year-old.

"He said he needs a break," Casey sniffles. "I asked him what he meant, but he just walked away. He walked away from me!"

"It's okay," Georgina sounds determined. "I'll speak to Brody; he won't let that happen. Let's go get him."

I hear them walk away and roll my eyes. Cooper ended his relationship with Casey? They've been together since freshman year.

"It's true," Cooper says from behind me.

I startle from the sound of his voice and spin on my heel to face him. "What's true, Cooper? That you're a stalker? I already gathered that."

"I broke up with her after first period." He reaches out to grab a piece of my hair.

"Don't touch me." I swat his hand away. "And why would I care what you do?"

"Well, I did it for you, sha."

"For me?" I raise my eyebrows in surprise. Then it quickly dawns on me… They're trying to fuck with me. I step into him and look up into his dark eyes. "Do your worst, Cooper. I don't give a shit about any of you. Try to break me."

I turn on my heel and head towards the school's main entrance and away from the dark eyed, dimpled demon.

"You're breaking me, KH!" he yells out behind me with a chuckle.

I pull out my phone and shoot Kimmy a text to let her know I'm okay and to meet me at my car after school. After I arrive to my last class of the day, I exhale a sigh of relief. I luckily don't have a single class with the assholes, but I have this class with Georgina. Great. I rush to a seat in the back corner, far enough away from her and her circle of fans.

"I may need to switch classes, y'all." Her screechy voice sounds like nails on a chalkboard. "I heard lice can jump over eight feet!" Her head turns to look at me. "None of us are safe."

"Is that how you caught crabs from Louis last year?" I snarl back as the class erupts into hushed laughs and smothered coughs.

It's a known fact Georgina cheated on Brody with Louis last year. The Golden Four found out and had him expelled. Brody didn't bat an eye and just kept right on dating the skank.

"No, that's how I got them from your father." She laughs, and her minions join in.

"I'll tell him to ease up on your mother, then. Should I send her a care package? She really shouldn't be spreading those things everywhere."

It's no secret Georgina's mother used to be a high-class escort. Then her rich daddy pulled her off the streets and made her a wife. They try to make people forget with their expensive clothing and big house, but I make sure to remind them when I can.

Everyone snickers quietly, and Georgina stares me down with a red face and murder in her eyes. Bring it, bitch.

The end of the day finally comes, and I rush out of class before Georgina can pounce on me again. I get to my locker and quietly stand in front of it and stare. What will it be for the first day? Worms? Dog shit? Honey? All these things and more have been in there before. I take a small step forward and slowly reach my hand out to spin the lock.

"No one fucked with it today." He will not leave me alone.

"Cooper," I growl. "You lost your right to talk to me the second y'all made my life hell. Understand?"

"What did we do?" He raises a brow and flashes me his dimples.

I'm unfazed … mostly.

"Stuck your hounds on me," I mutter and unlock my locker.

"Hounds? Sha, I do not own any animals." His face screws up in disgust. If I didn't hate him so much, I'd find it slightly adorable.

"Can you just get lost, Cooper?" I finally get my locker open and take a quick step back in case something jumps at me or explodes. When I see it's clean, I exhale a sigh of relief.

"Told you," he says smugly. "To answer your question, I can only get lost on one condition."

"What?" I ask, sounding exasperated.

"Go out with me."

"Have you lost your goddamn mind?!" I yell at him, attracting attention. Great, this is all I need to get back to Casey.

"Oui." He scrubs his hand down his face and convincingly looks put out. "But I won't give up. I have been waiting since primary for this."

"For what?"

"You, mon sha." He pushes off the locker beside me and winks. "I'll be seeing you tomorrow." Then I watch his retreating wide shoulders as he disappears into the crowd.

What the fuck is happening?

I get to my car where Kimmy is leaning against the passenger side. She has her arms folded and is looking out over the parking lot with a scowl on her face.

"Honey, who shit on your face?" I ask her.

"They've been watching you all day today," she grits out. Sure enough, I look to the back of the parking lot and see the four of them leaning against Brody's black Dodge Charger.

"Yeah, I noticed. I also have Cooper chasing me down for a date." I groan and open my backseat to throw my bag inside.

"What?" She spins around. "Why?"

"Thank you?" I raise a brow at her.

"You know what I mean," she waves me off. "He's with Casey."

"He told her he wants a break. I heard her crying about it when I escaped the cafeteria today. Only to have Cooper find me and confirm it."

"Oh, sweet baby Jesus," she curses in a hushed tone.

"Jesus ain't gonna do a damn thing for me. At least he hasn't yet," I mutter.

"I'll pray to him tonight. Usually he works miracles for young ladies who should go to church with their daddies." She looks at me pointedly.

I haven't been to church since my mama died, and I don't plan on returning. It's hard to listen about a God who watches over us but takes all the good ones and leaves the rest to torment each other down here. Sounds really selfish to me.

"I better get goin'," Kimmy says as she pushes herself off my car. "I got dinner tonight with Henry and his family."

"All right, text me later."

"Holla," she calls out on the way to her car.

I chance one more look across the parking lot, and sure enough, they are still all there, looking over at me. I can't help but feel like something big is about to go down.

DESECRATED FLESH

Kailey-Himari

TWO

My headphones are blaring out music as I try to rest all the random thoughts in my head. I can't seem to figure out what those four have planned for me this year. It's my last, so it must be a doozy. Maybe make me fall for one of them and then dump me publicly? Makes sense why they would send in the friendly boy of the group.

My music cuts off as my phone rings with an incoming call. I look at the screen and see an unknown number. Fuck that, I never answer unknowns. It's most likely one of the hounds, trying to get extra harassment in after school hours.

I hit ignore, and my music replays. Maybe if I go back to my regular attire tomorrow, they will leave me alone. But I don't really want to do that, do I? I like the feeling of taking back my confidence and accepting the femininity I've denied for so long.

The music cuts off again as my phone rings for the second time. This time it's not an unknown number, but still a number I don't recognize, so I ignore that as well. If they aren't saved in my phone, then I just don't give a damn.

Soon after that, my phone chimes with a text message. I open it up and stare at the unknown number.

Unknown: KH, why are you ignoring me?

What the fuck? I continue to stare at the text from someone who clearly knows me, but I don't have the slightest who they are.

Unknown: How can I convince you to go out with me if you won't even pick up my calls?

Oh, hell no, it can't be. How did he get my number?

Unknown: Listen, I'll give it to you straight. Date me, and you'll be safe at school. Ignore me, and things will go back to the way they were … maybe even worse.

Shit. Worse? How much worse could it get? I know the answer to this, and it's much worse. I could be physically harassed, and I don't think I could handle people touching me.

Me: Why, Cooper? I need a proper reason for all this.

Cooper: I told you. It's been a long time coming, and the time is now.

Me: And you're telling me I don't have a choice? I have to go out with you even if I don't want to?

Cooper: Don't want to? You sure, sha? Remember in primary, when you kissed me?

Me: We were seven years old and playing spin the bottle in the schoolyard. It hardly counts.

Cooper: Always counted for me. I'll expect your answer tomorrow.

Something strange is fucking going on.

My heart takes off in an erratic beat in my chest. What the hell does The Four want with me? And why now? I can't bother Kimmy because she's at dinner with Henry, and I don't have anybody else. I pace my room and chew my nails down to the skin.

This is not good. If I agree, then I will have Casey causing shit. And if I don't, he said things will get worse. Maybe I should ask him to clarify what's 'worse.' Yes, that's what I will do. It'll buy me more time to somehow figure out how to get out of this fucked-up situation I'm in.

A few hours later and I've permanently burned a hole in my rug. When my phone chimes with a text I nearly bounce off the bed in a rush to grab it.

Kimmy: Girl! Lance Kilmer is under investigation for suspicion of date rape on Tulane campus!

My heart immediately stops then thunders through my rib cage. I can feel the sweat roll down the sides of my face, and all the nerves in my hand have gone numb. Lance Kilmer, current running quarterback for the Green Wave, being investigated. Here I thought they were untouchable, that whole group.

Me: When did this happen?

Kimmy: Tonight! They've taken him down to the station for questioning. Three girls have come forward.

Me: Wow.

I don't know what else to say. My intelligence has gone out the window along with my heart and lungs. I can barely draw in a full breath, and my heart has been pumping blood at an alarming speed.

Kimmy: I wonder how the Landrys are taking it. He and Justin are best friends. Do you think Justin is involved?

There it goes again. My heart will fail me tonight. I can't seem to catch my breath, and my chest is feeling real tight. Justin and Lance, former heartthrobs of JFK Prep. They could have any girl they want, even been known to share a few. Before I can even stop myself, I lean over the bed and vomit on the floor. My stomach is a mess, and I'm fairly sure I'm having a heart attack. I can't answer her because I don't have one.

Thankfully, I didn't eat when I got home, so the vomit mostly comprises bile. I grab a towel from my bathroom and throw it on top of the puddle by my bed. I watch as my hands shake when I pick up my phone which has chimed in the last few minutes.

Kimmy: Hellooooooo…?

Kimmy: Damn it, girl, I wanted to gossip!

This is the last thing I want to gossip about. Kimmy doesn't know what happened to me the summer before freshman year, no one does. I have kept that secret so close to my heart and sacrificed so many things to keep it that way.

This town is a close-knit community. We look after our own even when they may be wrong. That's how I know someone, or many someones, will make this disappear for Lance. He will receive nothing more than a slap on the wrist. But those girls? They will lose everything, including their reputations. Coming forward with such information was a waste of time and a sure ride to Slutsville.

Me: Sorry, gotta make dinner.

Kimmy doesn't call bullshit on my lie, so I lock my phone. I don't want to think of that night, about the amount of alcohol my body consumed and the complete annihilation of Kailey-Himari. I was not the same after that night, and I won't ever be ever again. As the shadows creep in from the sides of my vision, I jump to my feet and race out of my room. I can't have these memories right now; I need to erase them.

I throw my shoes on and see that my papa is late getting home tonight. Probably for the best, because there's not much I could hide right now. I fly out the front door and jog along the sidewalk.

The last remnant of humid weather is fading as fall closes in. It's still balmy, and in no time, my clothes stick to my sweating skin. I need a distraction, and fast. For both freshman and sophomore years, I would dance to get rid of this feeling, but that was soon ruined for me too when he showed up for a visit. I had no idea his little sister was in the same dance studio. I thought I had my anxiety under control, but I don't, and I have no outlet for it.

I continue to run, but eventually, the feeling of my chest wanting to explode and my lungs struggling makes me stumble, and I fall across someone's front lawn.

My chest expands and contracts in rapid motion as I attempt to pull in air. Am I going to die out here of anxious asphyxiation? Is that even a thing? Probably not, but knowing my luck, I'll die from it anyway. The dusk sky shoots reds and oranges above my head as the last of the sun sets behind the oak and cypress trees. I don't know how long I lie here for when I feel tiny droplets of water hitting my face.

My chin is against my chest as I slowly rise to a sitting position. I need to get a hold of myself. I have to somehow forget what happened to me so I can live a normal life. This is the last year I will have the constant reminders, then I won't have to see his face in the halls each day, and I can finally heal inside. I just can't do it when his icy gaze finds mine with hatred brimming around the edges.

I get to my feet and drag myself home as the rain hits my hair and skin, running down my body in rivulets.

When my driveway comes back into view, I finally have a grip on my racing heart and breathing. I'm exhausted from the exertion I put my body through, and I just want to curl up in bed. I groan out loud when I see my papa's car parked there. He's going to have questions when he sees me in the state I'm in, hair plastered to my face and my clothing soaking wet.

I get into the house, and he immediately appears in front of me.

"Kailey-Himari, where the heck have you been? It's pouring out there."

"Sorry, Pa, I went for a walk earlier and got caught in it on the way back."

"Get on up those stairs and straight into a hot bath, young lady. You're going to catch a chill."

"Yes, Pa." I drag my feet up the stairs.

"Oh, Kailey?" he calls out from the bottom. "I like the outfit today. Probably looked a lot better dry, though."

"Thanks," I mutter and close the bathroom door behind me.

It's been awhile since he's seen me like this. For the first few years, he would constantly be on my case about looking and dressing like a lady, but I effectively blocked him out. Eventually, he let it drop, accepting what he probably suspects was just a phase. I didn't make it easy for him to raise me, and it's even worse he had to do it alone.

My mama was grocery shopping one day during the summer before freshman year. When she was walking in the parking lot back to our car, a hit-and-run driver killed her. The cops said she died immediately on impact, and they assured us they would find who did it. It's been four years, yet they still have no leads or suspects. Solidifying my apprehension about approaching the law enforcement of this town for anything.

That night, after learning about Mama, I went on a huge bender and drank more than my weight in hard liquor. It was my last night as the old Kailey. My innocence was stolen, and I was irrevocably altered forever.

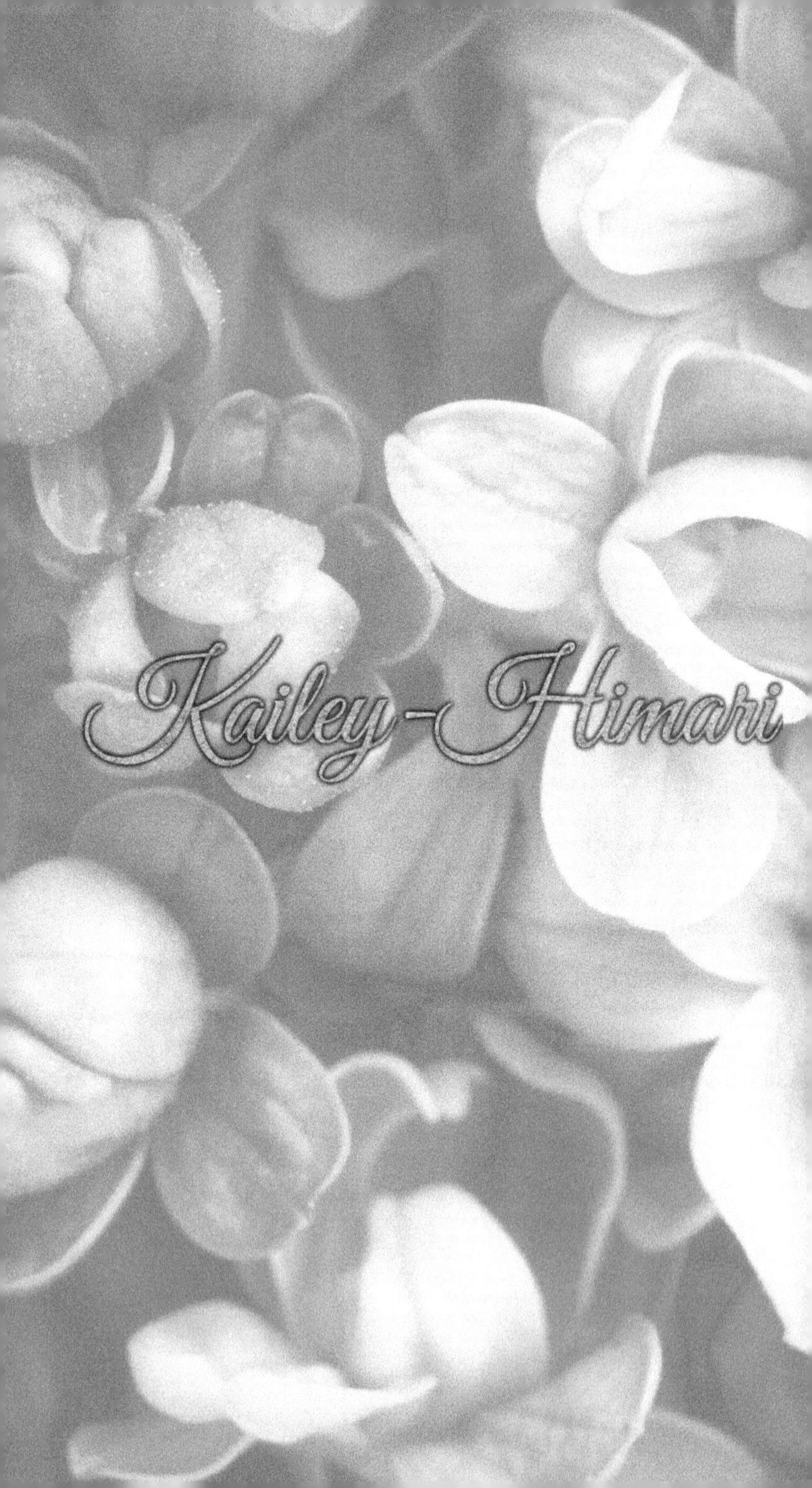
Kailey-Himari

THREE

"There ya are!" Kimmy calls out as I exit my car. "And the second day in a row of looking gorgeous."

"Sorry about last night. I fell asleep after dinner."

She waves me off and stands back to get a good look at me. Today I straightened out my waves and pulled them back into a high ponytail. I wore a pair of black leather pants and an off the shoulder, red sweater. I know red is loud and attention grabbing, but it used to be my favorite color to wear, and I wanted to feel a connection with the old me.

"You look beautiful in red." Kimmy's eyes shine.

"Thanks, girl." I bump her shoulder. "How's Henry?"

"He looks tired as all hell. He says he's being tested past his limits physically, but sheesh, his muscles." She fans herself.

I shake my head and laugh at her. "I'm glad his pain is your gain."

"Can you believe that stuff about Lance?" Her voice becomes hushed.

I don't want to talk about it. Just hearing the name makes my palms sweat and my heart speed up. "Crazy," I mutter.

"Henry says they took him out in handcuffs!" she scoffs. "He also said his family would get him out in no time."

Lance's father is a prominent lawyer in New Orleans. He

represents all the high-profile criminal cases in the state of Louisiana. Of course, he'll get off. It's a well-known fact around here about the group of people who are untouchable, the Golden Four included.

Speaking of, I see the four of them leaning against the brick as Kimmy and I walk by. I lock eyes with Cooper and feel my stomach bottom out as he lifts a brow and then winks. He's expecting an answer today. I avert my gaze and keep my head up, looking straight ahead. I refuse to look at any of them, especially the one with the ice for eyes and a heart.

My locker opens, and mercifully, it's still as clean as I left it yesterday. I pull out what I will need for the day then close it. Cooper is waiting as soon as the door closes, revealing his face. I gasp and cover my mouth as I startle.

"Sorry." He smiles apologetically. "Didn't mean to spook you."

"Oh, yeah? Then please pray tell, what were you meaning to do?" I snarl at him.

"Did you know when I was ten, my mother asked me what my absolute favorite color was?" He looks me straight in the eye, a slight smile ghosting his mouth. "I told her I liked the color dark green and light brown make, like moss on a cypress tree. She laughed and told me it was called hazel. I love the color hazel."

"You wanted to tell me a story?" I huff.

He laughs and acts surprised with himself, like he didn't mean to say that. "I like red on you. It's my new favorite color."

"You certainly display a character trait I assumed you had … noncommittal."

"It only changes when it pertains to you," he snickers and pushes off the locker. "I'll be waiting for you outside at lunch, unless you want to talk in front of everyone."

"Outside is fine." I roll my eyes.

His story runs through my mind as I hurry to class… Only changes when it pertains to you. I suddenly stop, and my breath catches in my chest. My eyes are hazel, a mix of dark green and light brown.

When we were ten, Cooper and I played for weeks straight, building sandcastles in the school sandbox. Could his story have been true? Or was he fucking with my head? I would bet anything on the latter, but it doesn't stop the niggle that's there, working its way to the front. Did Cooper have a crush on me when we were kids?

Thankfully, the morning goes by fairly quickly, and not one person has looked at me wrong. No snickers and nothing said as I passed. Even the hounds resorted to just glaring me down as I walked by them. It was a miracle.

It's lunchtime, and I have spent most of my morning trying to figure out what the fuck to say to Cooper. How can I tell him I want nothing to do with him but to keep the student body here at JFK Prep off me? It's not sane for me to date someone who helped torment me for years.

He may seem like the nice one, his dimples make him look innocent and his shaggy blond hair gives him a cherub look, but Cooper Fontenot is nothing close to being an angel. He's sin all wrapped up in a pretty, dimpled package.

I deduce he wants to meet in the spot we were yesterday. So I throw my stuff in my locker, then text Kimmy to let her know I can't make it to lunch. She sends back an eyebrow emoji, and I feel bad, but I don't reply. How do I tell her I'm speaking with the enemy?

I exit through the main doors then make an immediate right around the corner and down to the hidden alcove I was in yesterday. Sure enough, there he is in all his tanned, blond, dimpled, evil glory.

"Mon sha, you've gotten even more beautiful since this morning."

"Cut it out, Coop. What the hell is all this about?"

"Coop? Shit, how long has it been since you called me that?"

"Probably eighth year, before you decided to make my life a living hell. Then I called you something else."

My vitriol filled words do nothing to him as he tips his head back and roars out a laugh. Sweet Jesus, he is hotter than the fourth of July. I avert my eyes and try to remind myself of the stinking, rotting crawfish or the fish guts stuffed in my locker on multiple occasions.

"What's your answer, KH?" he purrs.

"You're so sure of yourself, huh?" I smirk. "The answer is no,

Cooper. I will never sink so low as to date you or have anything to do with the Golden fucking Four. Leave me alone, and let me live in peace."

"That was a mouthful," his eyebrows rise with surprise. "You know what this means, right? I've been holding the dogs at bay, but now I will let them go." He steps into me, our chests slightly brushing. "They are starving, mon sha. They will eat you alive."

"Bring it." I turn on my heel and head back inside.

How much fucking worse could it get? I've already lived through the worst thing. Bullying, I can handle. I rush back inside and spend the rest of my lunch standing in the girls' bathroom, praying I made the right decision.

The rest of the day goes by well. Nobody pays me much attention, and I can only hope they all got over their need to demean me constantly. Maybe, finally, this year I will be able to breathe.

DESECRATED FLESH

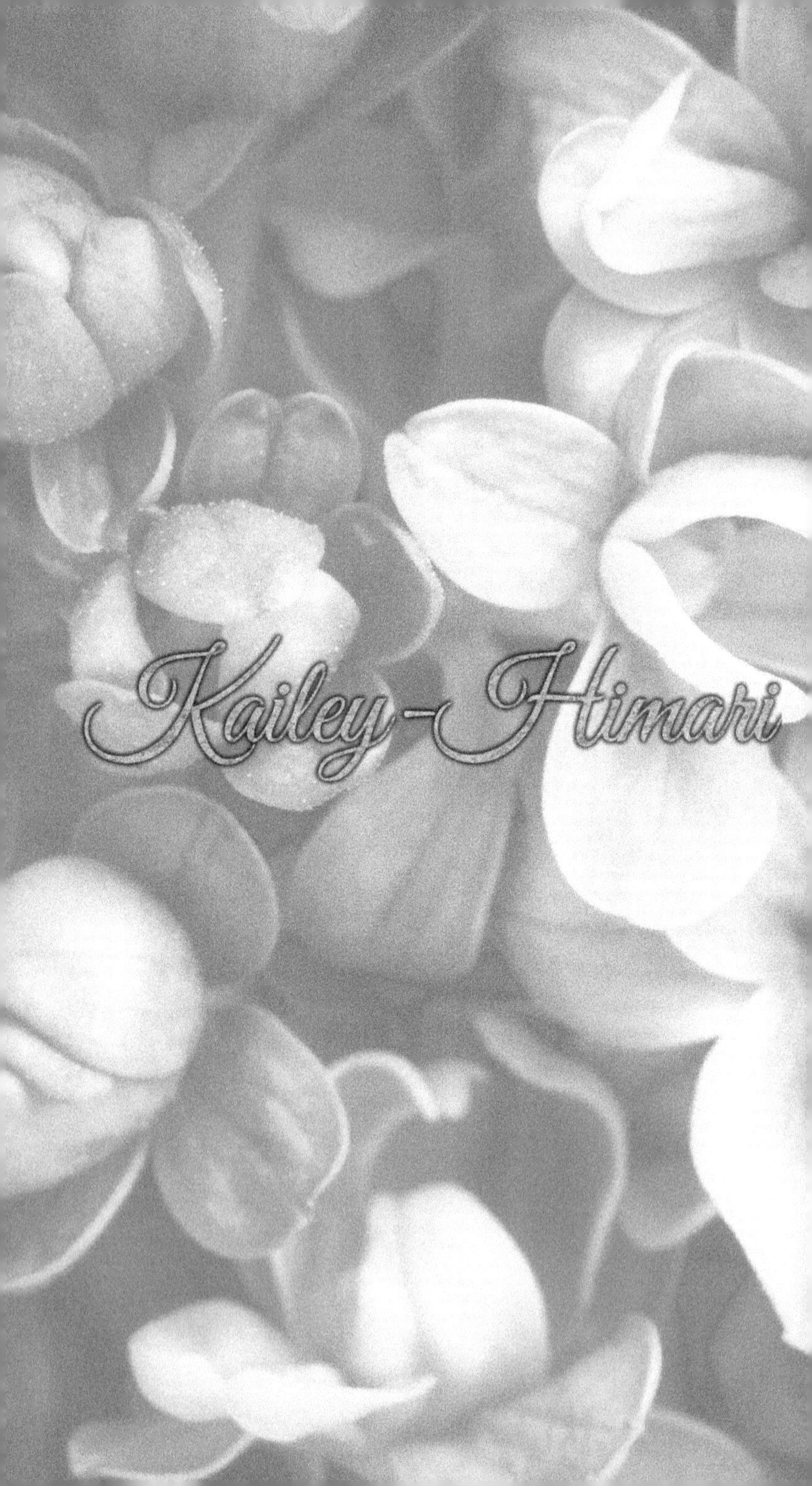
Kailey-Himari

FOUR

I was wrong … so very wrong.

The next morning, I arrive at school in a white sundress that just grazes the tops of my knees. My hair, I let loose in all its waving chaos around my face, and I even put on a white pair of stilettos that once belonged to my mama.

Today, I went the extra mile. I want to remind the student body here that I am a person too. I'm not some reprehensible creature living inside oversized sweats. This is my school too.

Again, I was wrong. It does nothing for me.

I'm being called loser and slut as I part ways with Kimmy and make my way to my locker. I hear Kimmy yelling at whomever she passes, trying desperately to defend me, but I know it will be of little use. The Golden Four has indeed freed the fucking hounds, and Cooper fucking Fontenot was right: They are starving.

Someone throws an opened condom at me, and it sticks to my arm. That's when I finally stop and acknowledge the surrounding people.

"Your mother should've worn that instead of having you." Casey, of course. Not only has she been let loose, but she has some pent-up anger from Cooper's dumping her.

"No, Casey," I turn and get into her face. Her eyes widen a fraction, and I see fear nestled in there. "Your mother should have a commercial sized box of these." I whip it off my arm and throw it at her chest. "Since she's shopping her daughters out to the highest bidders."

It's true, Casey's family is not the richest. In fact, they lost a lot of money when their Bayou oil money ran dry. Now, with six daughters, she's trying to pimp them out to the richest families in New Orleans, hence her dating Cooper Fontenot.

I watch her eyes narrow, and she growls in my face before abruptly turning and stomping off. I was lucky enough to catch the twinkle of tears clouding her eyes beforehand, though. Good.

Cooper's family works with Brody's family. Actually, all of their fathers work together, and they are multi-billionaires combined.

Money was never a problem in my household. Yeah, my papa runs a used car dealership, but he owns it, and he does well. Well enough anyway. My mama was a stay-at-home mom and devoted her time to her family.

I make it to my locker, and I am so fucking distracted, I don't smell or look closely. I open the door, and inside is a rotten fish with maggots crawling all over it and falling out of my locker. A guttural scream forces its way up my throat and out of my mouth. The smell is atrocious, and I gag into my forearm.

"Well, hell," Cooper's lazy drawl sounds behind me. "That is just disgusting. Is that your lunch, KH?"

Riotous laughter roars around me, and my vision tunnels to narrow right onto Cooper's face. I think he sees me on the verge of breaking, and his eyes show a glimpse of pity before he schools it and replaces it with an expression of bored indifference.

"I think we need to speak with your mother about the lunches she packs you... Oh, but wait, she's dead, ain't she? Now it all makes sense." The cruel words spewing from his mouth don't match his sweet and handsome face.

I slam the locker shut, not caring about the maggots spraying out from the impact. I turn and find the Golden Four—Brody, Cooper, Caine, and Zeke—are now standing there, staring me down.

"Yes, my mama is dead," I snarl into his face, uncaring of the audience. "But she loved me when she was alive. My father loves me so much it's almost suffocating, and lucky for me, I'm an only child. I don't have to deal with any siblings hating me. Can any of y'all say the fucking same?"

It's a low blow, but fuck them. I know—probably better than anybody else—how much these four resent their families and how little interaction they have with their siblings, save for Brody. He and his brother, Justin, are like two peas in a fucked-up pod. I know Cooper's older sister, Jeanine, stays away from New Orleans and rarely visits.

I flip my hair over my shoulder—a move I watch the hounds do on the regular—and turn my back on them. I hope they like the look of my retreating back, because that's all they'll ever get from me.

My first two classes are something close to hell. I have paper balls thrown at me, names thrown at me, and even someone's eaten apple core.

Where are the teachers, you might ask? Firmly in the pocket of the Golden Four, they refuse to intervene in case they might lose their jobs.

So, I endure but I don't cower. If anything, I become more incensed. It's my final year, this can't be the last experience of high school I get.

Kimmy is waiting for me outside of the cafeteria doors. I stalk up to her, practically stomping my feet. I have never felt this enraged before.

"Should we maybe eat somewhere else?" she asks as a group of students pass us and call me a filthy whore as they go.

"No!" I ground out. "I will not let them make me a victim anymore." I am vibrating inside.

"Okay." Kimmy looks unsure as she opens the doors.

The room falls silent as all eyes narrow in on me. I feel a sudden rush of fear as I sweep my eyes over the room. I don't see The Four, but I see their hounds, and they are looking at me with raw fury.

"Let's just line up and get some food." Kimmy grabs my arm in hers. "Allons."

It's spaghetti day today, and looking at the noodles is reminding me of what's slithering around in my fucking locker. Kimmy drops a tray in front of me with a plate piled with the shit. I take it and grab a chocolate milk just to appease her, then turn around to see the hounds standing in a line.

"Trash eats outside, in the bin," Casey sneers and Georgina snickers.

"Yeah?" I say through my teeth. "Well, you better run along out there."

"I have heard enough from you today!" Casey growls and quickly steps in front of me.

I know what she's going to do before she does it, but I'm just not quick enough to stop the assault. Her hand flies out, flipping the tray in my hands up and smearing it into my chest and stomach. I can feel the sauce seeping into my white dress.

The cafeteria erupts into rowdy laughter, and I can feel my cheeks heat and my eyes sting. I will not cry in front of these fleabags. My hand grips tight around the tray, and before I can even process my thoughts, I swing the tray out, and it collides with the side of Casey's face. I watch her head snap to the side before she plunges to the ground. With no further preamble, I run from the cafeteria and into the hallway.

I run down the hall to the one bathroom I know barely anyone uses. I know this because it's where I ate lunch during my freshman and sophomore year until I got my license and car.

I rush into the bathroom and throw myself into one of the two stalls, trying to calm myself down. As I suspected, my dress is completely ruined, stained with spaghetti sauce. The sight of noodles stuck to my chest makes me break. I let the tears out, knowing I'm alone in here, and no one can see me at my weakest. I need a moment to be weak because constantly having to maintain my strong front is exhausting.

I hear the bathroom door open and then shut with the click of the lock. Fuck, I should've thought of the lock.

"I know you're in here, KH," Cooper's voice rings out. "You left a trail of spaghetti all the way here."

I hear a few snickers, and someone else clears their throat. Are they all in here? The four assholes who have effectively ruined my life. Why the fuck did they lock themselves in here with me?

My chest rattles with the force of my heart beating. I hate the feeling of fear, and ever since that night. I fight it whenever I feel it creep up on me. Why are they in here? Are they going to hurt me?

"We're not here to hurt you, Kailey." I hear Zeke's rasp fill the room. His voice was always so soothing when we were kids. Now it makes my skin crawl. "Just come out so we can talk."

Zeke Boudreaux, captain of the swim team and computer club. Good looking and brainy. He's tall and has a lean swimmer's body, not too bulky but still toned. I watched one of his swim competitions, and it was surprising to see his body almost completely covered in tattoos. Both of his nipples are pierced, and he has another hoop in his nose. His face is not so bad either, with big green eyes, pert nose, and a Cupid's bow mouth. His black hair is usually cut into a faux hawk on top of his head. You'd never guess he was a genius by looking at him.

"Talk?" I hate how my voice sounds so small and weak right now.

"Sha," I hear Cooper against the other side of my stall door. "I promise we just want to talk."

I don't trust them. They are vile, evil beings, and they love seeing me in pain. I will not go out there of my own accord. They will have to force me out. I don't for one second believe they wouldn't. I know they would, but I will make sure they know I'm being forced.

I hear Cooper exhale, and he taps his fingers on the door. "I warned you, sha. You should've just agreed to my terms."

"I don't even understand why you would want to date that." I hear Caine's deep rumble filled with disdain penetrate through the stall. "Can't you just let this go? Fuck it. Casey has better tits anyway."

He's right, Casey has better tits—ass too. It doesn't bother me. My body is lithe from years of dancing, and I like it this way. Caine Leblanc would know. Last year when my clothes were stolen during gym, he was the one who ripped away my towel for most of the wrestling team to see.

He's the intimidating one, towering and so fucking muscular it looks like he lives at the gym. His skin is a deep, golden tan, showing his heritage—half Creole. His hair and eyes are the same dark brown color, and his wide cheekbones give most models a run for their money. All the guys are gorgeous, but Caine goes a step more. He is gorgeous, but he's mean. I've heard rumors about him and his preference for rough sex. I've seen the many fights he has in the hallways. Caine Leblanc is scary.

"I don't care about big tits." Cooper sounds offended. "Besides,

KH has had my sights since her hazel eyes found mine in that sandbox."

My breath catches, and I know my eyebrows have probably hit my hairline. I was right. Cooper had a crush on me all those years ago.

"Caine's right, Coop." Brody's ice-cold voice breaks through, sounding so fucking bored. "Are you sure you really want this?"

"Oui." Cooper still taps out a rhythm on my bathroom stall door. "I do. Pull out the big guns. I tried, mon sha. I asked you to come out nicely, so now I will have to force you."

Let him. I've been through worse, I've been through worse. As I wait for them to kick in the door and get me, I repeat the mantra in my head. What I don't expect is to hear my papa's voice reverberate off the bathroom walls.

"I will have it for you soon. Give me a few more days, please. I have a plan."

"I will give you two more days, Charlie, then I expect that money to be sitting on my desk. Are we clear?" That's Brody's father's voice. This is a recording.

"Crystal," Pa replies quickly before I hear his quick exhale of breath. "Thank you."

The line goes dead. What was my pa doing talking to Brody's father, and what money? I need to know what this is. I open the door and rush out into the bathroom's interior.

I meet his ice-blue eyes and recoil from the pure hatred reflecting in them. "What was that?" I ask.

"That was your dear papa begging my father for a few days longer on his loan. Half a million dollars is a lot to be behind on." His eyes don't change as he speaks. If anything, the hatred glows hotter.

"That has to be fake," I grit through my teeth.

"It's not. If you don't comply with us, I will make it public. Let the town know just how fucking desperate your father was for money," he snarls into my face.

He's not lying. I know when Brody lies; he gets a tick near the corner of his right eye. It's as smooth as a fucking baby's bottom right now, and if I don't date Cooper, he will make that recording known.

"Us?" My eyes widen. "You mean Cooper," I correct him.

"That was the original plan," Brody says, and Cooper's head swings around to look at him. Looks like he didn't know the plan had changed. "Now, you'll date both Cooper and Caine."

"Fuck that!" Caine roars. "What the fuck did I do?"

"I see what this is." I nod and pace, spaghetti drying and crusty on my chest. "You want to make me into the slut you've been calling me for years?"

Brody just shrugs his shoulders, but I see it in his eyes. He wants me humiliated. "They've been known to share anyway."

"When the girl is hot!" Caine spits out, his fury clear as day. "Casey is hot, and sometimes it works out, but this is different. I don't want the noodle."

Great, I'm glad he sees me as a noodle. I don't want anyone finding me attractive anyway. When I feel the noodles, I cross my arms over my chest in defiance. I cringe and remove my arms.

I'm hella not attractive right now, that's for sure.

Cooper has yet to say anything, but I see his jaw clenched tight. He looks pissed, and I fucking love that he is. Maybe I can make this worse for him, and I can get them to abandon this idea all together.

"Fine." I drop my arms and try not to have a smug look on my face. "I agree … if you throw in Zeke too."

Zeke gets a little smirk on his face, and his eyes light up. He's on to me. Of course he is, he's the fucking brains of the group. "Tsk, tsk, bebelle. You may as well take us all, then."

Cooper's jaw looks like it could crush concrete.

I look Brody up and down slowly and let the disgust I really feel show on my face. "Not in a million years."

I see the flash of hurt in his eyes, even if he is quick to cover it. "Georgina has the sweetest little pussy in this school. Why would I downgrade to something loose and fishy?"

Yep, that fucking burns. I swallow repeatedly to dislodge the ball in my throat and finally bring my eyes back to his. I shrug with indifference, but my insides feel heavy with humiliation. He really hates my fucking guts.

"Just Caine and Cooper," he grounds out then turns to unlock and leave the bathroom. "And, Kailey? Go home, and clean up. You look like you dove into a dumpster."

"Smells like it too," Caine sneers and storms out behind Brody.

Zeke throws me a pitiful smile then leaves me in the bathroom alone with Cooper.

"You had to do this the hard way." His eyes meet mine. "I wanted to make your life easier when I proposed this. I was fucking tired of seeing you pushed around and accosted with rotting seafood, but you just had to make it hard. Now you've pissed him off, and I have to somehow make it right. I'm doing this for you."

"Save it. I'm being forced, and that's that. I have to comply to protect my pa, but I will get to the bottom of that recording and find out the truth."

"I don't think you want that, sha." His eyes fill with remorse as he turns his back to leave the bathroom. "Go home, KH. I'll be picking you up bright and early tomorrow morning."

DESECRATED FLESH

Kailey-Himari

FIVE

I spent the night talking to Kimmy, telling her about the situation I'm in and tossing in bed, trying to slow my racing thoughts. This is not ideal; I do not want to be dating anyone, and especially not one half of the Golden Four.

I went from every guy avoiding me like the plague to dating two of the most popular. How will I have to do it? Do I hold their hands? Touch them? My palms sweat, and my chest beats out a quick staccato. Kiss them? I'm scared. I haven't been touched or kissed or dated before. Not by choice anyway, and this feels close to being the same as that. It's against my will.

Before that summer, I had regular schoolgirl crushes, and, if I'm being honest, it regularly rotated between The Four. We were always together. It was natural, but the steadiest crush I always had that didn't change was Brody.

He was always my constant crush with his big blue eyes, but over time—long after that crush had died—I watched as those eyes gradually narrowed with the strain of constant disdain. Not only did the boy I once cared for change in appearance, but his insides did too. He became angry, dark, and uncaring. So apathetic to his surroundings, no matter how many people suffered—how much I suffered—he always just watched with a blank expression.

The next morning, I forgo the new attire and revert to oversized sweats. If my new look caught their attention, then maybe my old one will make them change their minds.

I hate the thought of riding in a vehicle with Cooper, but I decide to just tolerate it because this situation will not last. I'll just constantly remind them of all the reasons they hate me.

At exactly eight, I hear Cooper's horn honk from my driveway. I'm already waiting by the door, my shoes on and my forehead resting against the cool wood. My only saving grace is my papa leaves early every morning, so he's not here to witness my walk of shame. I'll do as Kimmy says and keep my guard up, but cooperate so I can get the much-needed information about my papa.

I open the door and face the heathen waiting for me in his bright yellow Jeep Wrangler. Cooper is the loudest and most attention seeking of them all. It's why he's the most popular. Everybody likes him because they think he's this great guy with a killer personality. Heavy on the killer. He can be those things for sure, but he's also dark and can enjoy another's pain. He sure enjoyed mine.

I close my door behind me and watch as he gets out of the driver's side and moves around to open the passenger door.

"Sha, you look ravishing this morning." He winks at me.

I roll my eyes and get into the seat. "Whatever, Cooper."

His tall frame comes around the front of the Wrangler. He has on a white, sleeveless shirt and a dark pair of jeans. His hair is haphazardly falling over his forehead, and his black eyes shine mischievously.

"If you wore this outfit to deter me, then I must inform you, I liked you even in those." He points at my sweats.

"What game are you playing, Cooper?" I huff out. "What is all this?"

"I have a plan, KH, and I just want you to watch how it unfolds. It's fucking genius." He snaps his fingers and pulls out of my driveway.

"You shouldn't play with people's lives like it's a game, Coop," I stress. "What is this plan?"

"I can't tell you, KH." He shakes his head. "I can't tell anyone."

"None of the guys know what the fuck you're planning? They think this isn't some pretend game?"

"Who says I'm pretending?" He looks at me like I'm crazy.

I don't talk to him for the rest of the drive to school. It wouldn't make a difference; he's playing at some game, and you could bet your mama's life the others know about it. They rarely do anything without the rest knowing.

"How are we doing this?" I ask him as he parks the Wrangler.

"What do you mean?" He raises a brow.

"You want us to look like we are together, right?"

"I want us to be together, KH. Do what you want."

I take his advice, popping out of the vehicle and moving away from him as quickly as possible. Kimmy is standing over at her small, red Honda Civic, and as soon as she sees me, she rushes forward.

"Where's your car?" she asks as she hugs me close.

"Coop picked me up."

"Are you okay?" she whispers.

"Yeah, I'm okay."

"Sha," Cooper calls out. "Allons."

Her eyesight locks over my shoulder, and I turn to see what she's looking at. The Four have all arrived and are standing with Cooper as they watch us right back.

"I can't believe they are doing this," she grounds out.

"KH!" Cooper calls out. "School time, sha."

"How dare he force you to go be with him?" she practically growls.

"Cooper isn't so bad," I shrug.

"The Devil was charming too, boo. But never forget he was a fucking snake." She's got a point.

I hug her quickly then march over to the guys I hate with a passion. Cooper slings his arm over my shoulders and guides us ahead of them.

"Has she gone back to looking like a homeless person?" I hear Caine grumble behind us. "This is so much worse."

I feel Cooper shaking with laughter as I fight to hide my own pleasure. I'm glad Caine wants nothing to do with me; that was the plan, after all.

"Make the break with Connie before lunch," Brody's chilling voice breaks through. "Try to get a quick fuck in. After that, it's done."

"Would you break up with Georgina for that?" Caine asks him, sounding outraged.

"This has nothing to do with me." Brody's voice brokers no argument.

Caine brushes by Cooper, hitting his shoulder as he passes. His face is filled with thunderous fury.

"Why is he being forced?" I ask Cooper.

"Not sure," he shrugs and glances over his shoulder. "But it plays in to things perfectly."

I roll my eyes and swallow down the rest of my questions. I know I won't get full answers anyway.

We walk through the double door entrance, and I stiffen, preparing for the onslaught of verbal abuse. But the hallways are deathly quiet as Cooper keeps his arm around me and leads me straight to my locker.

I stare at it a while and dread opening it up to the mess I left it in yesterday.

"I had it cleaned out and your textbooks replaced when you left for the day," Cooper informs me and nudges me forward. "Check for yourself."

I enter the combination and open the door, stepping back slightly just in case he fucking lied. Because that's what they do, they lie.

This time, though, he was being truthful. Inside is pristine, with no maggots, nothing rotting, and smelling like a fresh daisy. My textbooks are brand spanking new, and there's even a short vine of purple wisteria.

That last item makes me suck in a breath of surprise.

"I didn't forget. That's your favorite, right?" Cooper says, sounding smug as hell. "You used to tie those up into your hair all the time."

I don't answer him, and I refuse to let the armor encasing my heart crack. He's using his knowledge of me to make me care, then crush my very existence. I won't budge.

I slam the locker shut and call out over my shoulder, "Wrong."

Wisteria is the flower my mama loved most. She planted a few vines in our backyard, and now they hang over the front of our gazebo, my absolute favorite place.

In primary school, there were two wisteria trees in the playground, and Cooper is right: I always tied them up into my hair. I hate that he remembers, leaving me with more questions than answers.

When the first half of my day is done and I have learned absolutely nothing, I text Kimmy and ask her where she wants to meet. Her text is instantaneous.

Kimmy: We're sitting with The Four.

Me: Pardon me?

Kimmy: I have been commanded, and you are being summoned.

My phone pings with another message.

Cooper: I got your lunch. Don't make me come get you.

I guess I really am being summoned, and it looks like I have to step foot back inside that cafeteria to face the hounds who attacked me yesterday. There's no fear, but I am wary. I'd be stupid if I wasn't.

I open the cafeteria door and look around. Some students look towards me, but mostly, I am unnoticed, which is fucking odd.

I know where The Four and their hounds sit in here. Their table is the biggest, located in the center of the room. It could easily sit fifteen or more, but only eight are ever allowed to sit there.

Today, it has the four assholes and Kimmy. Where are the hounds?

I do a quick sweep and find the four of them sitting at a smaller table in the back corner. Casey and Faith are consoling a crying Connie, but Georgina stares me down with a look that would cripple a weaker person.

I turn my head away and stroll to the middle table.

Cooper gives me a small smile and a wink. Zeke has his head buried in a large textbook, Brody is scrolling through his phone, and Caine is looking at me, similar to Georgina.

He hates me something fierce, and all I want to do is scream into his face. This isn't my fault. I didn't make this situation happen, so I would be as happy as a pig in shit if they'd just fuck right off.

"Sha, I got you lunch." I look down at the po-boy sitting on my tray with a carton of chocolate milk.

Kimmy has the same, sitting as untouched as mine. She looks at me from her spot between Brody and Zeke and raises a brow. I roll my eyes and sit beside Cooper, Caine on his other side.

"Thanks for lunch," I mutter.

"You should make her suck your dick for it," Caine snarls. "That's what we're supposed to be getting out of this, right? She must know how to at least suck dick. She's a slut, right?"

My eyes fly up and lock onto the icy-blues across from me. I don't know why I looked at him first. What do I think he'll do for me? He's the one who spread the slut rumors to begin with.

"Is that what you want, Caine?" Brody asks him, but his eyes never leave mine. "You want her to suck your dick?"

"I don't want her mouth anywhere near me," he retorts.

Kimmy and I stand up and turn to leave the table. I will be damned if I stay here and be treated like an animal. I have done nothing to these assholes, and I don't deserve this fucking treatment.

"Sit down," Brody demands, his jaw clenching. "Do not make me force you."

"This is fucking insane, Kailey," Kimmy hoarsely whispers. "Let's just leave."

"See, the thing about that is, Kailey's papa is in huge—"

"Fine." I sit down at the table and avoid Kimmy's eye. "Just go, Kimmy. I have to stay."

"Kailey-Himari," she hisses.

"I'm fine." I open the po-boy.

"Fine." She huffs before I hear the click of her heels as she rushes out of the cafeteria.

The cafeteria falls silent as I sit at a table with my most dangerous enemies, trying to swallow food and keep it down.

"Brody." Georgina's voice sounds from behind me.

"Yeah?" I watch as his eyes slowly leave mine and travel above my head.

"This has become too much. You want to destroy her? We can do it right now. Have it done with, and that's it. Everything goes back to normal."

I stiffen at her words and keep my eyes trained on Brody. He's the leader, and if he hands me over to her, I will put up the biggest fight. I am just about through with this shit.

"It's not my decision, Georgie," he croons to her. "Coop wants to date her. Caine wants her to suck his dick. So, I must oblige, and let her sit here with us. You can always come sit here too."

The way he says that sends a rush of anger through me. How dare he say shit like that? As if I don't have a fucking choice? Because you don't, I answer for myself.

Cooper places his hand on my knee and looks at me. His eyes are telling me to sit still and be quiet. Nothing I say or do will make this situation any better.

"Well, what about Casey and Connie?" She looks over at the table of girls.

"No," Brody shuts her down immediately. "You and Faith only."

Caine grumbles something under his breath and gets a stern look from Brody.

"I'm out of here." Caine abruptly stands.

"Stick around," Brody says to him. "You have to drive Kailey home."

"I'll drive her home," Cooper interjects. I'd rather go with Kimmy, but if I must choose between these four idiots, then of course, it's Cooper.

"No," Brody shuts him down. "Caine needs to get to know the girl he's dating."

"Whatever," Caine mutters as he storms out of the cafeteria.

The bell rings, finally freeing me from my lunch imprisonment, and I hop up from the table and skirt around Georgina. Her hand lands on my forearm, her nails sinking in.

"Listen to me…" she growls.

I rip my arm out of her clenched hand and spin on her. "No, bitch, you listen to me." I take a step into her face. "I did not make any of these decisions. Don't threaten me with shit, talk to your boyfriend, and never lay a hand on me again."

"Looks like you were told, *Georgie*," Cooper mockingly says her name. "Move along."

He gets up and slides his arm around my shoulders, guiding me out of the cafeteria.

"Ugh!" I exclaim after we leave. "I hate her."

"She hates you too," he shrugs.

"Because of y'all," I huff.

"Or because you're prettier, smarter, and catch the eye of every guy in this school."

"Are you dense?" I turn on him. "Have you not been in this school for the past three years?"

"I see everything, sha." Then he leans in and shocks the shit out of me by kissing my cheek. "You will have to go home with Caine. Don't worry, his bark is bigger than his bite." I raise my brow at him, and his shoulders slump. "Fine, that's not true. He definitely likes to bite. Just try not to provoke him, and he'll want it over with quickly."

I nod and turn to head off to my next class. "Oh, and sha?" I turn back to look at him. "Don't even think about kissing him. The first one belongs to me."

He is dense. I don't answer because he is so out of his mind if he even thinks there's a chance Caine and I would ever kiss.

The end of the day comes quicker than I would've liked, and I stand at my locker with a ball of dread forming in my stomach.

"You do not need to go home with him," Kimmy seethes beside me.

"I do, it's complicated," I tell her while I close my fresh smelling locker.

"Text me if he takes you down some country road," She orders me, her face completely serious.

"Okay," I nod.

I follow her out the front doors, and we both stop and stare at the matte black Ford Raptor with its music blaring. Caine is sitting in the front seat, his sight directed straight ahead, and his jaw clenched so tight I bet it could cut glass.

"Text me," Kimmy repeats. "That one is fucking dangerous."

I nod and head for the passenger door. Out of all four guys, I know Caine the least. He came during our eighth year when I was super busy with dancing. Then that summer came, and I backed away from them all.

I get into the truck and place my backpack on the floor in front of my seat. While I click my seat belt into place, I turn. I notice his leg jumping, like the mere presence of me irritates the fuck out of me.

Once the belt clicks, he's got the pedal to the metal, and we fly out of the parking lot. I don't think I have to worry about Caine taking me down any dirt roads. It's very clear he wants me out of his sight as soon as possible.

In no time, he's pulling onto my driveway and slamming on the brakes. I'm happy to get the hell out of this vehicle too.

I undo my seat belt and grab my bag. "Thanks," I mutter and turn to open the door.

Suddenly, Caine has his hand around my neck and his face in mine.

"Let's get one thing straight," he grounds out between clenched teeth. "I don't want you. I don't want you in my vehicle, and I definitely never want you on my dick. You got into one of our heads, and now I am forced to do this."

I lift my hand, wrapping it around his wrist, and squeeze. "Get your hand off me, Caine. I won't let you hurt me."

His hand comes away, and I rub my neck. "Hurt you?" he chuckles. "I don't hurt girls unless they beg me to."

"What?" My eyes narrow on his face. "What the fuck kind of girls are asking to be hurt? If they actually knew what being hurt was like, they would never ask for it." I open the door and jump out.

"A slut like you must know what I mean." The grin on his face is sinfully evil, but still so devastatingly gorgeous.

"No, I don't. I never asked for the hurt I got."

I slam his door and rush to my front door before he can see the tears spilling down over my cheeks.

I quickly get inside just as I hear his tires skidding out of my driveway. I'm never going to survive this year.

DESECRATED FLESH

Kailey-Himari

SIX

They left me here a broken mess with my shorts wrapped around my knees and my ripped panties laying on the ground beside me. Maybe I should be grateful they didn't take me with them. I could've ended up being the subject of their attention all night.

I'm still really drunk, and I turn my head to see a large puddle of vomit beside me, the smell of bitter bourbon and bile assaulting my senses.

When did I puke?

While they were … while they… A sob escapes me, and I finally feel the evidence of what happened between my legs. I reach down and wince as pain radiates up and inside me. My fingers swipe against something warm and sticky. I bring them back up to my face and see a mixture of cum and blood… A lot of blood.

The pain isn't only there, it's also in my rear as well. They violated me completely.

I try to sit up, but the pain is too much, and I feel myself turn on my side and dry heave onto the ground. There's nothing left in my stomach. All the alcohol that survived the first upheaval has soaked its way into my system.

Why did I do this tonight? Why did I have to come here while I was so intoxicated?

Because I wanted my best friend. I wanted him to take me in his arms and hug away the slicing internal pain I've had since I found out *about my mama.*

But when I got here, he was already preoccupied with Georgina, and her friends were occupying the other three. I didn't stand a chance. So I wandered off and continued to drink until they found me.

Why did I come down here with him? Why did I follow him? My head is pounding in the same rhythm as the pain down below. I need to somehow get home and sneak back into my house.

I know I should go to the hospital, but I can't let this get out. Too many people will ask questions. My papa would lose his mind and so soon after my mama's death. I couldn't do that to him.

I finally get to my feet and drag my shorts back up into place. The pain between my legs intensifies as I try to walk, and I end up falling against a tree. When I look up, I see the beautiful flowers of a wisteria— my mama's favorite. I reach out to pull off a vine and crush it into the palm of my hand.

I really believe the small vine of flowers gave me the strength to get home that night.

DESECRATED FLESH

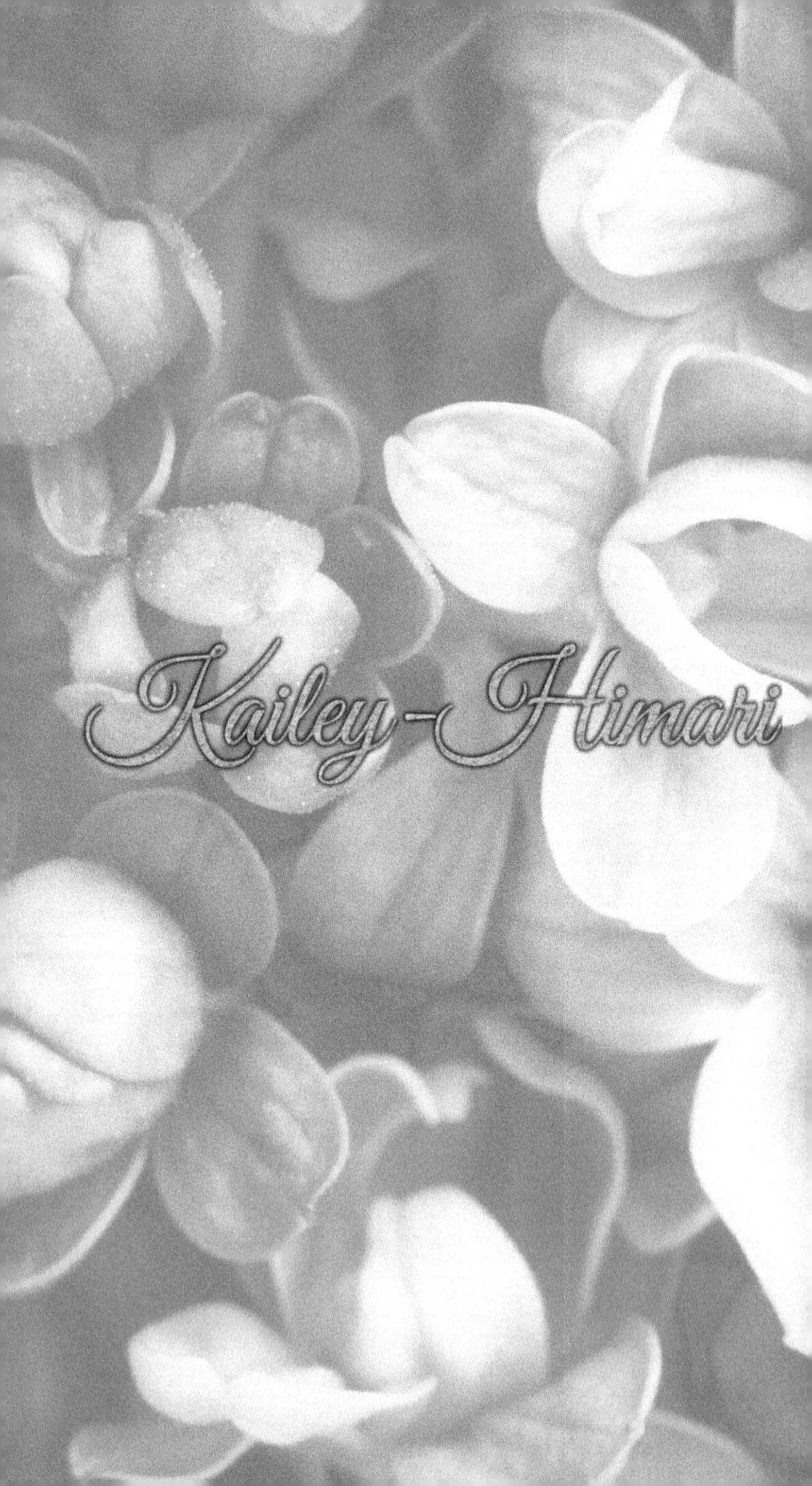
Kailey-Himari

SEVEN

The next morning, I hear the familiar beep of Cooper's car and exhale a sigh of relief.

Interacting with Caine yesterday brought back a lot of repressed memories I worked so hard to forget. The rough feel of his hand on my neck felt too much like *his* rough hand wrapped around my neck. I won't let him get to me, so I will damn sure be ready the next time he reaches to touch me. A swift kick to the boys should set him straight on what he can and cannot touch.

I ditched the sweats again today and dressed in something lighter to help with the dark mood that has ascended on me since yesterday.

I put on a yellow sundress with a light washed jean jacket on top and a pair of chunky ankle boots. My hair I swept up into a messy bun on top of my head, and I applied some gloss and mascara.

I walk out the front door and stop as I take in the sight of Cooper in front of me. He's in a pair of khakis and a black, long-sleeved Henley rolled to his elbows. There is a cap on his head and a pair of tanned boots on his feet. He looks like he belongs on the cover of a magazine.

I shake myself out of my perusal and grin when I see he's doing the same with me. I walk towards him, and he scrambles to open the passenger side door.

"Mon sha," he breathes as I brush by him to get into the seat. "You are a vision in that dress." He leans in and looks directly into my eyes. "Yellow is my new favorite color."

I chuckle at what he says then immediately roll my eyes. The bastard is really growing on me, so I need to be more cautious. I need to remember these guys know exactly what to say to reel me in.

I watch as his arms flex when he pulls himself inside the Wrangler. Cooper is deadly in how sexy he is. Like pure evil wrapped in a thin layer of angelic crust.

"How was the ride home yesterday?"

"What?" I ask. "Caine didn't give you all the complete details?"

"He did." He flashes me a grin. "But I want to hear it from you."

"It was just as you said. He made it quick," I mutter and watch the houses pass by.

"That's it?" he questions.

"Why? Did he say more?" My eyes narrow on him.

"No, his was a similar story."

I shrug and turn to look out of the window. I don't want to think any further about Caine's actions. He's not the type of person I would ever want in my life, so now that he's thrusted upon me, I have to avoid him and deal with it.

"There was one strange thing," Cooper murmurs as we pull into his parking spot at school.

I turn to look at him and see he's staring straight ahead. When I follow his line of sight, I see Caine standing with Zeke, no doubt waiting for the other two boneheads.

"What?" I prompt him.

"When I called to ask him if you got home okay, he seemed less angry and sounded a bit more remorseful. That's why I wanted to make sure he didn't try anything with you." He finally turns to look at me.

"Nothing happened, Coop. Stop overthinking stuff." I quickly exit the vehicle and do a quick scan for Kimmy.

"Goddamn, that dress really is gorgeous," Cooper says with his signature smirk.

I roll my eyes and continue to watch the driveway for signs of

Kimmy. The wind blows, and a lock of wavy hair comes free from the bun and brushes across my face. I feel his fingers lightly skim my cheek as he twists the wayward strands around his thumb and forefinger.

"Still as silky as when we were kids. I used to always love to play with your hair."

"I remember." I turn to look at him. "But that was a different time, Coop." I pull the strands out of his grasp and tuck them tight behind my ear.

"Yeah." He drops his hand and gives me a sad smile.

Finally, Kimmy's car comes into view, and I hasten away from the boy whose words and actions are clouding the reasons I hate him. I hurry towards Kimmy as she parks her car and gets out.

"Kimmy!" I yell out.

"Boo! Where y'at?" She waves with a big smile on her face.

"I'm okay. You?"

"I miss sex," she pouts, and I choke on laughter. "I got you something last night."

"Really?" I watch as she reaches into her jacket pocket and pulls out a small, red, flannel pouch with a short piece of leather cord attached.

"Give me your left wrist." I do as she says and watch as she ties the little pouch around my wrist. "There's a Voodoo queen a few houses down from me. I asked her to make me a protection Gris-Gris for you." She lifts my arm and presses the pouch into my mouth. "Breathe on it, and let it activate for you."

I do as she says and drop my arm. "You really believe in the Voodoo rituals?"

"Yes," she nods emphatically. "My mama couldn't have babies. She had a Voodoo queen make her a fertility Gris-Gris, and a month later, she was pregnant. I swear, they work."

"Thank you, Kimmy." I wrap my arms around my best friend.

"Sha!" I hear Cooper yell out and exhale a sigh.

"Go," Kimmy gives me a confident smile. "They can't hurt you while you wear that."

I nod and make my way back to Cooper, my Gris-Gris swinging lightly against my side. He watches me with a small smile on his mouth and lifts his arm to tuck me into his side. I don't fight him because I don't feel suffocated. The weight of his arm around my shoulders gives me a sense of protection, something I've rarely had.

We walk towards the other three, and I chance a look at them. Brody is the same as always, his face masked with a look of utter boredom, Zeke always has a playful grin on his mouth and a dangerous glint in his eye, and Caine looks slightly less irritated than yesterday. It's something.

We lock eyes, and he gives me a slow perusal from my feet to the top of my messy bun. When his eyes finally land back on mine, they don't hold the familiar disgust. Today, they look almost confused and pondering.

Not that I care.

Cooper leads me past them with a quick, "Mornin' y'all," over his shoulder. He leads me straight to my locker where there's a line of four bitches… I mean hounds—same shit, though, right?

"Coopey," Casey moans as she sees his arm around me. "This is becoming too much. You wanted a romp with the school slut, and you got it. Come back to something a little more proper."

Nope, not letting that fly. "Proper?" I look at the gathering crowd around me with mock confusion on my face. "Y'all, please correct me if I'm wrong, but is it proper to pimp yourself out to the highest bidder? Is it proper to find out a man's financial records before you go out for dinner? C'mon y'all, is it?"

A few muttered nos and snickers run like a wave around us.

"Gosh, I hate you so much!" Casey stomps her foot. "You're a dirty whore, and you should stay in your lane!"

"Honey," I lay it on real thick. "I didn't leave my lane." I look up into Cooper's amused, dark eyes. "He swerved into mine."

Cooper chuckles as he reaches down to take my hand. "Pleasant chat, ladies. But I think she said all there is to say."

He pulls me right through the middle of them, and they part with faces full of horror. *Woof, woof, bitches.*

I get to my fresh smelling, clean locker and pull it open. It's so damn nice to feel normal and not have anything rotting in here.

A body appears to my right, and I hear Cooper chuckle lightly from behind me. When I turn my head, I'm surprised to see Caine leaning against the locker beside mine, effectively blocking the person who owns it. Not that they'll complain, they'd rather be late than to ask him to move.

"Party at my house this weekend." He's not looking at me, he's clearly talking to Cooper. So I continue to disregard him and pull out my books I need for the day.

"Oh!" Cooper claps once. "A good ole Cajun fais-do-do."

"Nah, a small gathering, fool." Caine's deep voice resonates with a touch of humor.

"Small?" Cooper asks.

"Small," Caine confirms. "You can bring your little pet too." He pushes himself off the locker and strolls nonchalantly down the corridor.

"Pet," I repeat and shake my head. I guess that really is what I am.

"Pets are cute," Cooper says as he steps up close behind me and puts his mouth to my ear. "Like a little pussycat."

I'm not exactly sure what triggers it, maybe his closeness or the heat of his breath against my ear, but I tremble as my mind tumbles me back into the past when another pushed himself behind me and breathed nasty words into my ear. When the pain was so intense, I emptied my stomach while they desecrated my flesh.

"Kailey!" Cooper's voice breaks through the high-pitched wail surrounding us. It shocks me when I realize the noise is coming from me. "What just happened?"

He's now standing in front of me with his hands up and open wide. The look on his face is one of complete horror, and his eyes are as wide as silver dollars.

"Sorry," I murmur hoarsely, my throat on fire from the screaming.

I curl into myself when I notice I have the attention of several students and teachers who have stopped in the halls to watch.

"Can I come closer?" he asks quietly as he waves people on.

"Yes," I whisper.

He takes a few steps forward and stands in front of me, making sure not to make contact.

"What happened?"

Suddenly, my body is alive with anger. I stiffen and fist my hands at my sides. "What the hell do you care?"

His face hardens, and I see the sneer I've become accustomed to the past few years.

"Fine," he growls and storms off in the opposite direction. I feel a twinge of remorse as I watch his back retreat farther into the crowd, and I don't have the slightest clue why.

At lunch, I am miraculously left alone and able to sit and eat with Kimmy in peace. Maybe my Gris-Gris is actually working.

"They are staring a damn hole into the back of your head," Kimmy growls around a mouth of gumbo.

"Let them," I shrug as I attempt to exude a calmness I for sure ain't feeling.

After this morning and my outburst, I have been feeling jittery. The overpowering memories are causing a problem as they slowly unravel themselves from the prison I created in the darkest corner of my mind.

The warning bell rings, alerting us to the end of lunch. That means I'm already halfway through the day.

I get up from the table and turn quickly when I hear Kimmy's gasp. Standing just behind me is Caine, and when he's this close, he's like a freaking mountain.

"Same place after school," he mutters and then turns to leave. Great, he's driving me home again. Will this be routine from now on?

"What did that Hulk say?" Kimmy asks from behind me, and I giggle at her.

"Looks like he's dropping me home again."

"Bunch of heathens," she says as I walk with her out of the cafeteria.

The rest of the day goes by relatively quietly, and I am relieved to hear the last bell. But then I remember who the hell is taking me home, and the nerves once again flare up. This time, I vow not to let his hands get anywhere near me in the close confines of his truck.

"Miss Thang," I hear Kimmy say as she comes up behind me. "Your new posse just cornered me down the hall and told me to be at some party this weekend?"

"Caine's." I roll my eyes. "We're so not going."

"They made it sound like we didn't have a choice." Her eyes widen.

"Kimmy, if there's one thing I have learned in this fucked-up life of mine, it's we have choices. In this situation I am in with them, I chose not to have a choice. Feel me?"

"Not really." Her face screws up in confusion.

"One day, I will explain everything." I nod and walk with her to the front doors.

Just like yesterday, the matte black truck is waiting by the entrance, but this time his music isn't blaring. Still, his jaw is clenched tight, and his brows are low over his eyes.

"He's just a peach," Kimmy drawls, and I laugh.

"See ya tomorrow," I call out to her as I walk towards the passenger side of the truck.

His eyes flash towards me once, and then he quickly straightens out to face forward. I get in and quickly put on my seat belt, afraid for when he catapults us out of the parking lot, but to my shock, he waits until I'm belted. He also doesn't give me whiplash as we exit the parking lot this time. Small miracles.

"Look… I don't want this situation any more than you do," he says, his deep voice resonating in the truck's cab. "I don't know what Cooper is thinking, but this shit is going to end badly."

"Yeah." I nod because I agree with him, and yes, it's shocking.

He wasn't expecting my immediate agreement if I have to judge by the way he swerved us into the opposite lane.

"Yeah?"

"I have never wanted anything to do with you guys. Why wouldn't I agree?" I shake my head.

"I wouldn't say never," he mutters.

"What?" I turn to him. Did I hear him right?

"You used to be close to us. Well, not with me for very long, but the others? Y'all grew up together. You and Brody used to bathe together when you were kids. Zeke always had you playing a video game with him, and we could barely get the two of you off when we wanted to do something. And Cooper? He used to follow you around and do just about anything you wanted. Barbies, dolls, flowers, sandcastles…" he's listing them off on his fingers. "So yeah. You used to want to have something to do with us." He sounds almost like he's in disbelief that he said all that. I am too, but more disbelieving that he remembers all of that.

"Things changed."

I try to block the emotional tide threatening to drag me out into the bottomless ocean. I remember all of that. It's been a really long time since I thought about it, but now that he's brought up, I can't stop thinking about it.

My mama and Brody's mama were best friends. So Brody and I used to sleep together in a crib as infants at naptime. We did indeed bathe together, and we were pretty much inseparable. He confided in me so many things about his family, how his mama and papa fought like crazy but stayed married for appearances. He would stay over at my house to get away from the war zone.

Then Zeke introduced me to Grand Theft Auto—the video game—and I was hooked. We could sit in front of his wide screen and play for hours. His mama would always try to make us eat but rarely succeeded.

DESECRATED FLESH

And Cooper, he followed me anywhere. When I really wanted to be a girl and play with girl things, he never complained. He made flower crowns with me and played princes and princesses. Barbies too. He would be Ken, but he endured it. Our favorite, though, were sandcastles. He had a huge sandbox in his backyard, and we were always in it.

Caine came later. The beginning of eighth year, when my dancing was at its peak and I was in the studio more times than I was out of it. Those four would come and watch me, but Caine always brought me a Starbucks frappe for when I was done. I remember he always had his head in a true crime novel or a murder mystery.

"You always had a frappe for me." I don't realize I say it out loud until all the words are out of my mouth.

"Yeah," he murmurs.

He pulls onto my driveway, and I shake myself out of my memories. They will do no good to me now. The way things were is gone forever.

"Yesterday, when I dropped you off, you said something about being hurt," Caine says and stares at me, making it hard to look away.

"I didn't say it about me." I raise a brow.

"You didn't have to, Kailey. Did someone hurt you?" His eyes narrow.

"No." I shake my head and finally rip my eyes off him.

"Kailey," he growls. "Don't lie to me. You know how good I am at figuring shit out."

I know. All those novels taught him how to think like psychopaths, or he was actually always one himself.

I open the door and get out before he has time to continue his interrogation, closing the door behind me.

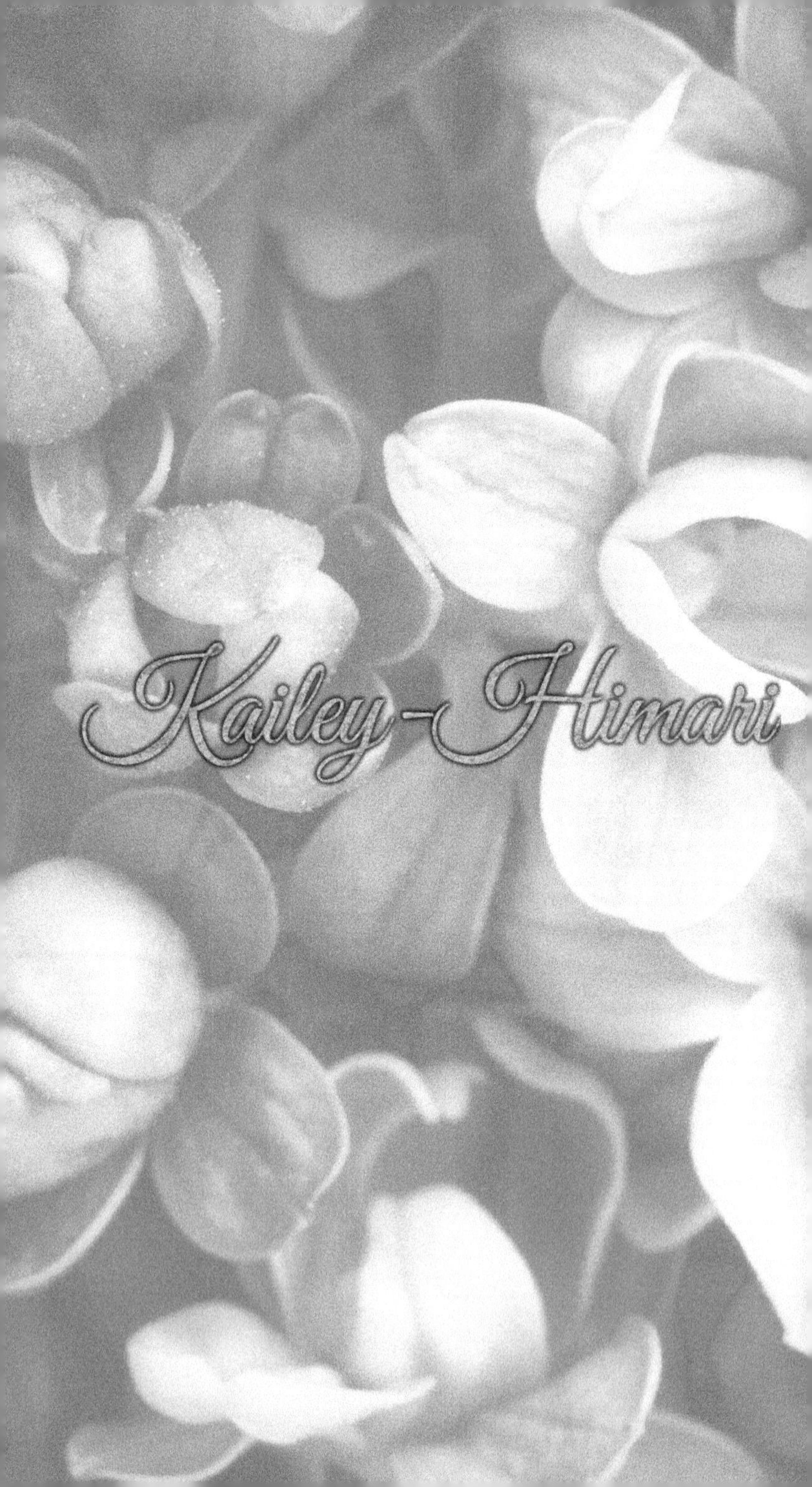
Kailey-Himari

EIGHT

"Why do you think they are doing this?" Kimmy asks later that night while we talk on the phone.

"I have an idea, but I don't have a clue how to figure it out." I sigh as the weight of my secret crushes in on me.

I pinch my Gris-Gris, still firmly attached to my left wrist, and try to calm my turbulent insides.

"Boo, I'm here if you need me. Ya know that, right?"

"Yes, I do." Because it's true. I'm just not ready to sully my papa's reputation, in case all of this is a ruse.

"It'll all work out," she assures me, and I nod.

"I should get to homework and some sleep," I mutter, and she agrees.

"Goodnight, Kimmy."

"Night, boo."

The sound of tapping wakes me up. I feel disoriented as I try to figure out where I am and what time it is. I spread out my school textbooks on my bed, noticing I am still in the clothes I wore to school earlier.

What time is it? I search under the books for my cell phone, and I am interrupted by the tapping again. Only it's not really tapping, it sounds more like hail hitting my bedroom window.

I finally find my cell phone and groan when I see it's already ten-thirty. I guess it's another late night for my papa. He usually wakes me when he gets home.

My window is assaulted again, so I sweep away the cobwebs of lingering sleep in my mind. What is hitting my window? I've only known one person to do that, and surely, it's not him … right?

I cross my room to my window. Everything is pitch black save for the yellow luminescence of the moon. I look outside and see a hooded figure. It's obviously male, but who exactly? I watch as his face turns up towards the window, but it's shadowed by the hood of his sweater. He must see my outline against the window because he lifts his hands out wide as if to ask, well?

I grab my hoodie off the back of my computer chair and throw it on as I make my way downstairs.

My curiosity is overwhelming my sense of self-preservation at this point. For all I know, it could be a serial killer. Or him.

That thought alone makes me stop dead in my tracks as fear moves like acid through my muscles, stopping them from working. It's been four years. Why would he come now? I take a few deep breaths and try to calm down. Plus, he's away at college, far enough not to just show up at my house when he feels like it.

Once I get a grip on the fear, I move to my backdoor. Yes, the guy outside is in my freaking backyard, not that it's hard to get in there, but what freaks me out most is that this guy knew which bedroom was mine. I open it up, and standing there on my back porch is the leading man in all my waking nightmares. Brody Landry.

"What the hell, Brody?" I hiss at him. He drops the hood down from his head, and I see the bruising under his left eye. "What happened to you?"

"No," he shakes his head and bends down so he's eye level with me. "What happened to you, Kails?"

"W-what do y-you mean?" I'm a stuttering mess as fear once again creeps over me and robs me of my speech and movement.

"I spoke to Caine tonight… He seems to think someone hurt you. Maybe before high school, maybe around the time you stopped talking to us." He paces the deck. "It fucking makes sense. I don't know why I didn't see it, but I was fucking livid with you!"

His final growl of frustration makes me jump, and I press my back against the door behind me. I have to get away from him.

"Nothing happened to me." I work hard to keep my voice steady and strong when all I want to do is unburden myself and tell him everything. My old best friend, the one I ran to with everything. "Caine is trying to cause a problem with our agreement."

"Was it your father?" He gets back into my face.

My mouth opens in shock, and I stare at him. "Papa? He would never hurt me."

He growls in frustration again and turns his back on me. "Why are you lying to me, Kailey?" he asks, his voice small.

"I'm not—"

"What the FUCK did I ever do to you?!" He lets loose a scream, and I jump at the noise.

"You need to go," I tell him as I watch the neighbor's porch light come on.

"Yeah," he snarls and turns to storm off towards the purple wisteria tree, planted there by Mama to frame her gazebo.

I hurry back into the house and lean against the door. What the hell was up with Brody? And where did that black eye come from? I know Caine likes to fight. He's a wrestler after all, but not just wrestling, he was always fighting someone at school. Could they have gotten into a fight?

I hear the garage door open, and I breathe a sigh of relief Brody left when he did. I don't know how I would explain to my papa that he was here or why.

I head into the kitchen and start putting together a sandwich for him. It's likely he hasn't eaten dinner yet. He comes into the kitchen, and

I turn to greet him, but the look of utter exhaustion on his face makes me gasp.

"Pa!" I exclaim. "Is everything okay?"

He waves me off and comes to kiss my cheek. "Just a day of paperwork and catch up. Nothing a good night's sleep won't cure."

I don't fully believe him, and that sends a wave of guilt crashing into me. My papa has never lied to me before, so I don't know why I'm questioning his reasons. It's Brody's fault, and that recording is constantly on loop inside my brain.

"How's school?" he asks me without really listening for a reply.

I know when he's distracted, like this when work is busy or a new season of cars is coming.

"Fine," I answer dismissively and hand him the plate with the sandwich. "Eat and get some sleep."

He nods and heads upstairs to his room. Yes, my pa works long hours, but I know he does it so he's not in this house. Too many memories of his true love, who he'll never see again. That's why I don't fault him for his absences or how little he pays attention to what's going on around me.

After my shower, I crawl into bed and cuddle with one of the many pillows. Why did Brody come here? He hasn't done that since eighth grade when his parents would fight.

He'd sneak out and hop the fence into my backyard. If it was late and I was already sleeping, he would throw the gravel from around the flower beds at my window. Then I would come down and we would sit in the gazebo and talk until he would leave, or we'd both fall asleep.

I sit up with a start. Could he be?

I jump out of bed, disregarding the fact that I am in booty shorts and a tank top. I run down the stairs and fly out the back door into the backyard.

The grass and sticks dig into my bare soles, but I carry on. I stand at the entrance of the gazebo. It's about 90 percent covered now by the low hanging purple vines. They look like beautiful, flowered curtains. I can't see inside, and I hear nothing, but I don't want to leave without checking.

DESECRATED FLESH

I push aside the cascading vines and step into the dark gazebo. When I was a kid, you could look up and see the stars through the open roof, but now it is completely blocked by wisteria.

My eyes adjust, and I scan the shadowed interior. The benches that run along each of the hexagram design's sides are bare. Of course, they are. It was foolish of me to even think he'd be here.

As I turn to leave, something on the bench closest to the entrance catches my eye. I walk over to it and see it's a short vine of wisteria. Most people would think nothing of it, it could've fallen off, but I know different. I pick it up and press my finger to the straight cut on the vine. It's wet and fresh, just cut within the last hour.

I don't realize I'm crying until I feel the tear slip down my cheek and drip onto the purple flowers. He would always cut me off a small strip every day to put in my hair and call me Princess Kails.

He must have stayed a bit after I went inside. Maybe he sat out here and waited for me, hoping I would remember. I'm overcome with sadness. The nostalgia makes me miss my old life, my normal life, my innocent life, and it makes me miss my old best friend.

But I am a different person now. Princess Kails has long died and is buried in the forest behind his house.

I throw down the wisteria and walk over it as I make my way back to the house.

R.I.P, Princess.

Kailey-Himari

NINE

I'm surprised to find Caine lounging against his truck, looking like a large cup of mocha coffee—just as hot too—the next morning.

He's wearing dark jeans, a black t-shirt, and a worn leather jacket. He has a baseball cap on his head, covering the top portion of his face, but his mouth is unobscured and sporting a cut lip. They had it out last night.

I stop on the bottom step of my front porch and look around.

"Your boyfriend has football practice on Thursday mornings. He summoned me to pick you up," he says, not with his usual hate-filled voice, more irritated.

"He's not my boyfriend," I dispute as I walk towards the passenger side.

He stops me with a hand to my stomach, and I instantly freeze. I'm so stiff, I'm sure I will crack if I try to move.

"What's with the new attire?" he asks as he runs his hand over my yellow, silk blouse. I left the top few buttons undone and let the lace of my tank peek out, and now I'm regretting it.

"You saying you like my homeless look more?" I snarl back at him, throwing his previous words in his face.

"And a skirt too. Is this leather?" He totally ignores my question and rubs the edge of the skirt between his thumb and forefinger.

I slap his hand away. "Get your hands off me."

"Why?" He wraps his arm around my waist and none-too-gently shoves me against the side of his truck, his torso pressing into mine. "Did someone hurt you? Are you scared I will?" He bends his head down to look into my face.

My heart rate skyrockets, and I feel sweat trickling down my spine. The very tips of my fingers go numb, and they feel like ice. The edges of my vision blacken, and I close my eyes to hold back the episode.

Please, I beg myself, not right now. It doesn't heed my pleas, and I am thrust through a black hole. Then I'm laid out on my stomach in the grass as my mouth fills with bile.

"Grab the bitch's hair and pull it up. I want to see her face as you fuck her tight asshole." His demand is punctuated with an evil tone.

My hair gets yanked hard, and my neck snaps back with a force that jars my brain inside my skull. The bile that was creeping up earlier now sprays from my mouth in a projectile mess and coats the ground with a foul scent.

"Stop," I moan, but it only causes them to laugh like I said something funny.

"He took a virgin hole, so now it's only fair I get one too," he growls into my ear.

The pain this time is nothing like the first. This feels like they've taken a knife and literally set it on fire then shoved it up my ass to the hilt.

My screams echo through the surrounding forest, but I know by the time it reaches the party, the music there will absorb it.

"Kailey!" I hear my name slowly breaking up my memory and pulling me back into the present. "Fuck! Kailey!" It's Caine's deep tenor that finally clears my vision in front of me.

His hat must have fallen off at some point, and his eyes are wide as his hands grip either side of my face. His touch causes tremors to begin throughout my body. As soon as he notices, he lets me go and steps back.

"What the hell was that?" he grounds out. "You're as white as a ghost, and your body is shaking so fucking hard. Kailey, what the fuck happened?"

"Just don't touch me," I say, my voice sounding weak and

breathless.

"Okay." His body deflates as he bends to pick his hat up off the ground. "I'm sorry."

I'd be shocked to hear an apology from him if I didn't feel so fucking weak and out of it.

The ride to school is quiet, and I can see Caine in my periphery, scanning me over every few seconds.

"I'm fine," I stress and continue to look out the window.

"You are not fine," he shakes his head. "You have classic PTSD."

"Excuse me? What are you? A doctor?"

"No, but it doesn't take a doctor to tell." His voice drops lower and fills with menace. "I'll figure it out, and then I will kill whoever did this."

"Why?!" I yell into the interior of his truck. "Why can't y'all just leave me alone?"

"A few days ago, ma petite, I would have agreed with you. But knowing what I know now, it changes everything."

"It changes nothing," I grit out between my teeth.

He just chuckles as he turns into the school parking lot.

"Listen," Caine says as he pulls into a spot beside Brody's Dodge Charger. "I won't say anything about what happened this morning to them, but you'll have to do something for me."

"Go ahead," I shrug him off. "I'd rather they know than do something for you." Disgust rolls through me.

"Fuck, you crazy? You think I would even want to touch you after what I saw this morning? I'm not that type of guy, even if you do look good in that top." I can see the start of a grin tug at his mouth. "But for right now, Kailey, you do not want him to know about this."

I follow his sight and see Brody standing beside a smiling Zeke.

"Fine. What do you want?"

"A name."

"No," I shake my head. "I can't."

"Fine, when?" He exhales heavily.

"Summer before freshman year," I say softly and wince as his head flies to look at me.

"The summer you stopped talking to us."

Before I can respond, there's a tapping on Caine's window. He presses the button to lower it without breaking eye contact with me.

"You guys have homeroom in the truck today?" Zeke's teasing tone breaks up some of the tension in the cab.

I open the door and round the front of the truck. "Mornin', bebelle. You look very nice today," Zeke smiles.

"Thanks, Zeke." I try to smile back, but I'm not sure how it looks.

I walk by Brody, and the weight of his stare finally has me looking up at him. "Mornin'," I say to him quietly, and he nods back to me.

"Kailey-Himari Richard!" I wince at the pitch of Kimmy's voice.

"Sounds like you're in trouble," Brody snickers, and I look back at him and catch a twinge of warmth in his eyes before he locks it away. "See you at lunch," he says dismissively and turns to go to the guys.

I jog up to Kimmy and wrap my arms around her. She's always been my anchor to this Earth without ever knowing why. I never told her what happened to me, but she's seen my episodes and knows without ever pushing me to tell her, just there when she knows I need it.

"You okay, boo?" She rubs my back.

"Yes, just a rough morning."

"Did that hulk do something to you?" I feel her body tense, and I try to restrain the laugh bubbling to the surface.

"Would you fight that hulk?" I giggle and pull back to look at her.

"I would damn well try!" Her fists lock up to her sides.

"He did nothing." She's still giving a good stink eye to the group of guys standing across the lot. "I swear." I grab her hand and pull her towards the front of the school.

"I spoke to Henry last night," she begins, and I already know where this is headed. "He said Lance was released from custody but pending the investigation, he's been suspended from Tulane and asked to leave the dorms. He'll probably be coming back here to stay with his folks, right?"

My legs freeze up, and I tremble. *He took a virgin hole, so now it's only fair I get one, too.*

"Kailey?" Kimmy looks at me with worry. "Are you feeling okay?"

"Um…" I sweat and look around frantically. I don't know what I'm looking for until he's standing in front of me.

"Kails." His ice-blue eyes scan over my face. "What happened?" He looks at Kimmy.

"She has these anxiety attacks sometimes." I hear her voice, but she sounds far away.

All I see is Brody standing in front of me, looking worried. Looking like Brody from four years ago.

"I'm going to take her to the nurse," he says and grabs my hand.

He pulls me forward, and I glance back to catch Kimmy's eye. She looks worried and anxious herself. I nod quickly at her to let her know it's fine and then stumble to keep up with Brody.

"Sorry," he mutters as he slows down. "What was she saying to make that happen?"

"I don't remember." I lie. Lie … lie … lie. It's all I do.

"What the fuck, Brody?" I hear Georgina as we pull up in the hallway with my locker.

I drop Brody's hand and walk around him to my locker. I don't owe her an explanation. She's not my problem. Besides, I didn't grab his hand.

"She's not feeling well. I was going to take her to the nurse."

"She's still as ugly as ever, but she looks just fine," she sneers in my direction. Bitch.

"Knock it off, Georgie," I hear Brody say to her. "Jealousy is a nasty thing."

I open my locker, and what I see inside causes me to fly back with a scream.

Someone has hung a dead squirrel by its head from the roof of my locker. My eyes lock on its dead and bulging ones, and I let out a garbled moan when I realize he was probably killed this way.

"Who did this?" Brody's low voice asks. He sounds calm, but I know that voice. He's livid.

"Looks like the whore made herself a few enemies," Georgina singsongs while the other three girls snicker. "Maybe someone is warning her to keep her filthy slut hands to herself."

So Casey and Connie are looking for retaliation against me for boys I don't even want. For a situation I had no choice in, what Brody forced me to do.

"You did this," he grits out between his teeth. He rips the squirrel down and lifts it up in front of Georgina's face, letting it swing.

"Kailey?" I hear Caine's voice, and then he appears in front of my face with Kimmy behind him. "What happened?"

"That was hanging in my locker." I point to the squirrel Brody throws in the nearest trash bin.

"Y'all psychotic bitches are resorting to torturing and killing animals now?" Kimmy screeches at them, and Connie is the only one who flinches.

"I didn't…" she begins, only to have Caine appear in front of her face.

"You're fucking twisted," he growls at her, and I watch as two fat tears roll down her cheeks.

"Get the fuck out of here." Brody grabs Georgina's arm and drags her away down the corridor.

Caine goes to my locker and pulls everything out, inspecting for anything else, rotten or dead. Kimmy wraps her arms around me, and we both cringe when the warning bell rings.

"You can go to class," Caine tells her then nods towards me. "I'll take care of her."

"You okay?" she asks me, and I nod.

She gives me one last squeeze then turns to rush off to her class, which is on the other side of the school.

"Here." Caine hands me a textbook. "Math first period, right? Or do you need that nurse?"

"I'm fine now," I whisper and accept the book, my eyes looking at my feet.

I know why I'm a target for the hounds. I've always known it was the guys. But today, they acted alone. They set up the most gruesome thing yet. I could take rotting carcasses, fish entrails, and bugs. To see that little guy swinging inside there, his life forcibly taken, made something inside me crumble. Just adding to my mountain of misery.

Caine walks with me to my class and waits by the door until I'm in my seat. When I sit down, I look up at him, and he gives me a quick nod. Then he turns and heads off to his class.

At lunch, I head towards the cafeteria. I feel a ball of dread tightening in my stomach, and once I step inside, I can see why. I look to the center table and not only see The Four but also the hounds. All four bitches are sitting at the table.

"Oh, heck no," I hear Kimmy's voice behind me. "We will not be sitting with them sick bitches today."

Georgina is sitting on Brody's lap, feeding him fries, and Connie is curled up against Caine's side. Caine has his arm around her shoulders, but his eyes are on me. He looks at me like he's disgusted and beyond irritated. Okay, whatever. Zeke and Faith are both bent over his phone, and Casey is trying her darnedest to get Cooper's attention.

I ignore the entire table and walk with Kimmy to the food line.

"Sha?" I turn to see Cooper. His eyes look sad, and his blond hair is curling a bit on his forehead.

He pulls me in for a hug, and instead of tensing at his touch, I like it. I relax into him and press my face against his chest, breathing in his scent.

"I'm sorry I wasn't there," he whispers.

"It's not your fault." My words are muffled by his sweater.

"You don't have to sit there today." He puts his arm around me and grabs my tray. "We'll eat out on the bleachers."

I look at Kimmy to see if she's okay with that idea, and I catch her looking at Cooper like he has two heads. I guess it is a little strange, him going against the others and hanging out with me. It really seems the girls have forgiven them.

"Don't you want to sit with Casey?" I stop and look up at him.

"No, I just want to sit with you and Kimmy here, if y'all will have me." Kimmy shrugs so I nod, and we follow her outside to the bleachers.

"I'll take you home today," Cooper says but then looks up at me. "Unless you'd rather Kimmy take you?"

"You can take me home, Coop." He's just being so damn nice… I can't help giving in.

Yes, it could be a trap. They could be gearing up to throw it all in my face. One epic throw-down in front of the school. But if I live my life like that—constantly worried—think of everything I would miss. Maybe my friendship with Cooper can be salvaged.

His smile is devastatingly handsome, and I give him one back.

"Yellow is definitely my new favorite color," he says as he looks at my shirt. I roll my eyes and hit my shoulder against his. "Just sayin'."

"What's up with Caine?" Kimmy breaks through our bubble. "I thought he was through with Connie?"

"Caine is … hard to understand. He has certain … interests Connie enjoys as well," Cooper struggles to explain without exactly explaining anything.

"Whatever," I shrug. I don't care anyway. Connie can have him and his piss poor attitude.

So why do I feel a little sad?

Cooper is humming along to a country song playing on the radio. His hair is a messy tangle of tawny waves, and his golden skin is vibrant. When he catches me watching him, his dark eyes smolder, and he shoots me one of those devilishly confident grins.

"You want me to serenade you, KH?" He smiles as I melt a little.

"No." I shake my head with a chuckle.

"Will you still come with me to Caine's party this weekend?" he asks as he pulls onto my driveway.

"I don't know…" I've never been to a high school party.

A part of me is scared to attempt it, but there's another part of me that wants to experience it before it's too late. The last party I went to literally ruined me.

"I'll stay with you all night. I won't let anything happen to you," he pleads, his eyes looking like a lost puppy's.

"Fine." I nod. It's not so much me giving in as it's me assuaging my curiosity.

"Yes!" He pumps his fist in the air and quickly leans over to kiss my cheek. His lips hit the corner of my mouth, and I gasp at the feeling.

He doesn't pull back as I slowly turn until there's less than an inch between our mouths.

"Is it going to be today, sha?" he whispers, his warm breath coating my lips.

"What?" I whisper back, keeping my eyes on his pillow soft lower lip.

His tongue comes out and swipes along it, leaving a sheen of moisture. There's an immediate reaction at the apex of my thighs, and I gasp at the foreign feeling.

"When you give me our first kiss." His mouth brushes mine with each word. "It's you who has to give it."

I'm hit with the sudden realization that I want to. It's not a feeling I'm familiar with. Usually, the thought of intimacy makes me hyperventilate followed by the sudden onset of an episode. But right now, I want to feel his lips on mine.

I close the distance between us and tentatively press my lips to his. His lips are so soft and plush. He doesn't push for more and lets me lead, which I am so thankful for.

I want more, so I press in harder and open my mouth to seal over his top lip, then his bottom. His breathing becomes erratic, but he lets me explore without probing deeper. I pull back, and my fingers immediately find my lips. That wasn't awful … at all. It was actually great.

Cooper's eyes run all over my face, and then a sweet smile pulls at the corners of his mouth. "Was that your first kiss, sha?"

I don't answer him. Instead, I grab his face between my two hands and bring him in again. This time he's running the show. He moans, and his hand grabs the back of my head to hold me in place.

I wait for that feeling of fear to creep up on me, but it doesn't. I relax and follow his lead. When his tongue swipes along my lips, I open, then he's inside. Tasting me and I'm tasting him. The way his tongue brushes along mine, the rough but smooth feeling, the warmth, all makes me moan a deep and tortured sound.

He pulls back and looks me deep in my eyes. "You okay?"

I don't know what's come over me because instead of answering, I'm diving for his mouth again. This time I want my tongue inside his mouth, feeling his ridges and teeth. His groan is long as we both become frantic.

His hand leaves my head and moves to my throat. Then he slides it along my collarbone. His skin feels so good running along mine. Then his hand grabs onto my right breast, and I freeze.

Slow tendrils of fear and disgust seep from the pit of my stomach, swirling up around my chest and burning through my throat.

Cooper pulls back when he senses the tension and looks at me with confusion.

"I'm sorry," I croak as I try to shake away the feelings. "I can't do this."

"It's okay, KH. I'm not pushing you for anything. Breathe," he soothes as he runs his hand down my hair.

The touch is innocent enough, but my body has already turned towards that night, so every touch right now feels like it belongs to them. I don't want my first kiss to be marred by their evil intentions.

"I've got to go," I say quickly and open the door.

"Wait." His hands rise into the air in surrender. "I have football again tomorrow morning. Are you good to get to school?"

"Yeah, Coop. I've been doing it for the past four years." I can feel the sensations quickening, and my skin feels clammy.

"Okay," he nods as he observes me.

"Bye," I say on an exhale before running up to my front porch.

Once I'm inside, I lock the door and slide to the floor. I can't hold it in any longer. The feelings bubble up quickly to the surface, and I sink into the black, inky pool of dread.

Kailey-Himari

TEN

"Kailey-Himari, what are you doing at one of these parties?" he calls out to me.

"Hey," I slur a little and hiccup. "Where's Brody?"

"Pool house. But I wouldn't go in there. They have chicks with them tonight." He snickers, and his friend joins in.

Both of them are smoking cigarettes, and I don't know if it's because I'm drunk, but I can kind of see why girls think they are so hot.

"I'm just going to go say, hey," I mutter and stagger towards the pool house.

"Wow, she's wasted," I hear him say to his friend, then they both laugh.

Whatever. If they knew what happened today, they would understand. I'm not telling them, though. I just want to talk to Brody. He will know what to say to make me feel better. Maybe he will make me that hot chocolate I like.

I get to the pool house and hear female laughter coming from inside. Caine's groupies again, I bet. All the girls love him because he acts like a dick and fights all the time. Only I know he's not that much of a dick. He can be thoughtful, and he's really freaking smart.

I get to the door and throw it open. I don't care, I basically live here. The first thing I see is Zeke with his hand up Faith's skirt and her head thrown back. Gross. I turn and see Connie, Caine, Casey, and

Cooper on the floor playing what looks like spin the bottle. So childish.

"Kailey!" Cooper jumps up and comes over to me. "Are you okay?"

"Yeah," tears fall off my cheeks. So not wanting these girls to see it. They are like sharks, so my tears would be like blood to them. "Where's Brody?"

"He's in the back..." I hear one girl say, but I don't stick around to hear the rest. I don't get along with them, but the guys have been hanging out with them more and more over the past few weeks.

I get to the door and open it. Inside, I see Brody in bed with Georgina.

Georgina is gorgeous with her auburn hair and big blue eyes. She's the typical Southern belle. He's over her in bed, and both are topless, soon to be without pants by the looks of it. My heart sputters then crashes to the pit of my stomach.

"Kails?" Brody jumps off of Georgina, who doesn't even bother to cover herself up. Why would she? She's perfect and already has full boobs. I don't even know when mine will come.

"Oh god..." I groan, covering my mouth with my hand.

I turn quickly and rush out of the room, jumping over the spin the bottle game.

"Kailey!" I hear Brody trying to give chase, but I'm faster and out the door before anyone can stop me.

Not that he even comes outside to find me. I guess this is how our friendship changes. He wants to date girls. It makes sense, and why would he even think of me in that way? I've been the girl who rolled in mud with him, climbed trees, and played cops and robbers. He will never see me that way, not the way I've been seeing him.

After what happened earlier, sneaking out of my room and drinking Papa's bourbon then catching Brody with someone else, I am about ready to give up. What's the point of being here when everything around me combusts and turns to ashes, floating along the wind away from me?

"There she is." I turn and see both of them are still smoking cigarettes in the same spot as before. "Why are you crying, pretty girl?"

"I..." a sob escapes, and I shake my head.

"Run up to the house, and make sure the party is okay," he says to the other with a smirk on his face. "Looks like Kailey needs a friend, right, sugar?"

I nod, then he nods his head towards the thick trees. He walks, and I hesitate. Why is he going into the trees?

"Come on," he waves his hand. "Just so we have privacy to talk."

Oh, that's considerate because I don't want Brody to come out and try to pull me away. I don't want him to see how upset I am about him and Georgina.

"Okay," I murmur and follow him through the trees.

Kailey-Himari

ELEVEN

I don't know how I got myself upstairs and onto my bed, but when the memory finally lets me go, that's where I find myself. Since the first year after it happened, I have not had this many episodes. I know what's triggering them… a lot of it is because of the guys being back in my life and the proximity they bring to what happened to me.

I need to get a handle on things and really crack down on what's happening with Pa. The longer I keep myself in this situation, the worse these episodes will be.

I get up out of my bed and leave my room. All the lights in the house are off, meaning my papa is not home yet. Lately, his days have been long, and when he finally gets home, he looks like hell.

I open the garage to make sure his car isn't here, and when I only see mine, I breathe out a sigh of relief. The door at the end of the hallway is his home office, and that's where I'm headed. He's barely in there since he's at work so much, but when Mama was alive, he was in there frequently.

I open the door, and the first thing I notice is how stale the air feels in here. At night, we usually open the windows and let the fresh breeze through the house, but this room has clearly been neglected. If the smell didn't give that away, then the thick dust on every surface certainly does.

I flick on the light and look around. The pictures on the walls are still the same. Us in Japan for a vacation to meet some of my mama's family, us at the Grand Canyon, and even one of me riding my bike without training wheels for the first time.

I sit at his large desk and open drawers. The first few are empty save for a few pens and empty file folders. The bigger drawers at the bottom contain files of car sales from ten years ago. He's locked one of the middle drawers, and no matter how much I wiggle it around, it stays firm. Something tells me I need to see inside this drawer, so I go back up to the top drawer and pull out the envelope opener I found there. I jam it into the lock on the drawer and twist it hard. I hear a crack and see I've damaged the lock and some of the surrounding wood, but good news … the drawer slides open.

The drawer literally has two sheets of papers inside. Why would he need this to be locked up? The longer I sit in here, staring at those sheets, the more apprehension I feel. What have you been up to, Papa? I pull out the papers, noting how shaky my hands are. I need to know, but I want nothing to change. He's the only family I have left. Ignorance is bliss.

I don't read them here; I don't want to disturb the surface dust and give away the fact that I've been here. If he really is in trouble, I will somehow work it out with Brody and help my papa. But if I find out Brody was lying, I will make his life a living hell.

When the door to the garage opens, I shut the door to the office. I hurry down the hallway and slip into the kitchen before he makes it there. I fold the two pieces of paper and stick them into the waistband of my skirt to open the fridge.

"There's my little lady," Pa says, sounding all kinds of tired.

"Papa, I'll make you a sandwich."

"It's okay," he waves me off as he puts his briefcase down and loosens his tie. "I grabbed a burger on the way home."

"How's the dealership?" I make conversation, trying to calm my jittery nerves.

"Busy," he exhales. "Looks like I'll have to hire a few part-timers so I can be home in the evenings."

"Charlie Richard." I place my hands on my waist. "You should've done that long ago. You look like literal death."

"Thanks, sweetie," he chuckles and ruffles my hair. He finally takes in my outfit, and his brows hit his hairline. "Do you have a boyfriend?"

"What?"

"You've been different since school started. A good different. I just wondered if it was for a boy."

"Please, Pa." I roll my eyes. "I did this for myself. Boys are never worth a female's effort to look good. That's why she should always do it for herself first."

"That's my baby." He nods and leaves the kitchen. "I'm going to sleep like I look, literal death."

I chuckle and shake my head. My pa is a charming Cajun man. He's funny and still has golden looks that haven't aged too much. He could easily have another wife, but he loved my mama too much to move on.

The papers resting against my back crinkle, reminding me of their existence and taking the good mood with it.

I walk slowly to my room, my back crinkling the entire way there. I want to see what these say, even though I know not every answer can be on two sheets of paper. Either I will have to continue looking or bring what I find to Brody. The latter is the last thing I want to do.

Once I'm in my room, I crawl up onto my bed. I pull the papers from out of my skirt and sit there just looking at the folded pieces for a bit. I'm so nervous I can feel the bile swirling its way out of my stomach. The burning sensation of fear is almost all-consuming.

I quickly unfold them and lay them both flat. It takes me a minute to understand what I'm reading, but once I do, I'm confused about why it was locked up. It's sensitive information, but most people have these kept in a folder with a will or estate value.

The first sheet is a life insurance plan for yours truly. According to this, if I were to have an accidental death, I am worth two hundred and eighty thousand dollars. I set it aside and pull the next one in front of me.

This is a life insurance plan for Sara Richard. Hers is significantly more at five hundred and thirty thousand dollars. Makes sense. When we lost her, we lost a certain way of life, and I know money doesn't replace that, but it helps. If I was younger than what I was, it could've been used for a nanny or extra childcare.

I fold the papers back up and tuck them into my side table. For now, the information will stay with me. I don't see the significance of telling any of them about it. But like I thought, I have to dig around a bit more. If my Pa is having money trouble, I think I would see more proof. There was nothing in his office alluding to that. No statements, no past due notices, nothing.

Tomorrow officially brings the end to my first week of senior year, and it already feels like an entire month went by. The amount of shit that's happened and the current situation I'm in is overwhelming.

I make a promise to myself here and now… I will find out everything about Brody's accusations, and then I will save myself from their evil clutches.

Then I picture Cooper's face, and my heart palpitates. If he's sincere, I may just want him to stay in my life. But if I find out this is a game, and he's the ringleader, I will make him wish he never knew me.

The next morning, I find I have a little extra pep in my step. I get to take my damn self to school today. Never thought I'd be this excited to do so. I open the front door, humming a song when I stop at the scene in front of me. Sitting in my driveway is a matte black Dodge Charger, and leaning against it is none other than Brody Landry.

"Heard your boy has practice today. Figured you weren't wanting Caine here after seeing him back with Connie at lunch yesterday."

"I can drive myself," I grit out between my clenched jaws. "Get off my driveway."

"Now, now, Kails." He tsks. "Let's keep this cordial."

"Brody, get lost," I huff and move towards my car, which he has effectively blocked in with his.

"Don't make me come get you, Kails. You know I will. What will the neighbors think when they see me carrying you? Even better …

when they hear you scream? I'll tell you though, this…" he grabs his dick through his jeans and pumps it, "will fucking love it."

I stand transfixed, my mouth slightly ajar and my core pulsing in unexpected need. I can't look away from his hand squeezing his junk, and it's only when he chuckles I realize what I must look like.

"Fuck," I hiss and move towards his car. Pick your battles and all.

"Good girl," he purrs, and again, I can feel myself get heated.

The first few minutes of driving are quiet. He hasn't turned on the radio, and he just keeps drumming his fingers on the steering wheel. But I will say this: he smells absolutely divine. His cologne is like a mix of musk and smoky wood, so intoxicatingly good.

His black hair against his pale skin shines like he's run some gel through it, and his bottom lip has been firmly stuck between his teeth. It's been his nervous habit since we were kids. I don't think he remembers I know that.

"Can I ask you something?" he finally breaks the silence.

"Do I have a choice?"

"No." I wave him on. "Where did you go that night when you found me in bed with Georgina?"

"What?" My heart is literally lodged in my throat and pounding out a deafening rhythm into my ears.

"The night we had the party, literally the last night you spoke to me. I couldn't find you."

"I don't remember," I mutter.

"You were extremely drunk, I could see it in the way you swayed on the spot. Why did you run, though?"

"It probably embarrassed me, seeing you naked with a girl for the first time," I shrug, my voice sounding so small.

"Hmm," he nods. "I heard you retaliated, though."

"Retaliated?"

"Got back at me, with multiple guys too." He side-eyes me as he drives.

"Why would I retaliate, Brody?" I turn to look at him. "I didn't care."

"Just what I heard," he shrugs, and that's the end of the conversation.

DESECRATED FLESH

Kailey-Himari

TWELVE

The last day of the school week drags on. It's finally lunchtime, but it really feels like my day should be ending.

I follow Kimmy into the cafeteria and smell jambalaya right away. We stand in the line, and I have Kimmy behind me giving me the play-by-play of what's happening at The Four's table.

"Looks like Connie isn't sitting there today," she whispers. "No Casey either. Brody and Georgina look cozy, though."

I don't know why that makes me feel angry, but I do.

"Cooper is looking around. Okay, he's spotted us. He's coming over now."

"Sha." His honey voice spreads over me. "You got to school okay, I heard."

"Yeah," I say and nod at him. "Did you tell Brody to pick me up?"

"No, I actually told him to let you drive yourself. Sorry." He smiles a little and shrugs.

"It's fine. How was football?" Coop is our star quarterback. When we have games, he's who everyone comes out to see. He has a full scholarship to Tulane. He's that good.

"Coach is riding us hard this year. He wants State again."

"You'll get it, Coop. Just like every other year you've been on the team," I tell him.

"Have you been keeping track of my football career, sha?" He leans forward and places a sweet kiss on my mouth.

"Cooper!" I hiss at him and look around the cafeteria.

The table with the guys looks mostly preoccupied, all except for Caine who's staring a hole right through my head.

"Let him stare," Kimmy growls. "Maybe he should try a little harder if he wants it that bad."

"Amen, sister!" Cooper gives her a high-five, and both of them laugh.

"Can you not?" I shake my head and grab my tray of jambalaya. It's unnerving how Kimmy is accepting of the fact I may or may not be dating more than one boy.

"Come sit at our table today." Cooper looks from Kimmy to me, knowing it's a packaged deal.

That's when I notice a new face striding into the cafeteria. He looks too old to be a student but too young to be a teacher.

"Who is that?" I ask.

Both Kimmy and Cooper turn to look at the male now grabbing a tray at the lunch line. Some teachers also eat the cafeteria food when they stay during their lunch hour.

"Oh, shoot!" Kimmy exclaims. "I totally forgot to tell you, that's our new guidance counselor, Oliver Ballon."

"He used to go to high school here. He's fresh out of college," Cooper adds on.

"Did Mrs. Gregory retire?" I ask them.

"Not sure," Kimmy shrugs, and Cooper shrugs with her.

I watch the new guidance counselor as we move with the line to the end. He has a shaved head and skin the color of hazelnuts, dark gold. As if feeling my eyes on him, he looks up, and I am caught in the liquid, metallic pools of his eyes. I've never seen eyes like his, light steel-gray orbs swirling around black pupils. His jet-black brows pull together as he continues to look at me, his full lips slightly turned down in thought.

"Allons, boo," Kimmy chuckles as she pulls on my arm. "You're making him uncomfortable as you hold up the line."

"Shit," I curse and hurry to follow Cooper to the table.

I place my tray down, and with little thought, sit down beside Caine. Nobody notices since they are in deep conversation about the fresh addition to J.F. Kennedy.

"Ballon used to go here like six years ago," Caine says around a mouth of jambalaya.

"So he's what? Twenty-four?" Georgina purrs as she watches him sit at a table with a few other teachers.

"Around that. He was a few years older than Justin when he went here," Brody answers then rolls his eyes at her. "Don't waste your time. I heard he's gay."

"All the gorgeous ones are," Kimmy murmurs from beside me, making me giggle.

"What are you laughing at, cow?" Georgina sneers at me.

"None of your business, bitch," I throw back at her as Caine chokes beside me.

She leans forward on the table right across from me, slapping her hands down. "Listen, you whore—" She doesn't get to finish her sentence as Brody pushes her off his lap and onto the bench seat.

"Knock it off, Georgina. Quit starting shit," he growls at her.

"Aargh!" she exclaims as she gets up from the seat and storms off with Faith following close behind her.

"Now you've done it. You won't get your dick sucked for at least a week," Caine snickers.

"Good thing you're having a party tonight. Maybe I'll find a willing mouth or two until she calms down," Brody replies while looking at me.

Right, the party I agreed to go to with Cooper before we made out in his Jeep.

"Kimmy, you could come too," Cooper says.

"Can't. I've got a Skype date with the hottest football player I know." She smiles widely at him.

"How's Henry liking Tulane?" Cooper asks her. "I can't wait until next year."

"He says it's tough, but he's enjoying himself."

They chat about college football, the pressure, and the scouts for the NFL, but I tune them out. I can't seem to get those gray eyes out of my mind. If he's taken over Mrs. Gregory's job, then it's only a matter of time until I'm sitting in front of him.

I have been seeing Mrs. Gregory once a month since I've been here. She was helping me deal with my mama's death and the workload of high school. It was her I confessed to about the bullying, and she helped me pick out a university and major that would get me away from here.

"Earth to KH," Cooper breaks up my thoughts.

"What?" I look around the table at everyone staring at me.

"I'm picking you up tonight at eight. Be ready." Cooper raises his brows.

"And dress in proper clothing," Caine butts in as he gets up from the table.

"Fine." I lift my chin in the air. "Cooper, I will need a pair of your sweatpants."

Caine groans and leaves the cafeteria behind Brody. Kimmy leans over and kisses my cheek then disappears as well.

"I can't wait to see you wearing my clothes. You can have whatever you want." Cooper smirks, and I squirm at the reaction my body is having to him.

I get up and flick his ear. "I'll see you at eight."

I take my tray and walk it back to the food line. I rarely do this. We usually leave them at the tables, but I need one last look. I walk by the teachers' table, and as if sensing me, his head pops up from his bowl of jambalaya. Our gazes lock again as I slowly walk by. What is it that's pulling me to him? He's like a magnet my eyes just can't pull away from.

He's the first to drop his head and continue to eat. I get to the line and drop my tray in the dirty pile before turning my back to leave the cafeteria. When I reach the double doors, I risk one final look back. There are those eyes, watching me as I leave. Once in the hallway, I release the breath I'm holding.

Get it together, Kailey-Himari, I chastise myself. That's a fucking teacher.

I guess my hormones have finally caught up with me. After years of not being able to think of boys, I'm being bombarded now.

It happens in the fourth period. I have my head down, reading the pages we were given, and the door opens. I don't look until I hear my name. It's the secretary from the admin office, and my teacher points me out to her.

"Kailey-Himari?"

"Yes?" I look at her.

"Could you come with me?" The surrounding kids whisper and some snicker.

I grab my bag and put everything away inside. "Bring it all with you, you may not be back today."

The whispers become ohs like I'm in trouble, and I roll my eyes as I walk to the front of the class.

"What is this about?" I ask as I follow her down the hallway.

"Guidance requested you."

My heart gallops against my ribcage, and I can feel sweat gathering under my shirt. Mrs. Gregory always called for me in the mornings, so I wasn't prepared for this.

I continue to follow her straight to Mrs. Gregory's—Mr. Ballon's now—office. "Thank you." I smile at her before she nods and heads back to the main office. I take a deep breath and knock on the door.

"Come in." His deep voice penetrates through the door. It's a man's voice, and it sounds commanding.

I open the door and stick my head in. "You called for me?"

His eyes come up and meet mine. I may imagine it, but it looks like they widen in shock for a split second. He clears his throat and stands. "Kailey-Himari?"

I come inside and close the door behind me. "Yes, sir," I nod.

His nostrils flare slightly, and he gives me a quick once-over. "While we're in here, you can call me Oliver."

I raise my eyebrows and nod. I have never called a teacher by their first name.

"Have a seat." He points to the chair on the other side of his desk, and I do as he requests. "Kailey-Himari, is that Japanese?"

"Yes, my mama was Japanese."

"It's nice." He smiles slightly, and my heart picks up again at the sight. He is truly a beautiful man.

"Thank you."

"I called you here so I can make introductions. I can see you were a student Mrs. Gregory saw on a monthly basis. We will continue those meetings."

"What happened to Mrs. Gregory?" I ask him.

"She took a leave of absence; she has an ill family member." His deep tenor is doing something to my insides.

"Oh. I see."

"So, Kailey-Himari, I read over your file—"

"While we're in here, you can call me Kailey." I repeat his earlier sentiment and watch as those gray eyes swirl just a little darker.

"Okay." He clears his throat. "Kailey, I read here about your mother. I am sorry about that. How are you coping this year?"

"It's still difficult, but I'm managing."

"And I read you were also being bullied by some students. Were you not sitting with a few of them at lunch today?"

So he saw me, he noticed me. "It's better this year," I nod.

"They've made amends?"

"Something like that," I mumble.

"In this room, you can tell me anything, okay? Judgment free zone."

"We worked it out." I nod at him.

"All right." He sounds reluctant to let it go. "How about I see you every two weeks? It's your final year, and we should monitor your grades and start applying to colleges."

"Every two weeks?"

"Yes, I think it would be beneficial if we got to know each other so you can feel comfortable talking to me."

I don't think I will ever feel comfortable talking to him like I did to Mrs. Gregory. I wasn't attracted to her. She didn't make me want to find out how her lips would feel pressed against mine or what she looked like under her shirts.

"Kailey?"

"Sorry what?" I shake my head.

"Is there anything you want to discuss today? Maybe you have some questions about me?"

"You used to go to school here?" I ask.

"Ah," he chuckles. It's so smooth and dark as it ripples over me. "That's already made its rounds, huh? Yes, I graduated from this school five years ago. Went to college and came back here as soon as there was an opening."

Five years older than me. That's not too bad. It makes him twenty-three. Not a crazy difference. I shake out my head again because I shouldn't be having these thoughts about my guidance counselor.

The last bell rings as I stand. "Thank you, sir."

"Oliver," he corrects me with a small smile. "Before you leave, I want you to know you can come here anytime. If there's something you need to talk about, you don't have to wait for our appointments."

"Okay, Oliver." I test his name out on my tongue and decide I like it. "Have a good night."

"You too, Kail."

Kail, he's given me a personalized name. I bite into my lower lip and smile at how much I like the sound of it. I give him a small wave and head out to my locker. He's just as gorgeous as the Golden Four, but he's a man.

"I've been given permission to drop you home." I hear Kimmy's voice behind me, and I turn with a laugh. "They are mighty protective of you."

"Cooper, you mean." I shake my head and smile.

"No, it was Brody today." She raises her brow as I shrug her off.

"He's just controlling. By the way," I turn back to my locker. "I met with Mr. Ballon today."

"No way!" she squeals. "Tell me, is he just as gorgeous up close?"

"Yes," I hiss at her and laugh when she squeals again.

"Let's get you home so you can prepare for your very first high school party." She coos as she wraps her arm around my shoulders. "But first a pit-stop at my place so you can borrow an outfit and some makeup."

"Okay," I agree. I was nervous about this party, since the last one I was at left me raped and discarded in the woods.

But now, knowing I have Cooper to take care of me, I'm feeling excited.

DESECRATED FLESH

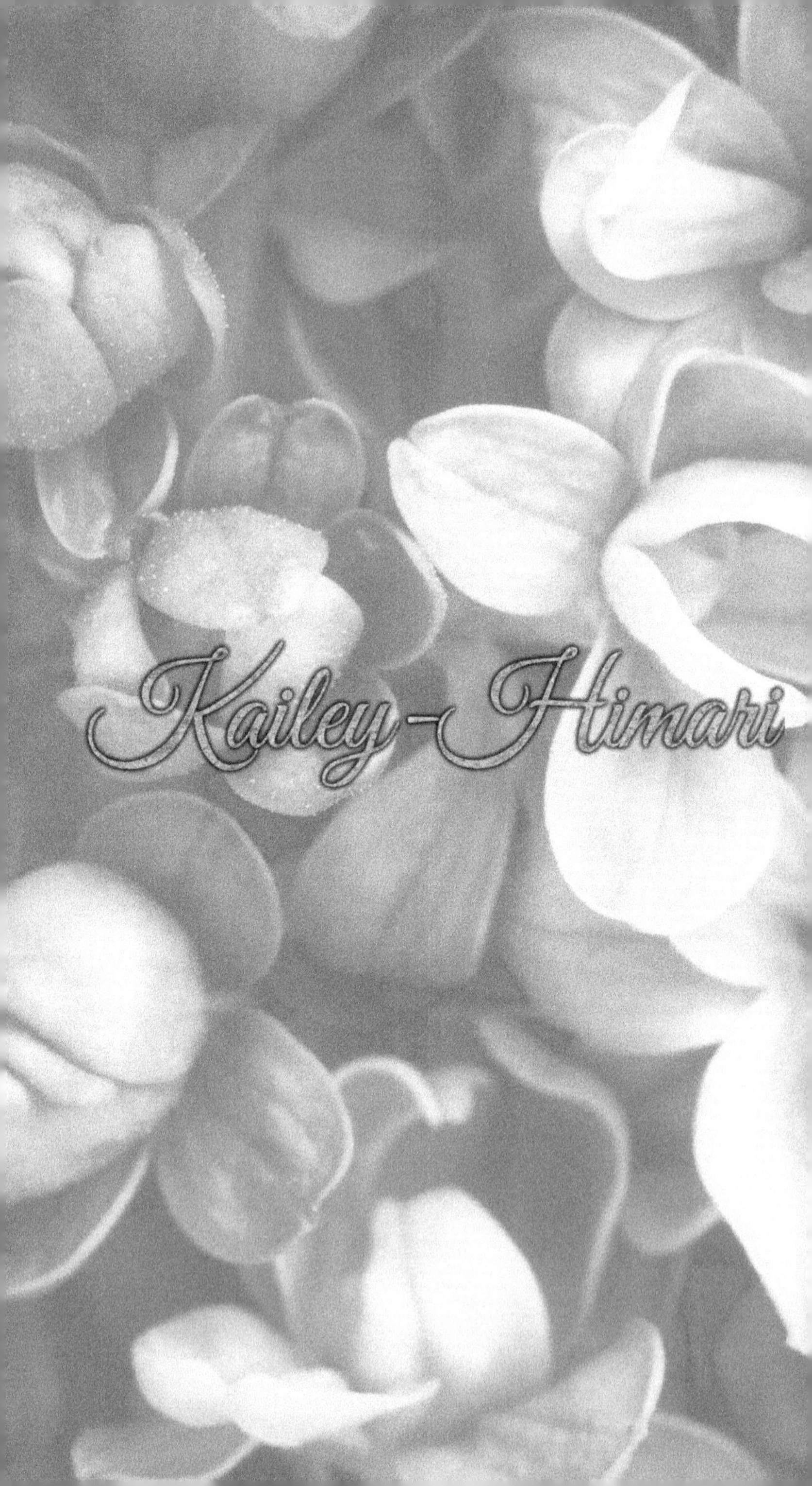
Kailey-Himari

THIRTEEN

I'm dropped off back home with a killer outfit and shoes I'm sure will actually kill me. Kimmy gave me some ideas about hair and makeup then told me to 'take no prisoners.'

My hair ends up a mass of curls that bounce and shine in a half up, half down hairdo. For my makeup, I give myself a smokey eye that brings out the green in the hazel and a dark red lip that emphasizes the pouty shape. Finally, the leather corset top coupled with a white, flowing skirt that hits just above the knee with a slit to mid-thigh and a pair of red bottoms to break my neck.

I leave a note for my father about where I'm going and tell him to eat and sleep. Eight o'clock on the dot, I hear the horn of a familiar Jeep and take a deep breath as my stomach flips in anticipation. This is it. I can do this. I've come a long way, and I refuse to let what happened to me cripple me as a victim forever.

With a quick check to my corset top and a fluff to my hair, I open the front door and step out carefully onto the porch. I sway a little in the heels but take my time shutting the door and locking it. When I turn around, Cooper is standing at the bottom of the stairs with a shocked look on his face.

"KH," he breathes. "You look amazing."

He doesn't look so bad himself. Tonight, he's wearing a pair of gray slacks and a black, long-sleeved Henley pushed up to the elbows.

His hair is slicked back and looks darker from the gel in it.

"You look fantastic too, Coop." I give him another once-over.

He leans in and places a sweet kiss on my mouth. As soon as I feel his lips on mine, I step in closer to him and grab handfuls of his shirt, keeping him close. His groan spurs me on as I lick the seam of his mouth, moaning when he opens, and our tongues tangle together. I pull away and watch him look at me with hooded lids and wet lips. I can't help but think my hormones are now in overdrive. How many guys do I even want right now?

"Let's go before I forget what we're supposed to be doing and do what the fuck I want us to be doing." He turns and opens the passenger door for me.

"Was that supposed to make sense, Cooper?" I snicker and get in the seat.

"Yes, to us guys who have pined over a girl for years and are finally getting their chance." He winks and closes the door.

Pined over for years? That can't be true. They were bullying me for years.

That thought simmers off my lusting thoughts, and I right myself before he gets in. I can't soften up now. Forgiveness can't be given easily for something that has been happening for so long.

Caine lives on a sprawling estate near the bayou. The cypress trees here look beautiful and haunting, hanging low with their vines dragging along the ground. His house is the largest among The Four, but I know he hates to be there, especially if his parents are home.

His father is an angry drunk—much like Brody's—and his mother is a recluse who locks herself away. Caine once told me he was raised by nannies and preferred them to his mother. He is an only child, bred for the continuation of the family name. He said if he'd been a girl, he's sure his parents would have aborted and tried again. The thought is depressing.

We drive up his winding driveway. On each side are rows of cypress trees creating a daunting tunnel. Finally, it opens up at the end to a large manor home stretching on for what seems like forever. Leblanc Manor, as it's come to be known. With the sun setting, the twinkling lights coming from the multiple windows make the place look serene and majestic. Very few know how far from the truth that actually is.

We round the driveway and stop in front of the large wrap-around porch. Two men stand at the entrance, and two others hurry to each car. A Leblanc party is always known for its extravagance whether it's held by the parents or the son.

We exit the car, and I watch as Cooper hands over his keys to the valet then walks towards the front. The two men move aside as soon as they see Cooper, bidding 'Mr. Fontenot' a good night. They don't bother giving me a second glance, and I can't help but feel relieved. I can only hope that's how the rest of my night will be.

Cooper grabs my hand and looks at me with an excited grin on his face. He looks adorable, so I give him one of my own.

"Sha…" He stops just in front of the double entrance doors. The music is blaring, and I can literally see the doors vibrating with the beat. "Just stick with me, okay?"

"Okay," I agree. That was the plan this whole time.

He squeezes my hand and opens the door. The heavy beat of a hip-hop song rushes at me, and I feel like I'm slapped in the face by the level of noise released. When I get my bearings, I look around. A lot of students from school are here. They look drunk, and some are practically dry humping each other to the beat of the music. I can see some older people here as well, college age. No one wants to miss out on a Four party, except me. I was all too willing to miss out on every one of them.

Cooper continues to lead me away from the thumping bass and passes the half-naked couples all over the place. We get to a large kitchen, and I suck in a breath at the pure opulence of it. Everything gleams from the lights reflecting off the shining surfaces. The white and gray marble floors are waxed to perfection, and the matching stone tops are pristine and clean. The white cabinets shine, the stainless-steel appliances sparkle, and the eggshell white walls top off the white perfection. This kitchen is easily the size of my family room and kitchen combined.

"Caine's place is over the top," Cooper grumbles as he grabs a few beers from the fridge. He offers me one, and I shake my head.

"Miss Perfect doesn't drink?" I hear a sneer behind me and turn.

Standing there are Caine, Brody, and Zeke. Caine has his usual resting bitch face on, Brody just looks bored and irritated, and Zeke smiles at me with a wink.

"No, I don't," I shake my head.

"Have the drink," Caine says.

"No," I stand my ground. I haven't drank since that night four years ago, and that's not changing tonight.

"Have. The. Drink. I. Said," Caine punctuates each word forcefully through his teeth.

I don't let his attitude faze me. I refuse to let him scare me into doing something I don't want to. "And I said no," I shrug.

"When was the last time you drank?" Zeke asks quietly.

"Before freshman year." I avoid eye contact.

"That party?" Brody cuts in. I nod and lift my eyes to his when I hear him chuckle. "Makes sense. I heard you were a slut that night."

The words cut through my chest and slice directly into my heart. I feel like I'm bleeding out all over the immaculate, shining floors.

"Fuck the drink," Cooper says softly and leads me out into the backyard. I vaguely hear them whispering and snickering behind me.

Once we get to the backyard, the sounds of the cicada's thrum through me, and I close my eyes to gather my emotions.

"To be fair, I remember that night. You were pretty wasted." He leans against the railing. "When you ran from the bedroom and into the night, we were shocked. Brody ran out behind you a few minutes later, but you were gone. When we got up to the main house and asked around for you, a few guys commented that you were giving out free blowies in the woods. Crushed my little black heart." He says the last part quietly.

"None of that is remotely close to the fucking truth," I say. The anger lacing my words not only surprise Cooper, but me as well.

"What is the truth?" he asks.

"Maybe one day, Coop." I plead with my eyes for him to drop it.

"Let's get back in before they come looking for us."

He grabs my hand again and leads me through the house.

Everyone has congregated in the family room where the music is the loudest, and The Four are sitting at a table with people gathered around them.

"I knew they would pull this one out." Cooper grins as he rubs his hands together.

He leads me straight through the crowd—everyone parting for one of their kings—and right up to the large round table. The Four aren't the only ones sitting here. The hounds are as well, and as soon as Casey sees my hand in Coop's, she rolls her eyes and clenches her jaw.

But those bitches aren't the reason my breath is locked up, and my fingers are numb. Sitting right beside Brody is none other than Lance Kilmer. He looks up from their conversation and locks eyes with me. His face practically glows with perversion as he looks me over. The vomit threatening to coat everyone is being held back by sheer will.

"Kailey Richard." His disgusting voice hits me over the music. "You look ravishing."

I want to leave. Cooper looks at me with a question in his eyes as he tightens his hand. I can't have any of them find out what happened. No one would believe me.

"What's wrong?" Cooper asks against my ear. With Lance watching, every touch or wisp of breath makes me want to pass out.

"Where's the bathroom?" I ask him.

He points back out the way we came, and I take off out of the room. Is he here as well? I lean my back against the wall and try to calm my breathing, letting my head tip back. I should've thought of this. Kimmy told me he was home. I should've known he'd show up. This is his type of scene. A lot of young girls for the picking.

"Bebelle, I knew you weren't needing the bathroom. Your face was as white as a sheet." At the sound of Zeke's voice, I open my eyes, and I'm stunned to feel a tear slide down my cheek.

He slowly makes his way to me, afraid I'll run maybe, then leans against the wall beside me. "He's cruel because you were the first girl to hurt him, and probably the last."

"What?" I look at him with my confusion clear.

"Brody, and what he said to you earlier." They think that's why

I'm upset? It's better than the truth.

"Yeah, just hard to hear it," I nod.

"You should come back now," he motions back towards the room where my veritable nightmare is sitting. "They'll come looking, and I think it's better me than Brody or Caine." Or Lance.

"Okay," I sigh. He gets up off the wall and walks back to where I hastily left.

We get back to the room, and Faith is waiting right beside the entrance. As soon as she sees Zeke, she tugs him to her side and literally hisses at me. Fucking ridiculous. I roll my eyes when she grabs his face and sticks her tongue down his throat. Good stuff, bitch.

I slowly reach the table, after a forceful pep talk with my fear, and find Cooper sitting across from Lance.

"Sha." His hand comes out to grab mine. "Sit with me."

He pulls me onto his lap, and his arms go around my waist, his face in my hair. I catch the ice of Brody's gaze on me as his lip turns into a sneer. I will have to accept that he will always hate me.

"Who's first?" Zeke asks as he sits and pulls Faith onto his lap. She shoots me a look of disgust and flips me off.

"You piss everyone off," Coop chuckles into my ear. I want to laugh along with him. Hell, I'd love to smile right now, but I can feel Lance leering.

"Me." Lance jumps at the bottle laying on its side in the center of the table. "There's a certain someone I'm hoping for." Thank God he doesn't look at me because everyone is watching him.

He spins the bottle and I watch—internally praying—as it rotates. Please don't land on me. It slows as my palms sweat, passing me once, twice, slowly on three, then barely inches by me to land on Connie. The excitement in her eyes is clear as she licks her lips and looks at Lance expectantly.

"Caine, brah," Lance smirks at Caine. "You okay with this?"

"It's the name of the game," he shrugs nonchalantly, but I can see he's tense and eyeing Connie as she looks like the cat that got the cream.

Connie gets up from her seat and stalks towards Lance who leans back in his chair and spreads his legs wide. She steps between them, placing her hands on Lance's shoulders, and his hands come up to grab her ass. I quickly look at Caine who's watching the scene like someone bored out of their mind.

When I turn back, it looks like they are sucking each other's face off. It's sloppy; nothing about it looks attractive.

"Gross," I shudder, and Cooper squeezes me as I feel his chest vibrate with laughter.

I look back at Caine again as Connie and Lance continue to go at it and find him looking at me. His tongue comes out to run along his bottom lip, and his eyes are darkened with lust. Does watching his girlfriend make out with someone else do it for him? To each their own, I guess. They finally break apart, and Connie's red lipstick is smeared all over both of their faces.

Georgina does a slow clap as Faith giggles in Zeke's lap. Weird bunch of people. It's unnerving, how they don't mind passing each other around.

"My turn," Brody says, and he bends over the table and spins the bottle. He gives me a haughty look as he sits back down in his chair.

The bottle spins, and as it slows, I wonder how I will feel if it lands on me. When we were best friends, I always imagined what Brody's kiss would be like. Was he a soft kisser, passionate, or was he the type to devour a girl's mouth? I used to wonder about that a lot, but not anymore.

The bottle slows and stops between Faith and I. Caine smirks and shoots me a look full of mischief.

"Looks like you get to choose," he snickers at Brody.

"That's an easy decision." Brody rolls his eyes and motions for Faith to come to him.

Zeke looks unaffected and pats her butt as she gets up out of her seat. This shouldn't surprise me given the fact they've been playing this since eighth grade, and Brody not picking me is actually a good thing.

Cooper rubs my thigh soothingly. Maybe he thinks I'm offended. It's sweet that he cares. Faith leans down, and Brody gives her a chaste kiss on the mouth.

"Wrong choice, if you ask me," Lance says and throws me a wink. I gag, and Caine barks out a laugh.

Caine reaches for the bottle and spins it hard. The thing skips a few times as it's spinning. Cooper stops paying attention to the bottle and is running his nose up and down my neck. I tense up, not because of what he's doing, but because of the pair of eyes that have barely left me since I've sat down. I don't want to be in the same room as Lance.

"Well, well, well," Caine says smugly. I look at the bottle and see the neck pointing straight at me. It literally couldn't be any more perfectly on me. I look at Cooper behind me, and he's hiding a grin on my shoulder.

"Go on then," I shoulder bump him. "Caine is waiting for your smooch."

Caine rolls his eyes. "Get over here, Kailey."

I look around the table. The girls are all looking at me with matching smirks, figuring I won't do it, and the guys just look plain bored. Except for Lance... He looks like he can't wait to see it. Makes sense. He'd want to see a girl look totally unwilling in sexual encounters, being a rapist and all.

"The longer you take," Caine licks his lips, "the longer the kiss."

"Fuck," I grumble and get up out of my chair.

I stride over to him in record time because I don't want his lips on me for any longer than they have to be. I bend over towards him with an exaggerated pucker and close my eyes.

He laughs as he lifts me up onto his lap. My skirt's slit slides up to my waist as I straddle him. I watch him with surprised eyes as he looks to the slit and slowly rakes his eyes up my body, stopping at my lips. I feel him harden between my legs, then he presses up into my thin, lacy underwear.

Nope, this is fucking uncomfortable. Everyone is looking, and I don't have to play any game I don't want to. This isn't fucking kindergarten. I shake my head and try to get up off him, but his hand shoots out and wraps around my throat. I instantly still and look at him in shock. He doesn't squeeze, he's just holding it, but I don't underestimate any of The Four. I know he's more than capable of snapping my neck.

"Kiss me, ma petite, and make it good." I shiver at the graveled tone in his voice but don't move to kiss him. His eyes narrow, and his hand tightens in warning around my throat.

Fuck it. I lean in for a quick peck, but Caine has another idea. Maybe Connie really pissed him off, and he's taking this opportunity to fuck with her. As soon as my lips touch his, he keeps me still with his hand around my throat and forces his tongue into my mouth. The heat of his mouth, the taste of expensive bourbon on his tongue, and the hardness of him between my thighs causes a shiver to wrack my body. Everything feels heightened, and Caine has just overloaded my senses. I try to control my body, but it's no use. I feel myself rub along his hardness, and he groans fiercely into my mouth, devouring me like I'm his last meal.

"You can't be fucking serious," I hear Connie whine as I try to pull away from his mouth.

He has a firm hold on my throat still and doesn't let me pull back too far. Our lips are still brushing, and our labored breaths are mingling. "I think I finally see what Cooper meant." His words make his mouth press into mine.

"Let me go," I say to him, my voice raspy and rough from arousal.

He nods and releases me. I get up off his lap and look down at the evidence of how much he actually enjoyed that. I avert my eyes quickly and walk back over to Cooper. He holds his arm out as I plop back down onto his lap.

"Told you," Lance chuckles while slapping Brody on the shoulder. "You chose wrong."

"That's it," I growl and get up out of Cooper's lap. "I'm out."

"Sha." I hear Cooper, but I'm already halfway across the room and back out into the hallway.

"Why are you leaving in such a hurry?" Lance's voice halts my retreat, and I turn back to look at him.

"Because you're here." I try to sound strong, but the fear seeps out and causes my voice to crack.

"Thought you'd be happy to see me," he drawls as he slowly walks towards me. "With our history."

I back up, but he continues to come forward. I don't want to turn my back on him because just the thought of what he's done behind my back before makes me want to pass out.

"Lance, stay away from me," I warn him, finally working some grit into my voice.

"Oh, my girl toughened up?" he chuckles.

"I am not your girl." Bile burns a path up my throat.

"You don't think so?" His eyes flash with intensity.

I hasten backwards but end up stumbling on the sky-high heels and falling against the wall. He takes that opportunity to stalk forward and grab my throat, exactly how Caine had earlier. Only difference is Caine did it with passion, Lance is doing it from a vile place.

"I think we need another trip to the woods," he growls into my ear then licks the shell. "Give you a reminder of what I'm capable of."

I push against his chest, digging my nails in when he grips me tighter, and I can feel my air supply dwindle. I grab onto his arm with both of my hands, but he's so strong.

"This is how I like to see girls, barely breathing and at my complete mercy." He grinds his pelvis into my stomach, and I can feel the truth in his statement.

My vision grows gray and fuzzy around the edges, and my lungs strain from the lack of oxygen. The more I struggle, the harder he grows and presses it against me. It's like I'm stuck in one of my flashbacks, and I can't change the outcome of what's happening. His other hand slides up my thigh, and he cups my mound in his hand. He clenches his fingers, and pain courses through my body.

He licks across my cheek and pushes into my mouth. I can't stand his scent or the taste he's leaving inside my mouth, so I clamp my teeth down so hard onto his tongue, and instantly I taste his blood. He jumps back with a roar, giving me just enough space to run and escape him. I rush out onto the front porch, and the two security guards startle.

"Are you okay, miss?" one asks with genuine concern in his eyes.

"Could you please call me an Uber?" I keep looking behind me, but Lance hasn't followed me out. Not with these men out here.

The security guard calls me an Uber, and I sit on the porch to wait for it. My phone vibrates in my bra, and I pull it out.

Cooper: Where are you?

Me: Sorry, called an Uber. Looks like high school parties just aren't my thing.

Cooper: I could've taken you home.

Me: It's okay, I'll call you TMR.

Cooper: K.

His response sounds like he may be slightly pissed I left, but I can't seem to find a fuck to care right now. One of my rapists accosted me again, and I barely got away. I am thankful I didn't drink. It's what ensured I had a level head and complete control over my body. I barely got away as it was.

My Uber pulls up, and thankfully, it's an older woman. I'm just super skittish about men right now. I thank the security and get inside.

I can feel the waves of fear clinging to me as I shake in the backseat. The rest of this weekend is going to be torture, and I only have myself to blame for putting myself in this situation.

Kailey-Himari

FOURTEEN

The smell of foliage and the saturated feeling of humidity clogs my senses. The earth is damp, and when my fingers press in, they leave behind deep notches. My nails gouge out the dirt, and they become firmly packed with debris from the forest...

I get home, and the house is completely still, a silent structure housing a man broken by despair. The walls absorb his sadness and disperse it throughout. It's so palpable, I can't avoid it while I am inside their confines. The porch protests as my carefully placed footsteps carry me to the front door. The pain radiates from every pore, every cell in my body, preventing me from moving at a normal speed...

The stairs to my room are a formidable enemy. The lift and haul of my legs causes immense pain, and it's nearly impossible not to make a sound. Fortunately for me, the bourbon that has laced my papa's blood is encasing him in a soundless bubble as I moan and groan my way upstairs...

The water pelting my skin feels scalding and abrasive. When my fingers tentatively touch down below, I have the overwhelming urge to vomit. The pain is too much, so potent the water alone is making me nearly pass out. The cloth I use to press against my wounds comes away a bright red and soaked through. I know the intelligent thing to do is to go to the hospital, but I can't bring myself to cause my papa any more pain...

The feel of threaded fabric rubbing across my over sensitized skin makes sleep impossible. The echo of their voices drowns out all thoughts, and sleep becomes punishing, just beyond my fingertips...

The next day, my whole body radiates with pain, but now there's something inside me that wasn't there before. Something growing and festering as time moves forward, like a malignant tumor slowly destroying who I am... Fear.

Cooper: *KH? I heard about your mom. Call me.*

Zeke: *Kailey, I'm sorry about your mom. I wish I knew yesterday when you came by.*

Caine: *I'm sorry.*

Brody: *Kails? Please call me back.*

Brody: *I heard about your mom.*

Brody: *Please don't ignore me.*

Brody: *What you saw last night meant nothing. I don't even know why I did that.*

Brody: *Kailey... Please.*

His messages stop after nine days of being ignored. My mama's funeral is on the tenth day. The church service is agony. I can barely sit, and walking is still difficult. The rain starts while I am trying to stay standing, looking at the casket being lowered. I'm devastated, but I can't bring myself to cry, not like Papa. There's a festering mass inside me that's slowly taking over, and I'm in a constant state of fear. I haven't been out of the house since it happened, afraid I would see them, and it would happen again.

I can see the guys in my periphery, but there's one set of icy blues willing me to look at him. I don't. I don't want to see them, don't want to be near them, and the thought of pretending and trying to go back to normal is impossible.

"Kails!" he screams out to me as Papa and I walk away. "Please!" His voice sounds agonized and tortured. But what the hell does he know about those feelings? He has no idea.

"Baby," Papa looks back. "Why are you ignoring Brody?"

"He has new friends," I shrug, my voice monotone and distant. "It's time we moved on."

That was the beginning of the new Brody as well... My malignancy spread to him too.

DESECRATED FLESH

Kailey-Himari

FIFTEEN

The rest of my weekend is spent in bed with the covers firmly around my neck. I feign sickness to keep Papa off my case, and I ignore the pings and rings of my cell phone. The constant flashbacks make it difficult for me to function, and I know the one person to blame it on. Lance Kilmer laying his hands on me, his breath heating my skin, and his proximity spiraling me back into the blackness of fear and pain.

Monday morning comes all too soon, and I have to find the will inside me to get up and get to school. I need to bottle up the turmoil and try to find the strength I gained in the last few years.

I dress in a pair of dark skinny jeans and a black v-neck sweater. I pull my hair up into a messy bun and forgo makeup. I can't bring myself to care too much about my appearance, not when all I can see in the reflection is his tongue on my skin and his hands on my body.

The ride to school is quiet. I should question why no one was waiting for me in my driveway, but I can't muster up the want to care. Cooper is probably pissed about the party, and maybe he's changed his mind. A slightly unsettling feeling flutters inside me at that thought, and I know it means I enjoy his company … again.

The parking lot is full by the time I get there, but I see Kimmy waiting for me as usual. I park and get out, knowing Kimmy is about to give me a tongue lashing.

"Boo!" she hollers as she gets closer. "Please tell me your phone was dead, dropped in water, and stomped on." She stops in front of me with her arms crossed on her chest.

"Sorry, Kimmy. I wasn't feeling so hot this weekend. I just slept and ate." My hand is on her arm. She immediately relaxes and drops her arms to her side.

"You sure? Is everything okay, Kailey?" Her concerned eyes roam over my exhausted face.

"I'll get better." I nod and tuck her arm in mine. "Promise."

As we walk to the front entrance, I feel Kimmy stiffen up again. "What the hell is that creep doing here?"

I follow her line of sight, and my eyes land on the Golden Four with none other than Lance Kilmer. Of course, they're watching us, and Lance has the audacity to raise his hand and wave his fingers at me. The sudden onset of fear is all-consuming, and I drop Kimmy's arm to run inside the school. I can hear her yelling for me, but I can't stop. I burst through the front doors and run down the corridors with one destination in mind.

My feet skid to a halt in front of the door and I don't knock as I storm inside. He jumps up from his seat and hurries around the desk to my side.

"Kailey?" Mr. Ballon looks at my obvious distress and closes the door behind me. "What's happened?"

"I need to get away from him. He's following me."

"Who?" He holds my biceps in his hands and bends slightly so we are eye level. "Who is following you?"

"Something bad happened to me … before. He's back." I know I sound unhinged, and my words are rushed.

He guides me to a chair and forces me into it. "Take a deep breath."

"I can't have it happen again, I'll die." My hands cover my face.

He crouches down to peer up into my face. "Kail." His hands rest on my thighs and oddly enough, his touch is comforting and calming. "I need names."

"I can't," I whimper and shake my head.

"Okay, start by telling me what happened."

"It was the summer before freshman year," I begin, saying the words already feeling liberating. "My friend was having a party at his house. I was planning to go, but earlier that day, a hit-and-run driver killed my mama. I drank a lot after I heard, and I ended up showing up at the party. Something made me upset, and I ended up talking to a couple of guys I thought I knew, but turns out not as well as I thought. They were older than me, and I felt special at that moment. They led me into the woods, then both of them…"

"What happened, Kail?" He's absently rubbing my knee, and I can't help but feel calm.

"They raped me," I whisper. "Brutally, I was in terrible shape after."

"Did you tell the cops? Go to the hospital?"

"No," I shake my head. "The cops wouldn't have helped me. These two come from prominent families and the hospital would've called the cops."

His hand wipes down over his face, and he looks me in the eye, his steel-gray eyes filled with anger and sadness. Thankfully, I don't see pity in their depths.

"Do they go to this school, Kail? Is it one of them?" I know who he's talking about, and I know he thinks I'm covering up for them.

"No, Mr. Ballon. They used to go here."

"They graduated already?" he clarifies.

"Yes," I nod.

He looks thoughtful for a few seconds, and then his eyes widen a fraction.

"Listen, Kailey. I need you to hear what I have to say and then answer my questions honestly." He reaches out and takes my hand, his thumb rubbing along the back of mine. "The year I graduated, we had a tremendous scandal here. Two sophomores were accused of raping three girls at a house party. There was an investigation, but the girls eventually dropped charges amid rumors they were paid off or coerced to do so. Those two guys were Lance Kilmer and Justin Landry. Are these the same guys who did that to you?"

I maul at my bottom lip. If I say yes, everything changes;

someone besides me will know what happened, and I have to trust him to keep my secret.

"Kail," he says softly. "What are you worried about?"

"Scared, Oliver," I correct him in a hushed voice. "I'm scared, not worried."

"It's Lance, right?" Oliver stands up and begins pacing in front of me. "He's been back home since the rape accusation at Tulane. He's the one following you?"

"He was at a party I went to on Friday—"

"Did he touch you?" He cuts me off with a growl.

I swallow thickly and nod. "Yes, he grabbed my throat." I place my hand exactly where Lance had his. "And other places."

"Look, Kailey, you're eighteen, and I can't force you to turn him in, but think about how many other girls he could do this to. How many he has done this to since you."

"And look at how many times he's gotten off," I argue. "It would ruin my family's reputation if I was made to look like a liar. Brody is Justin's little brother. They're close; he would never believe me, and he would make my life a living hell all over again."

Oliver leans against the edge of his desk and crosses his legs at the ankles. As he's thinking, I take the time to check him out. He has on khakis today, but you can tell he doesn't miss a single leg day at the gym. His blue polo shirt sits snug on his shoulders and biceps, detailing the toned muscles of his arms. I can't believe I'm crushing on my guidance counselor right now, but at least what happened with Lance hasn't broken me again.

"I will have a word with the principal about allowing over-aged men on school property, especially those who are under investigation for rape. But I still need to figure something out for you when you leave these grounds." He's mostly muttering, but I hear every word.

"I'm fine at home," I say quietly, even though that's not entirely true. My pa is rarely home, and the thought scares me all over again.

"I'll figure it out. For now, you need to get to class. Give me your phone." I do as he asks and watch as he programs his number into it. "Now call me so I have yours."

I do it and watch as he saves my number on his phone. "Why are you doing this, Oliver?" Using his first name is easy now that I've bared my soul to him.

"It's my job."

"Not to do this much," I counter.

"I'm a good person?" He makes it sound like a question with his brow raised.

"You are," I agree and get up out of my seat. "I should get to class."

"I'm here all day if you need me."

I nod and exit his office, closing the door behind me with a click.

"Kailey." I hear a deep voice behind me as I navigate through the halls to my first period.

I turn and see Caine closing in. "Yes?"

"You left early on Friday. Lance left not too long after you. Is there something we should know?"

"Hold on," I put my hand up. "We? Who's we?"

"The four of us. You're supposed to be dating Cooper, don't you think you should have told him about Lance?"

I walk up to him and look him in the eye. "Excuse me?"

His brows crash together in confusion. "He said you were seeing each other."

"Over my dead fucking body. He's a rapist," I grit out in anger. I'm angry they believed him, and I'm angry Lance is building a large, intricate web of lies.

"Those are just allegations—"

"He's a rapist!" I scream and then cover my mouth in shock at my outburst. I shake my head and rush off away from him and towards class. He's calling my name, but I refuse to speak to him any further.

Lunch is spent in my car with a concerned but quiet Kimmy. I see her furtive glances, and I huff in irritation. "What is it?"

"What happened this morning? Where did you go?"

"I just got overwhelmed. I'm sorry."

She reaches out and pinches the Gris-Gris on my wrist. "Is it working? Are you safe?"

Actually, now that I think about it, things could have ended really badly with Lance on Friday but they didn't, and today, I found someone to help me. "It's definitely working," I nod to her.

The rest of the day goes by with little drama. It's the quietest it's been my whole time here at JFK Prep. When the last bell rings, I head to my locker and grab my stuff to head home. My cell phone pings with a message. When I see the name, I feel a smile grace my lips.

Oliver: Please text me if anything seems off tonight, no matter how small.

Me: Okay. Thank you.

I tuck my phone away and leave the school. I feel bad I didn't wait for Kimmy, but I just want to get home and crawl into bed. My head is down as I walk to my car, but I stop when I see a few pairs of feet in my path. I look up and see the Golden Four standing in front of me.

"Do I need to remind you of our terms?" Brody's crisp voice asks.

"No." I shake my head.

"Why did you leave early on Friday?" he questions. I try to steal a glance at Cooper, but his jaw is clenched, and he's staring firmly at his feet.

"I wasn't feeling comfortable," I murmur.

"Your comfort wasn't part of the deal," he growls, and I look up at him in surprise.

"What happened to you, Brody?" I step into him. "What made you such a fucking asshole?"

"You will spend the time you are supposed to with Cooper, and now Caine as well."

I look at Caine with surprise, and he answers me with a smirk. "Whatever." I shake my head and try to move around them.

Cooper blocks my way, and I look into his face. He's hurt. It's radiating out of his eyes and straight to my heart. "You need to tell me what's going on. I keep hearing conflicting stories."

"What do you mean?" I ask. My heart is feeling heavy for him.

"Lance. He says you two have history, and you're picking up where you left off."

"It's not true. I want nothing to do with Lance." I shake my head.

"She believes he's a rapist," Caine interjects. "I believe her when she says she's not seeing him."

I look at him in confusion. Why is he defending me? "I want to get home. Can I get by, please?" I look at Cooper.

"I'll be picking you up in the morning." His voice sounds softer, but his eyes still hold a lot of hurt.

"Sure," I shrug, and he finally lets me by. I get into my car, and without a backwards glance, I leave behind the school and the four guys so hellbent on watching me burn.

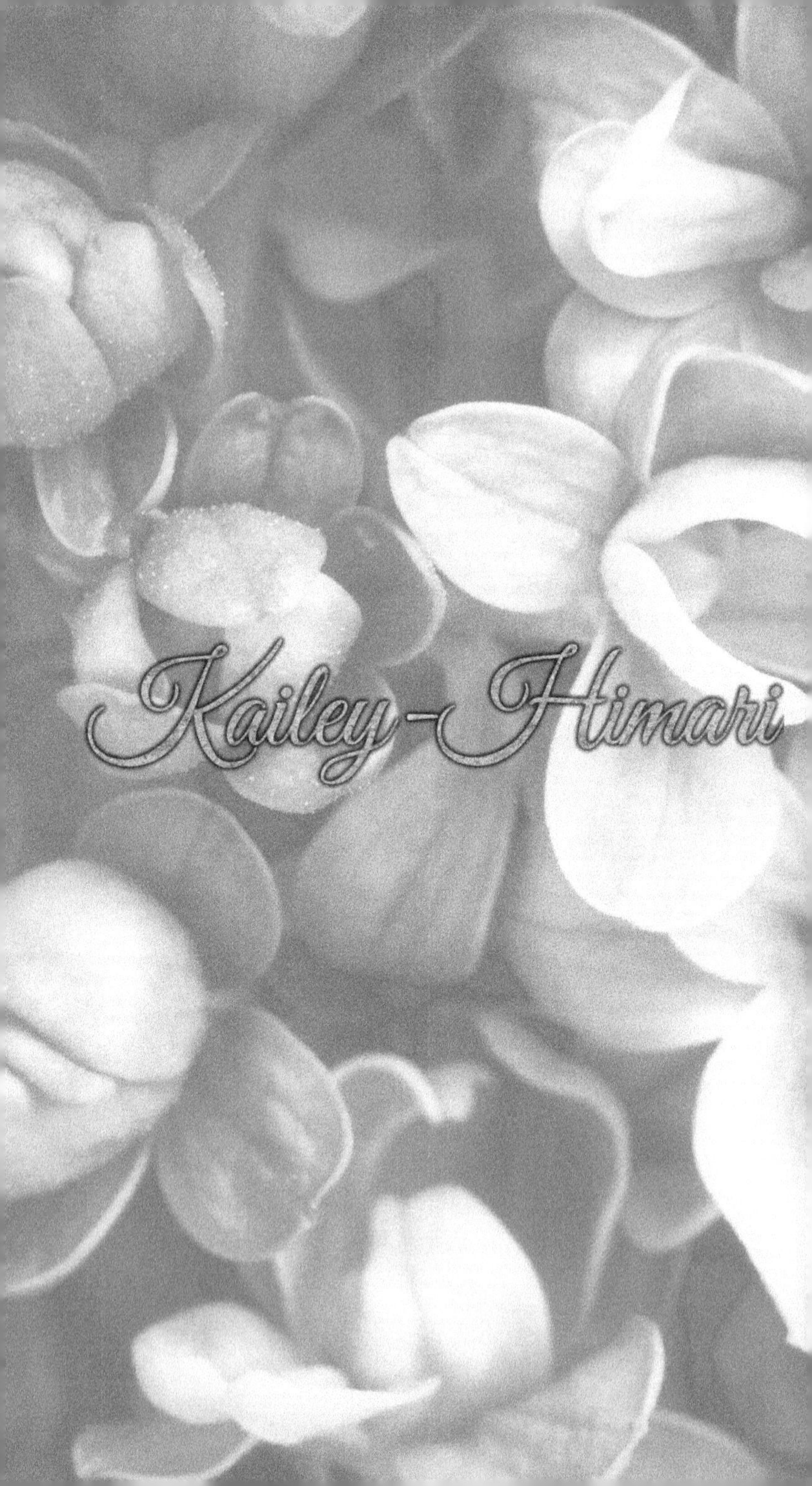
Kailey-Himari

SIXTEEN

I sit on my porch, rolling a vine of wisteria between my fingers while watching the gazebo. Looking at it still hurts, like that structure is the embodiment of her spirit. I have a hard time going in there, but I want to, especially on hard days. I wonder what she would think about how my life turned out. How would she see her daughter nowadays, and would she be proud?

The breeze blows by my face, lifting my mass of waves up off my neck and tickling my cheeks. I used to come out here and believe the breeze was her, caressing me and reminding me she loves me. Now I'm more cynical. I guess it's hard to believe she's still here when I know she belongs in heaven with the angels.

Papa hasn't been out here since she's been gone. The lawn gets taken care of by a company who's been told not to go near the gazebo. It's sad, but no one goes near it anymore, almost like we're afraid she'll actually be in there to reprimand us for the way we're living. Especially me. I think she would be disappointed to know I missed out on so much. Homecomings, junior prom, and basically every high school social event. She was excited for me to start high school and always spoke about how much fun she had with her friends and all the boys she danced with at homecomings. Papa was her prom date, her first and only love.

I wanted that for as long as I could remember. Watching Mama and Pa love each other and laugh together made me realize true love was real at a young age. My first veritable crush was Brody, and I had always hoped I could have that with him. I would imagine it vividly until I saw it with the others as well. My crushes then became on rotation, and I couldn't even fathom who to choose by seventh grade. Then Caine came into the mix, and he won me over too with his honesty and sincerity. Four boys who ruled my heart and all my fantasies until that fateful night. After that, true love washed away with the salt of my tears and the poison of my fear.

"You're a liar." The voice startles me, and I jump out of my seat.

"Cooper!" I snarl. "Don't scare me like that. Why are you calling me a liar?"

He points to the flower in my hand. "It is still your favorite."

I sit back down with a huff and watch as he comes up to sit beside me. "What are you doing here? You know normal people ring the doorbell, right?"

"We used to jump your fence when we were kids. Now it's a fucking breeze to get over. I'm not sure how I ended up here, KH, but this is where my feet took me."

We both sit in silence, watching the gazebo. He was here the week Papa had it built and watched the chaos in our backyard. All of them were. They knew how much Mama loved it out here and how well she tended it. Looking at it and all its disarray of vines makes me feel ashamed I didn't maintain it.

"Those vines need to be trimmed," he states into the silent evening.

"Papa has been busy at the dealership, and I don't want to go near it."

"I see." He leaves it at that. "How's the dealership?"

"Is it really true, Coop? Did he borrow money from Brody's dad?" I ask him.

"Yeah, sha. It's true."

I know Cooper could be lying to me just to keep up the farce, but I feel like he isn't. I know Cooper; he's not a liar. He's cruel and brutally blunt, but he's not a liar. I also know how much he can hold back, sharing half-truths and giving people the runaround. It's hard to trust if what he's saying is the full truth.

DESECRATED FLESH

We've never been a rich family by this town's standards, but we were extremely comfortable. We have a large home with a large backyard and three cars in the garage. I never want for anything and even have a credit card at my disposal. So I can't imagine Papa needing that money. It all seems to be an elaborate lie to bend me to their will. But why?

I know after what happened that summer—when I turned my back on them and refashioned my life as if they weren't ever a part of it—did reprehensible damage. I can even understand the hate they must carry in their hearts because they didn't have a single clue why I did what I did, but to make up such a life altering lie seems far-fetched. Then again, I see Brody's ice-blue eyes in my mind, the pure hatred that simmers in them, and the cold, emotionless tone when he speaks to me. He would make it up.

Cooper sits quietly beside me, letting me think while he watches the gazebo as well. We would lie out there, the five of us, and play truth or dare. We would climb to the top on the hottest days and sunbathe until our skins were a dark golden brown. My mama would bring us out sweet tea and cucumber sandwiches while we listened to music and laughed at the latest gossip.

Soon after, I became their gossip, and the gazebo was left to weather and age without the warmth of human kindness. *I'm sorry, Mama.* I hope she can hear me wherever she is, and I pray she sees how hard I'm trying to make her proud. I wish Papa was home more, and I wish he would attempt to sit out here and try to remember life is more than a business or money. He has a family here with me.

I feel Cooper's eyes on me, and I close mine to take a deep breath. The guilt rises as I remember the hurt I saw in their depths. I should've called him to say I wasn't feeling well, or instead of running out, I should've told him I wasn't feeling well. Maybe he would have left with me, and all the shit that went down with Lance wouldn't have happened.

But it's all just what ifs. All that shit happened, and I can't change it. I want to apologize to him because I know he deserves it, but the words don't form in my mouth. I feel like if I apologize to him, then I'm bowing to him. I deserve a million apologies from them, but I doubt I will ever hear even one.

Having Cooper make the effort to come here, the effort he's put in from the start of this, and the way I feel drawn to him are causing me to doubt my actions. Would it be so crazy to open my heart back up to him? Can I trust him with its worn and tattered pieces?

DESECRATED FLESH

SEVENTEEN

I watched her from the side of the house like the stalker I am. I was in love with Kailey-Himari in seventh and eighth grade, then I hated her for most of high school… until now. Coming here unannounced, jumping her eight-foot-high fence, and then staring at her for fifteen minutes, made me realize I'm in love with her again. I knew it was a possibility. How much can one person change in four years? In her case, not at all yet completely at the same time. She's still KH—mon sha—but she's also different.

Her light brown hair is still thick and flows in unruly waves around her shoulders and down her back. Her eyes still have that mesmerizing mixture of moss green and light brown, swirling together and held in by a dark green ring. Her skin is the color of the creamiest coffee, and her full, tempting mouth pouts when she's deep in thought. All of that remains the same, except in those eyes I see a mountain of pain and an ocean of hurt, her spine is rigid like she's always prepared to fight, and she has an edge to her that screams she's no longer a victim … which means she was one at some point.

Caine insisted she was attacked, and he thinks her father was the culprit, but I'm not so sure. I never got to know the KH who lost her mother, but I know they were a close family. When I mentioned this to Caine, he was adamant I was wrong and he was going to get to the bottom of it. That surprised me because he would never do that for anyone besides us brothers, the four of us. It was then I knew he was feeling something close to what I was, and when he realized it, he hopped back into bed with Connie to erase it. Until his party, when he had her on his lap and his tongue down her throat. I know my brothers better than anyone else, so I saw the shock that lined his features after, even if no one else did. He was a goner the second he tasted her.

I've had this plan in motion since the beginning of the summer. At the mall, I saw her and Kimmy, and it felt like kismet. I watched her throw her head back and laugh, the full hearty laugh of someone who was genuinely happy in that moment. I saw her light, and I saw her darkness all in those few minutes, and knew I had to have her. I knew the guys would fight me, tell me I was insane and try to dissuade me. Brody was the hardest to convince. He's hated her with a passion, the fire only burning brighter every year. I know why his hate is so deep. It's because his love was so fierce for years until she disappeared, and he blamed himself. Most of the hate emanates from what he feels for himself, and projects it at her. When she caught him fooling around with Georgina, I watched both of their hearts break.

I got my way, with some stipulations. They would blackmail her and eventually force her to find information about her father. They haven't asked yet, but they will. They feel like KH's father is preparing to come for Brody's father in an attempt to break away, but Mr. Landry owns Mr. Richard. Brody wants to know what he has on his father, and he thinks KH will get that for him. After I've fucked her senseless, of course. I don't know what happened between them, only that Mr. Richard needed money and had a hard time paying it back, but I think Brody knows more. We all have secrets the others don't know, so I don't push him.

Having Caine share KH was unexpected, but I will admit it makes things easier. I think us four need one girl to tame us and keep us as a family. Pussy has a way of separating and breaking brotherhoods, but not if it's one we all love and cherish the same, and I think sha is just the girl to do it. After four years of our torture handed down by the girls, she's stronger, resilient, and downright feisty. I always knew her backbone was made of steel, and I'm glad she proved me right. The guys see it, and they respect it even if it is begrudgingly.

The silence is thick around us as I sit beside her and watch her twirl the flower her mother loved between her fingers. When she skipped out on that party early, I was angry … livid. Caine got to make out with her, felt her straddled on his lap, and had his hand wrapped around her throat. I wanted my turn. I wanted to dance with her, feel her body move against mine, and I wanted to taste her again. Caine is sure something triggered her, and she fled in fear. I didn't believe him until I saw her this morning.

"Sha," I clear my throat, trying to tamp down everything I'm feeling. "What happened this morning?"

"Nothing." Her response is quick, an automatic defense mechanism.

"Don't lie to me, please," I beg her. "I want to help."

"It's hard for me to trust you, Coop," she whispers, her voice shaking. "Any of you."

I understand that. After what we put her through, she probably feels like this is one big elaborate prank we're pulling in our final year. I don't know how to convince her otherwise without telling her how I feel and even if I did, I don't think she'd believe me.

"What can I do to prove you can trust me?"

"I don't know if you can," she answers honestly.

"I don't believe that. We have a history, KH."

"Part of that history was you and the Golden Four making my life hell," she retorts, her voice laced with venom.

"That's true. I can't deny it. But can you also believe for many years I had feelings for you? That right now I am exactly where I want to be?"

She sucks in a breath, and her wide eyes scan over my face, looking for a falsehood. "I want to," she finally says in an exhale.

"That's a start," I nod.

"I miss my mama," she begins, her voice shaking with emotion. "I wish she was here, and I could tell her everything. I also think if she didn't die, my life would be completely different."

"How so?" I ask.

"The day she was killed, I made some poor decisions, and it paved the path I would take that has brought me to where I am right now."

"Where you are right now is bad?"

"Not everything, but most things, yes. My pa is rarely home, he has a bed at the dealership he sleeps on some nights. We used to be a family. He would rush home to be with us, and the love in this home was potent. School has been the worst experience for me. I can't trust anyone; even Kimmy gets half-truths and avoidance from me."

"I'm sorry, Kailey-Himari," I say her full name so she knows I'm sincere. "I'm sorry for the role I played in all this."

"Why are you guys after my papa?" Her voice is small. "Why are you dating me? Is it to punish me for what he's supposedly done?"

"No," I shake my head. "I'm dating you because I want to, always have. Brody may have some issues with your father, but that has nothing to do with how I feel."

"And Caine?" She raises a perfectly manicured brow at me. "If you care, why am I also having to date your friend?"

"Valid," I nod. "Would you understand if I said life would be easier if we shared the same things equally? There would be no jealousy and nothing to split us apart."

"I'm confused."

"I know, and I promise you will understand soon enough." I reach my hand out to take the wisteria from her. She watches me closely as I tuck it into her waves and smile at the memories it brings with it. Sandbox castles and a beautiful princess with flowers in her hair.

We both stand and look at each other pensively. She's so fucking beautiful it hurts. I step into her, and my heart races when she doesn't back away. I don't want to scare her off, but I need to taste her again, feel her in my arms, and have her body pressed against mine. I run my fingers along her jaw and towards her full lips, tracing them lightly. They part, and her breathing becomes ragged. I know I have the same effect on her she has on me.

"Can I kiss you, sha?"

She inhales sharply at my request, and her eyes skate back and forth between mine. Finally, she nods, and I exhale the breath I'm holding in anticipation. I don't give her any time to change her mind as I swoop in and claim her cushion lips with my own. I pull her top lip between mine lightly and then do the same with the bottom. I want to go slow, ease her into this because I know she's inexperienced with guys. Something us four did purposely all throughout high school. If anyone showed interest in her, we shut it down with rumors of her whorish ways.

Her tiny hands come up and press against my chest. I pull back, but her hands fist into my shirt's material and she drags me in closer. Her mouth opens, and I strike instantly, my tongue gliding against hers and tasting what has become my sweet addiction. How did I ever think kissing and sex were great before this? I can't even compare her to anyone else because she is that far into her own league. Her soft moans and delicate whimpers make her sound timid and shy, but the grip she has on my shirt and the way she's pressing her pelvis against mine is such a drastic contrast. She wants me too.

My hands skim down her back, pressing lightly along her spine, causing her to arch into me more. She hums her approval, and her hands unclench from my shirt to travel up my chest, along my neck, then sink into my hair, pulling lightly. My hands skim along her lower back, flirting with the top of her ass. I wait for her to object, and when she doesn't, my hands grab her luscious ass by the handful. I squeeze hard, the sensation probably bordering on pain, but to my surprise, she jumps up and wraps her legs around my waist. I groan at the feeling of her center pressed against the bulge in my pants, and like a pubescent boy, I almost come from the pressure alone.

I tear my mouth from hers and run light teasing kisses along her jaw, sucking into my mouth the sensitive skin underneath her ear. I sit back down on the chair as she straddles me, grinding lightly and sending the sensations floating through me into overdrive. If I don't stop this soon, I won't be able to stop.

"Sha," my voice sounds pained and raspy. "As much as I want to do this all night, I am getting to the point of no return. I've wanted this for so long, and I can't control myself with you grinding on my cock and feeling your skin."

"I'm sorry." Her voice is airy and charged with lust.

"Don't be. I'm in heaven right now. I just don't want to push you into something you're not ready for, and if I continue doing this, I will make a fool of myself when I come in my pants."

The delicious tint of pink coating her cheeks is mesmerizing. "This is new to me." She lays her forehead against mine. "I've never wanted this before."

That tells me everything Caine said is correct. Our girl has been hurt, but to what extent? And by whom? I want to press her for more information. I want an explanation so I can dole out the punishment, but

I know KH… If I press too hard, she will clam up, possibly forever. I have a lot of work ahead of me to gain back her trust by showing her how much I care for her. Tonight gives me the assurance I needed to know she feels the same. The current I was feeling between us was mutual.

"I'm glad you chose me," I whisper back.

"My mind hasn't chosen you yet, but my heart has other ideas," she mutters, and I find myself on cloud nine from her words.

Her heart wants this. I can work with that. I know I have a lot on my plate, I'm dealing with football scholarships and keeping a high GPA, then I need to convince KH to trust me, and the most time-consuming will be convincing the guys she's the one… For all of us.

It's not like its unfamiliar territory for us. We've shared before, and we've doubled down in the bedroom too. The girls were all too willing to be passed around between us, and sometimes shared. The unfamiliar territory is introducing KH into that role and eliminating her from the outcast list we have her on.

She shifts on my lap, and my painfully hard dick presses tighter against my pants. I will have to jack off so many times later just to relieve the blue from my sac. I grab her waist, halting her movements, then kiss her lightly on the mouth. When I came here, I wasn't expecting this. I just wanted to let her know I wasn't going anywhere. What I've been telling her this entire time is fact. I want her, and I want her to be mine.

She leans back and holds my face between her hands. "What about Casey, Coop? If I do this, there will be no back and forth. I know it sounds strange to say I want you to stay true to me while I date your friend as well, but I didn't come up with this situation."

"Casey is already out of the picture, sha. She was never really in it. We had our fun, but that was it. I never saw a future with her."

"But you see a future with me … and Caine?" Her nose scrunches adorably.

"I think you're woman enough to handle us, yes." I bop her nose with my finger.

"And he'll still want Connie too?" Her eyes bore into mine, looking for any deep, hidden truths.

"Maybe have this conversation with him?" I ask her gently. "I can't speak for him, but I think after the party at his house, he might just agree to your stipulations."

At the mention of the party, her entire body tenses up, and she gets up off my lap to stand. Again, I can't help but think Caine is right in his assumption of something triggering her there. Was it Caine and his dominating ways? If so, she will have to get used to that and more. Caine is not a gentle lover by any means. He likes his sex dirty and rough.

"Is everything okay?" I ask her.

"I'm just a little tired." She runs her fingers through her mass of waves. "I should probably get some sleep."

"Sure." I stand up and peer down at her in front of me. I reach my fingers out slowly and brush them against her cheek. "I'll pick you up tomorrow, cool?"

She nods and curves her cheek into my hand. "Yeah."

I brush a light kiss to her forehead then step down from her porch.

"Coop?" she calls out.

"Yeah?"

"Use the front door. You're not a heathen." Her grin is back in place, and mirth is dancing in her eyes.

"Au contraire, sha. I am a complete heathen … facts." I wink at her then round the corner of her house to hop the fence.

I clearly have my work cut out for me, but I just need to keep reminding myself the prize is so fucking worth it.

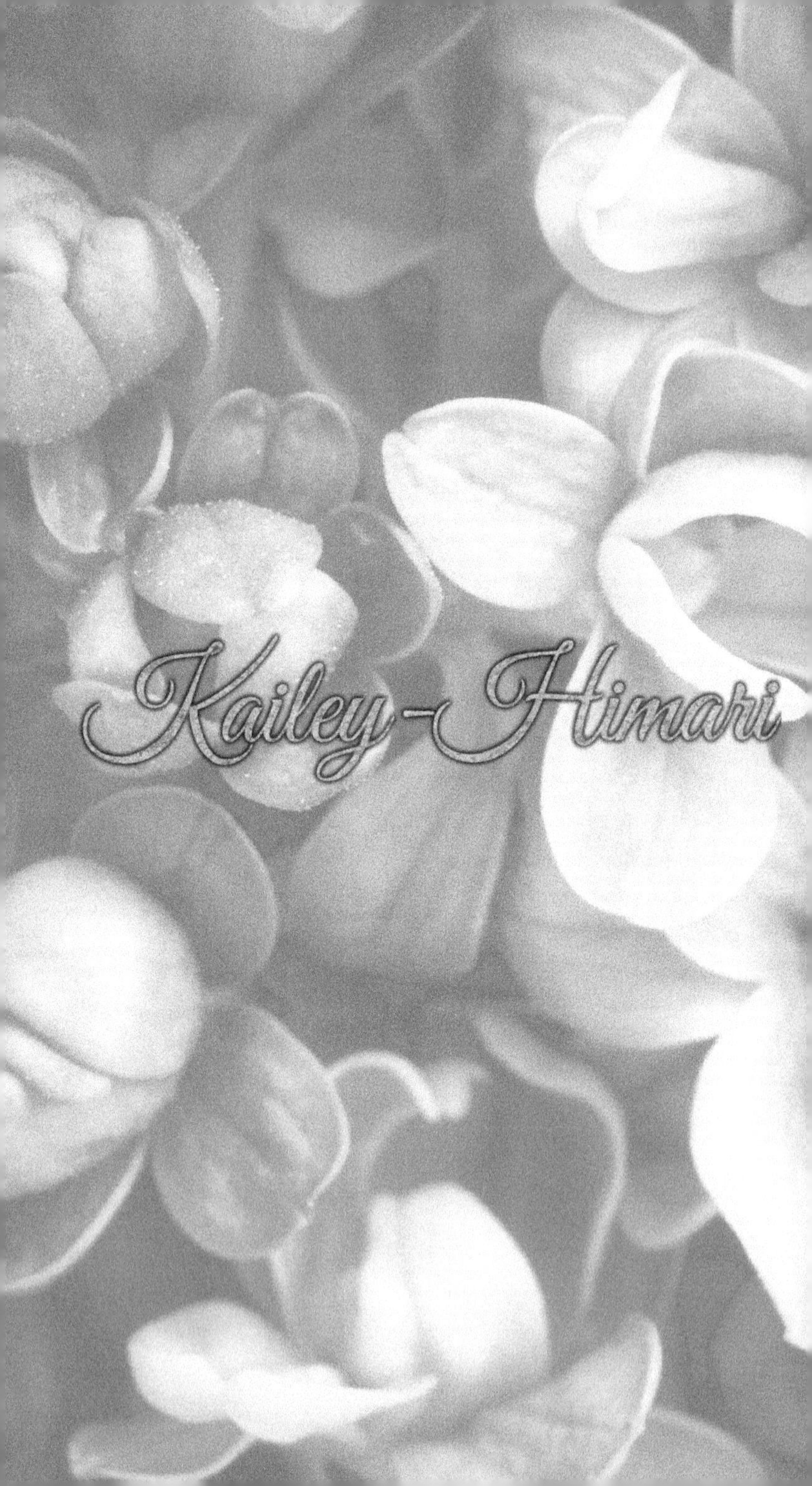
Kailey-Himari

EIGHTEEN

I am holding Cooper's hand as we bypass the three guys looking at us curiously as we make our way into the school.

"Shouldn't you say good morning to them?" I ask him as I look over my shoulder.

"You want to go back and say it?" His grin is taunting.

"Heck, no." I shake my head, and he laughs.

"Thought so. Besides, let them work to earn that from you." He smiles at me warmly.

Can I just say 'dating' Cooper is like standing in direct sunlight? It's warm, and the blinding light sears through your eyelids from the concentrated solar radiation. I love it.

"Miss Richard?"

I turn towards the voice and see Mr. Ballon leaning against the wall casually. "Yes, Mr. Ballon?"

"Could I see you in my office before classes start?" He pushes off the wall, and I can't help but imagine his abs flexing as he does.

"Uh, sure." Cooper has a confused look on his face as he looks between me and Oliver. "I'll see you at lunch?" I say to him.

He nods and leans down to plant a firm kiss against my lips. When I pull away, Oliver is looking between us, also perplexed. I guess that's my new superpower, causing confusion.

I follow behind him as he leads us to his office. Once we're inside, he closes the door as I sink into the chair across from his desk. He doesn't move to his chair. Instead, he takes the chair directly beside mine, our knees brushing.

"How are you?" he asks as he leans forward, bringing his face closer to mine. I notice the light dusting of scruff on his face, perfectly lined up and giving him a dangerous looking edge. His steel eyes look over my face, trying to find the answers to his questions.

"I'm trying to be normal," I answer honestly. "I want to date, and I want to move on from what happened to me."

"I guess you're dating Cooper Fontenot?" His brows crease in the center. "He has connections to both Lance and Justin. Is that something you've considered?"

I don't know what makes me do it, but I lean forward in my seat as well, our mouths a few inches apart. "Do you think I shouldn't date yet?"

He doesn't move an inch. In fact, he quickly draws in a breath as I watch his eyes darken. He's looking at my mouth, and I can't help the grin that ghosts my lips.

Suddenly, he sits back and looks at the floor, his hands scrubbing down over his cheeks. "Not at all. Maybe dating is a good thing, but take your time. Don't let anyone rush you, and make sure you avoid triggers. I would also try to stay clear from any social gatherings that may include Lance and Justin."

"Triggers," I repeat as I fiddle with the hem of my shirt. "Like what triggers?"

"Maybe speaking with me about that isn't a good idea. People determine their triggers with a therapist."

"Well, I will never see a therapist about this," I say, holding my chin up with determination.

"Triggers are the instances that happen right before the onset of extreme stress and anxiety. Could be anything, people, places, or things."

"Intimacy and my rapists so far," I mutter.

"Makes the most sense." He nods as he moves around in his seat. "Have you been … ah … intimate since then?"

"I haven't had sex yet, but I have kissed and fooled around." Is he blushing?

There's a flash of something in his eyes. Is it jealousy? It can't be. I'm just not used to reading people's emotions since I've been avoiding most of them for years.

"Oliver," I say and watch as his eyes flick up to look at me. He really has gorgeous eyes. "Thank you for everything you're doing to help me and with how understanding you are being."

"Kail," he leans forward again. "I will admit I am worried about seeing you dating Cooper and hanging out with that group."

"Thanks for being worried, but I think I'll be okay." I smile at him and stand up from my chair. It brings his face level with my pelvis, and I can feel heat spread across my cheeks. He doesn't move right away, so I take a small step to the side as he snaps out of his thoughts.

"I'll check in with you this week. You can text me or call me if you need anything."

"Thank you." I grin and open his door. When I look back, he's leaning back in his chair, looking deep in thought. The crinkle between his brows looks adorable.

I close the door just as the first warning bell rings. Guess I won't have time for a locker drop off before class.

"Boo!" I hear Kimmy yell out from down the hallway. "I'll see you at lunch!"

I laugh and wave as she rushes by to her class.

"It won't last," I hear from behind me. I turn to find Casey right behind me with a nasty sneer on her face. "He's doing it because Brody is making him. I heard the entire plan... You have something they need on your father, so Cooper volunteered to date you to find out."

I shake my head and walk away.

"Did they play the recording for you? That was part of the plan, to force you and make you have to date Cooper." I stop and turn to face her. How the fuck could I ignore that? She knows literally everything that's happened.

I stalk back towards her, feeling all the pent-up anger releasing throughout my limbs. I've put up with this shit for four years. I'm done. Her eyes widen, and she swallows thickly as I grab her arm then force her into the bathroom behind her. The last bell rings, announcing the beginning of the first period, but I have a bitch to interrogate.

"Kailey!" she squeals as she tries to pull her arm out of my grip, but I'm determined and filled to the brim with all-consuming anger. "You're hurting me!"

"Shut the fuck up!" I growl into her face. She does as I say and keeps her trap shut. "Now you are going to tell me every little thing they have said about my papa, regardless of how insignificant you think it is."

"Okay," she whispers, as her bottom lip trembles. I bet I look all sorts of disturbed right now. "Brody would complain to the others about his father bothering him. Saying things like 'Mr. Richard is falling through the cracks', or 'Richard is up to something.' Brody has to figure it out if he wants the company, or else his father will give it to Justin."

"Justin was always going to inherit that company; he is the oldest," I grit through my teeth, catching her on a lie.

"That was true until Justin started having ties to the rape accusations. Their father decided the company going into his hands could tarnish the Landry name." Fuck, that makes sense. "He left Brody with one assignment to prove he could handle the responsibility."

"Finding out what—if anything—Papa is up to," I mutter.

"Look," she looks around the bathroom nervously. "What you said before about my mother and how she's trying to marry us all off to wealth, it's true, and she has her sights set on Cooper. No one else will do. I also have to prove myself. I have nothing against you personally."

"Whatever," I roll my eyes. "What else did they say?"

"They would make you fall in love with Cooper so they'd have all access to your house, and therefore, your father," she shrugs. "Sounds like your father has fucked-up something with the Landry's."

"Did you hear that recording?" I sneer at her and watch as she pales a bit.

"No," she shakes her head profusely. "They made sure not to do that in front of us girls. But I don't know how much Georgina knows. Her and Brody are tight."

"Right."

Suddenly, the bathroom door flies open and hits the wall with a resounding bang. Both Casey and I scream like hyenas and turn to face an angry Caine.

"Get the fuck out," He growls at Casey, and I watch as she scrambles by us both. Once she leaves the room, he immediately locks the door and turns his narrowed eyes on me. "What the fuck was going on in here?"

I refuse to look any more scared than my scream already portrayed and pop my hip. "Depends. how much did you hear?"

He's across the room in no time with his hand wrapping around my throat and my body slamming into the wall. "Don't toy with me, ma petite." His hand tightens around my throat and effectively blocks my air supply.

I open my mouth, but his grip is tight, so trying to speak becomes difficult. This should be a trigger, right? I shouldn't be feeling turned on right now, right? Why is it when Caine does shit like this, I am aroused, but anyone else and I want to sink into a pool of fear?

"I should make you get on your knees and stuff my cock so far down your fucking throat," he rasps out against the shell of my ear. I can't help it … a breathy moan escapes me, and the look of surprise on his face would be amusing if I wasn't so turned on. "You like this, don't you?"

His fingers loosen, but his body presses in against mine. All his hard ridges sinking into my soft body feels almost euphoric. Caine's big body is something to behold, so when it's molding into every dip and curve of mine, it makes thinking impossible. His hand travels down the column of my throat and in between my breasts. The whole time his eyes are trained on me.

"Ma petite," he rasps and licks his full lips. "I came in here to scare you into telling me why you were discussing your father with Casey, but now I think I have another tactic."

"Class has started…" Before I can finish my sentence, he flips me around and presses his groin into my ass. I can feel the panic rise inside me, dousing my arousal.

"Wait…" my voice even sounds panicked.

This position and his breath hitting my ear is all too familiar, and I can feel the black pool of dread threatening to drown me.

He flips up the long skirt I'm wearing and reveals my ass in a black thong. The groan that leaves his mouth sounds almost agonized, but I can't concentrate on that because I am actually in agony.

"Please, Caine," I beg him to realize I'm not enjoying this. I want to tell him, but I can't seem to form the words through the mind-numbing fear pumping throughout me.

"That's right." His voice sounds mocking almost. "I knew I would have you begging me at some point."

Why does he sound like them? How did his deep rasp become Justin's light teasing voice or Lance's sharp and cold one?

"Caine, stop," I plead and try to pull away.

"No. Get it together, Kailey, because we both know you want it." *You know you want it.*

I struggle against his hold on me, the force of my panic tearing down coherent thought, and my fight-or-flight reaction kicks in. Caine groans again as my ass hits his bulging erection, and the grip on my hips is bruising as he crushes his hardness into me farther. His right hand slips down over my ass cheek, and glides between my legs. When his fingers press into my underwear just over my center, I cease the struggling and close my eyes to wait out the rest of the assault.

"You are so wet." His voice holds a hint of reverence in the rasp. I am? Why would I be wet against an assault? "Fuck, Kailey, you're soaked."

His fingers curve inside the edge of my panties and swipes through my folds. Nothing about Caine is gentle, and right now his rough fingers are spreading me open, finding that little bundle of nerves. As soon as his finger lands on it, the sensations send me to my tippy toes.

That's what it's supposed to feel like? I never knew, never explored for myself because the thought of doing that would make me feel nauseous. But right now, I am feeling the opposite, and by the evidence coating my thighs, I am indeed soaked.

His fingers continue to swipe through my folds and come back to concentrate on my clit with acute accuracy. My limbs start to feel a gathering energy, sort of like lightning skating across my skin, and my lower belly begins to burn and tighten. My breaths are coming out in quick pants, and I can feel something building inside me.

"Come for me," he growls in my ear, sounding threatening. Regardless, it works, and I come all over his hand as my hips jerk erratically.

My first ever orgasm has left me feeling boneless, with my face and shoulders propped up against the tiled bathroom wall.

"I didn't even have to do this…" He inserts a finger inside me, and I tense up, expecting pain, but my core clenches around it, and I moan as my orgasm dwindles down.

He turns me back around to face him, and crashes his mouth to mine. Before I can react, he's forcing his way into my mouth and devouring me from the inside. His mouth wrenches away, and he shoves my shoulders, making me fall to my knees.

"Take it out." He jerks his pelvis into my face, and I see the significant bulge. He grabs a handful of my hair, pulling sharply. "I said take it out."

I reach forward with trembling fingers and undo his button then slowly release his zipper. Caine isn't wearing underwear, and his exceptionally large, angry looking cock almost smacks me on the forehead. "Grab it."

"Caine—" I try to reason with him, but he cuts me off by pulling harder on my hair.

"Stop talking and do something more useful with that mouth." He looks angry and captivated at the same time. "Or do I need to force you to do that as well?"

I swallow down the lump forming in my throat and reach forward to wrap my hand around him. My fingers don't meet around his girth, and I panic. How will this go in my mouth? Will he really stick it down my throat? The skin on his shaft is velvet soft, like lamb skin. I glide my hand up and down and revel in the small jerks it makes in response.

"Lick it." His voice is raspy and low.

I want to protest, but when I look up and see fire in his eyes, I back down. If I don't do this, it'll just get worse. I lean forward and lick the wide mushroom top. The drop of moisture tastes salty. His guttural groan of approval has me going in for another taste. It's not horrible, but I still can't imagine this fitting in my mouth.

As if reading my thoughts, he says, "Open your mouth."

"No." I shake my head firmly, even though he still has a fistful of my hair.

"Did I ask you?" he retorts, and to my utter astonishment, grabs his dick and slaps my cheek with it. "Open your mouth now."

At the sound of his demand, my mouth opens almost of its own accord. I say almost because I'm mindful of it, yet stopping it feels impossible.

Before I can take a proper breath, his cock is hitting the back of my throat, and my lips feel stretched past their limit. He stops there, moaning as my throat works to swallow around him, and my lungs attempt to gather air.

"Fuck," He hisses, and he moves back slightly, only to slam back in again. I gag forcefully around his flesh, feeling almost certain I'm about to puke. I try to pull back, but he doesn't let me get far, his fist pulling my head closer. "I'm thinking of making this a morning ritual." As long as I get what preceded this, sure.

He continues to fuck my mouth roughly, only letting me gasp mouthfuls of air here and there. My cheeks are soaked from the tears caused by vigorous thrusts down the column of my throat, making me gag.

He thrusts one last time, and I feel his cock jerk, then the warmth of his cum spills into my mouth. The taste is not fantastic, and I gag again at just the texture, but I'm glad it's over.

I try to stand, but he pulls my hair, making me look up at him. "Did I say you were done? Put it back."

The degradation should be enough to cause me shame, but I'm aroused again, and the sensations between my legs are humming throughout my body. I feel like a traitor to myself and everything that has happened to me. I should never feel good about being forced to please a man, but I do as he says and put his cock away.

"Good girl." His deep rasp coats over me, and the praise makes me feel like I'm glowing. It's pathetic.

He releases his hold on my hair, and I stand, groaning from the soreness in my knees. I lean back against the tiled wall and wipe my fingers across my sore lips. His eyes watch my every move and darken the longer he's staring.

"Come here." He reaches forward and pulls me into his arms. "I want to taste myself in your sweet mouth."

He bends and kisses me. Not the same way as earlier, though. He's taking his time, savoring me, and it's sweet. When his lips leave mine, I try to chase after them for one last taste, but he chuckles and holds my face between both of his hands.

"Now tell me what you two were talking about. And, Kailey? Don't leave anything out, or we do this again. Rinse, repeat."

I'm tempted to lie just so we can do it again, twisted I know. He chuckles, probably seeing the indecision in my eyes. "You liked it, admit it."

"Some of it." My voice is croaky, and I'm in need of water.

"No, you liked all of it. That will be the last lie you utter in this bathroom. First period is over in fifteen minutes, so I suggest you make it quick before we miss second period too."

"Casey stopped me in the hallway to tell me about the grand scheme you guys have concocted. Cooper is to date me so he can dig up anything he can about my pa." I cross my arms over my chest. "She even asked if you guys played the recording for me."

"How did she know…?" he trails off and turns his head to the side in thought. "Go on."

"This is Brody's chance to prove to his father he can take over the company. No wonder he stuck both of you on me. He needed to make sure when one of you fucked-up, the other could carry on."

He grabs my face in one hand, pinching my cheeks together and causing my lips to pucker out. "Watch your fucking mouth, or I'll really fuck it next time."

Really fuck it? He nearly beat a hole through the back of my neck. What does he mean really fuck it? His tongue comes out to swipe across his bottom lip, and I can't force my eyes to look away. The intensity of want I feel almost knocks me over. His face comes in closer, and he licks me from my jaw to my ear. I moan and press my body into his.

"Good girl," he whispers into my ear and then bites it hard. I whimper at the pain, but my hands snake up and under his shirt to rest on his perfectly formed abs … all eight of them. "Now get to class, ma petite."

He pulls away and goes to the sink to wash his hands. "Caine…"

"Now, Kailey, or I will fuck you over this sink, and I promise you, I will be the only one who enjoys it."

Prick.

DESECRATED FLESH

NINETEEN

It was never supposed to go that far, but I saw the submissive in her, and my instincts took over. Her words were saying no, but those eyes were screaming at me to do the filthiest things to her. I've never had a girl—or guy—so willing.

Once her brain realizes what her body likes, I am going to have a fucking field day because little Kailey-Himari—ma petite—likes it hard and depraved.

The bathroom door bangs shut behind her, and I finish washing my hands. I better get out of the girls' bathroom before the period finishes, or I will have to waste time explaining why the fuck I'm in here.

The hallways are empty, and I continue on towards the library. He's going to be pissed about my being late, but maybe I can placate him with my recent discovery.

The heavy ring of keys jingle in my pocket as I pull open the library doors and slip inside. The librarian looks up from her current novel—however many shades of some color—and gives me an appreciative look. I don't have time to tie the bitch up today, and even if I did, I think I found someone my dick wants more because he doesn't stir a bit. I walk by without sparing her a glance. Her shoulders slump, and she sticks her nose back into her book.

The library has a scattering of students here and there, but mostly, it's empty. That's why when we plan at school meetups, we specifically pick this time.

The one dark oak door standing at the far back of the library is always locked, and no one has a key except the four of us. This room is ours and will stay that way until we have children or successors to take it over.

I stick the largest ancient key into the keyhole and listen as the old lock tumbles and turns to permit my entry. The three of them are seated at the large, matching oak table, watching me as I come in.

"You're late," Brody says in that cold, detached voice of his.

"With reason," I retort as I sit in my designated seat. "I found Casey having quite the heated conversation with Kailey in the girls' bathroom."

"Let the bitches fight it out," Brody waves it off.

"Casey knows about the plan and the recording. Any idea how?" I shoot back, and I rest my elbows on the table.

"That's impossible," Cooper protests. "She was never around for our meetings, and I never told her a thing."

"I'm sure someone else told her about it. Someone who was at the house during our meeting." I lock eyes with Brody.

"Georgina," he says without emotion. "I will deal with her. What happened with Kails? What does she know?"

"She knows the plan to date her and extract info. She knows we were always going to play the tape, and she knows this is a test from your father to see if you are worthy of the company."

"So she knows way more than she should, but not even close to all of it." Brody's eyes land on Cooper. "Talk to Casey, and get the complete truth from her. Now tell me what you found out about Charles Richard."

"His business is on its last legs, he has debt mounting again, and he's never home. According to Kailey, he sleeps most nights at the dealership, or so he tells her." Cooper speaks evenly. "She has no idea about the money issues and the situation surrounding her mother. Doesn't even suspect anything."

"We need more," Brody replies. "Caine," he looks at me. "Get close to her."

"On it." I've already begun.

"I think it's time I hacked his financials for the dealership," Zeke interrupts. "We can't let him go to the same extremes as the last time he hit rock bottom."

"Maybe if he kept his fucking nose clean, he'd be fine. Instead, he's sniffing it all away." Cooper rolls his eyes. "But I agree with Zeke. We can't let him go that far again."

"I really don't care if he does." Brody is fucking heartless.

"Well, I do," Zeke retorts, surprising us all. "I'll look into it tonight."

"Fine," Brody waves him off. "Lance is in hot water right now, and I think it's best for us to stay away. If he shows up at another party, we have to escort him out. Justin has had enough of his reputation tarnished by this asshole, and when he gets home for the holiday break, he won't be happy if I have let the fucker do the same to me."

"How's his case going?" Cooper asks.

"He'll get off, but it'll cost his daddy way too many zeroes." Brody looks at me with a gleam in his eye. "That's the downfall of liking rough sex, right, Caine?"

I don't say anything because there's no point. I'm not a rapist. I know when a girl wants me and when she doesn't. So I shrug my shoulders and wait for him to carry on. No one has ever accused me of rape because they always leave satisfied, like ma petite.

"The runners," Brody looks at each of us. "How much profit came in this week?"

"We are at 30 percent more than last week," Zeke says as his fingers fly over the keys on his laptop. "Next week's projection looks to be at forty. The new product seems to be a favorite."

"And my father's?" he asks him.

"Down 20 percent this week," Zeke answers with a grin.

"Sweet," Cooper chuckles.

What our fathers don't know is their proteges—beloved spawns—are working tirelessly to fuck them over and crush the very businesses they hope for us to take over. We don't want to take anything over; we intend to replace theirs with our own. Brody's father runs drugs and loans, Cooper's father has a clean up business and deals with security detail, Zeke's father specializes in whores of all ages and genders, and my dear ole pop controls all hired deaths with his team of trained assassins—all of this under the guise of a multibillion-dollar business conglomerate.

For the last four years, we have been building, training, and controlling our own futures. Securing our power and picking away at our fathers'. Fuck them for giving us assignments to test our responsibility. We only follow along to avoid detection. By the end of this year, all avenues our fathers used to make money will belong to us.

Zeke has freed children and teenagers from his father's clutches this year, causing a huge dent in the man's revenue. He doesn't have a single clue it's his own son. Zeke is building himself a tech security company and building a militia with Coop, biding his time until we strike.

Cooper has slowly built a group of trustworthy guys and often teams up with Zeke on security jobs. This year alone, he has stolen four large accounts belonging to his father. He was the one who thought of hiring mercenaries and using them as runners. We run drugs right now, yes, only to fuck with our fathers' street cred. Once we succeed, we won't let drugs into our turf again.

Brody has successfully taken his father's business of drugs and weapons to its knees. He literally sells the drugs and guns at a loss to us just to fuck over his father. The pressure is mounting, and Landry Sr. is attempting to pass it off to Brody sooner rather than later.

I made sure every newly hired assassin on my father's payroll was conveniently placed there by me. So the guys he trained and honed for the last four years belong to me. They only know loyalty to me and don't take orders from my old man. I've been allowing it until the time comes when we can burn everything to the ground.

"We have to conclude this shit with the Richards and move the fuck on. It's taking up too much time." Brody scrubs his hand down his face. His disdain for Kailey and her father is heavy.

"This isn't just a project for me, Brody." Cooper leans across the table. "I will keep her."

"Whatever," Brody dismisses him.

We all stand as the meeting comes to a close, and the bell for lunch sounds. Brody is the first out the door with Zeke trailing behind him, his nose in his laptop.

Cooper watches them and shakes his head. I know he's planning something with Kailey, and at first, I was against the whole thing. I didn't trust her. The girl who was once one of us then just turned her back without a second thought. I think if someone can turn their back on family, on lifelong friends without remorse, then they're heartless fuckers. But something happened to her, and I know it was the night her mother died, but there was something more. I'm so close to figuring it out.

"I love her," Cooper says to me quietly. "I always have, even while I hated her. KH was my one bright spot when I was always surrounded by my shit family."

"Then I will be the one to tell you," I look him in the eye. "I just hooked up with her in the girls' bathroom then made her tell me everything Casey said."

His grin is instant, and I swear his eyes light up with mirth. "Good."

"You just said you loved the girl." I look at him like he's crazy.

"And I love you too. I'm glad you're seeing her for what she can be."

"Can be?" I look at him, completely perplexed.

"Something we can share forever." Then I watch as he walks by me and through the library.

It's common knowledge Cooper and I share occasionally. It's our thing, and we're the least afraid of swords crossing and all that bullshit. So hearing him say he wants me and him to share Kailey forever sounds almost perfect. I just don't think she plans on wanting us beyond the situation we're forcing on her.

But we can hope, right?

Kailey-Himari

TWENTY

The bell rings, signaling the end of second period and my discomfort. I need a bottle of water and something to rid the taste of Caine out of my mouth. Not that it's a foul taste, just that it's a reminder of what I let him do to me and liking it.

I gather my things and head to the door. Standing just outside is Cooper, leaning against the wall with a wide smile on his face. Would he stay smiling if he knew what happened an hour and a half ago?

"Sha," he breathes as he gathers me into a hug and inhales the scent of my hair. "You smell like Polo."

"Huh?" I look up at him with confusion.

"Caine's choice of cologne." The smile is still plastered to his face, and I can't tell if it's fake or not.

"About that…" I begin. "Caine and I—"

"I already know, sha. But it warms me to know you want to tell me."

"You already know?" It literally just happened. What did Caine do? Pull Cooper out of class to brag about sticking his enormous dick in my mouth? Am I that much of a game to them?

"I see your face slowly getting angrier and angrier." He tries to calm me down. "But it's not like that. We both have feelings for you, and if you want to explore us both, we are okay with it. You already know this."

"Yeah, but to discuss the things we do like I'm a toy—"

"We didn't discuss the things you did," he cuts me off again. "Just that something happened. But we can discuss those things if you want… Hell, next time I'll join in."

I can feel my face burning red under the words he just said. A part of me feels intrigued, but a larger part of me feels like that situation just might be my biggest trigger yet. I walk beside Cooper towards the cafeteria. His arm is slung over my shoulders. Standing outside the doors is a nervous looking Casey.

"Kailey, you head inside and find Kimmy. I'll be with you soon." He leans in and plants a firm kiss to my lips. I feel myself opening up under him, and he groans into my lips. "Go before I embarrass us both out here."

I do as he asks and shoot Casey a warning look before entering the cafeteria. She better not try anything with him. He's mine. The thought should be enough to worry me. The possession I feel is overwhelming, but I can't help it.

Kimmy is waiting for me in our usual spot next to the line of food. She's looking at her phone with a scowl.

"Tell me," I say as I sidle up next to her. "Who's doing what now?"

She startles at my voice and shoots me a look. When I laugh, she joins in and taps her shoulder against mine. "Henry has been quieter than usual. I want to believe it's his grueling football schedule, but I can't help thinking maybe he found a hot college girl."

"On god, girl, if that boy even thinks about another set of titties, I will hurt him. None will ever be as nice as yours."

She scoffs and shoves at my shoulder, making me laugh out loud. "When the heck did you get so crass?"

"This was always me." I point to my head. "It's just recently I've let her out again."

"Gosh, keep her out. She sounds like a hoot!"

It's true. This is me. I used to chill with boys, talk with boys, and joke around with them. I had a crass sense of humor before, and I can feel it coming back to me. I know I have Cooper to thank for it.

"What's going on with all your boys?" she asks as we grab our food.

"They ain't all mine," I scoff. "Cooper and I guess Caine as well, but the other two are nothing."

"Girl, you are as blind as a bat," Kimmy scolds as she grabs a bun. "Brody is murderous at anyone who looks at you, and Ezekiel's eyes always find you in any room you share. Cooper is obviously head over heels, and Caine looks about as fond of you as a gator when he finds himself a baby deer."

"Honey, you are the blind one." I walk behind her as she approaches the table with Brody, Zeke, and Caine. It's become a normal thing now to sit with them.

"Hello, boys," she croons, and I snort.

"Hi, girls," Zeke says as he looks at us, his smile wide. He and Cooper have always been the sweet ones.

Brody barely spares us a glance, and Caine just watches me with intensity. The things we did in the bathroom suddenly flood my mind, and I feel my neck and face heat. He chuckles and pulls me down to sit next to him.

"You smell like me," he says with his head in my hair, not unlike Cooper earlier. "I'm taking you home today."

"Okay," I whisper and begin to eat. Fighting them has become futile, and I'm not sure I want to anymore.

Cooper saunters into the cafeteria solo, and I look behind him to see if Casey enters. She doesn't, and I breathe a sigh of relief. I don't want her complicating things. I feel like I am just getting back to who I used to be, and if I end up losing Coop and now Caine, I will be lost for good. I know it sounds strange that I will lose myself over guys, but if it weren't for them, I would still be stuck inside that bubble of fear.

Cooper sits on my other side, effectively locking me in between him and Caine. The innuendo is not lost on me as Caine toys with my hair, and Cooper rubs his hand along my thigh. I wait for that sinking feeling of fear. Being between the two of them should do that, but it doesn't. I breathe out a sigh of relief and chance a look at Coop.

"Everything okay?" I ask him.

"Oui, sha, everything is just about perfect." He looks over my head to Caine, and I watch him smile.

"Brody," I hear Georgina's whiny voice. "This weekend is my birthday, and I have a yacht docked and ready to be filled. My eighteenth is important, so I will need you to escort me."

"Sure, whatever, Georgie." He rolls his eyes.

"It's a society formal, Brody. You know I have been planning this birthday since I was thirteen. You always agreed to do it."

"Georgina," the warning in Brody's voice is clear. "We will all be there."

"All?" Her pretty face crumples into a sneer. "Surely you mean just the guys."

"And their respective dates."

"You'll be happy to know you can save a place at the table because Coop and I will be sharing a date," Caine taunts.

"Oh, dear god," Georgina moans. "That will be the talk of the decade. Please don't let them do this to me," she begs Brody.

"Who am I to tell them who they should and shouldn't date? Remember how we didn't let them tell me?" He sneers at her and dismisses her with a wave of his hand.

What does he mean they didn't let the guys tell him? Did the others try to dissuade him from dating Georgina? I look at Cooper, and he leans in to kiss me softly.

"Gosh," I hear Kimmy sigh. "I really hated the thought of her dating you, but it looks as sweet as honey."

"Dating both of us," Caine corrects her and turns my face to claim my mouth. He's rough, and his teeth nip hard on my bottom lip.

"Slut," Georgina coughs into her hand.

"Watch it, Georgie," Caine warns her. "You say anything else about my girl, and I'll make you watch as I burn your yacht down."

Her quick inhale of breath tells me she believes Caine would do it. Not that I doubted his words for a second.

"Well, I'll say I'm hot and bothered," Kimmy chuckles as she fans herself. "You think Henry would agree to such a relationship?"

"What?" I laugh. "Him and the football team?"

"Exactly," She nods. "All that muscle…" Her eyes turn dreamy, and I laugh at her.

"Henry would break noses if they even looked at you," Cooper chuckles. "I remember what he was like last year."

"Dang it," she pouts, and the three of us laugh at her.

"Besides," Caine drawls. "It takes a certain type of woman to handle more than one."

His words transport me back to the forest, the smells and the sounds of their grunts as they forced themselves wherever they wanted. I can hear my name faintly in the background, but my mind is transfixed on the forest floor, the mud seeping into my clothes and the smell of blood.

His hand wraps around my neck, pulling my head back as he plunges into me. Lance stands in front, jerking himself off while he meets my eyes, and instead of feeling any kind of remorse, he's clearly getting off on the pain reflected there.

The sound of Justin's flesh slapping against mine and the sound of Lance's hand around his cock becomes in sync, the rhythm echoing around the forest.

"Please, Justin," I try to speak around the grip he has on my throat. "Please stop."

"Almost … done …" he groans deep with one final slam into me. "Now it's his turn. You can handle it."

The vision is fading, but the pain is lingering throughout my body. My legs, my throat, and especially where they desecrated me. The pain radiates through me with each pounding footstep.

"What happened?" I hear someone ask. "Not the nurse's office. Bring her in here."

Thankfully, I succumb to the blackness, and the pain numbs for now.

TWENTY-ONE

I see Caine Leblanc running towards the nurse's office with a groaning, semi-conscious Kailey in his arms. He looks frantic, and Cooper Fontenot looks no better, chasing behind after them.

"What happened?" I ask as I step out of my office, making him come to a complete stop. If I find out he hurt her, I'll lose my job and possibly my freedom when I'm through with him.

"I don't know…" he shakes his head. "We need a nurse—"

"Not the nurse's office. Bring her in here." I open my office, and both boys come in with an unconscious Kailey. "Lay her on the couch."

They do as I say, and we all stand in a line looking down at her. "Why did you want us to bring her in here?" Caine asks, his eyes narrowing. "She needs a nurse."

"Explain what happened," I demand. "Every detail, and then I will decide how much to tell you."

"We were eating lunch… She was relaxed … but then she stiffened up, and she let out an anguished scream. Like she was in pain. Caine grabbed her face, but she wasn't looking at us. It was like she was somewhere else. She kept crying and moaning like someone was torturing her." Cooper's voice cracks with emotion, and I can't deny he really cares about her. "What happened to her?"

"I can't discuss anything about Kailey with you guys," I try to explain. "She's had a rough past, as you guys would know, having a hand in it."

"We were in her past!" Cooper yells. "There was no trauma."

"We don't know what happened after that summer when she stopped talking to us," Caine says quietly. "We never questioned it, didn't fight for her. Something happened that summer."

I don't say anything further and place my hand on his shoulder. He's freakishly strong, and the bulging muscles under his clothes only prove that.

"I got her from here. I'll speak to her afternoon classes, but I have to ask you to leave. Something triggered her, and I'd rather her not have another episode as soon as she wakes up."

Caine turns to look at me, his face stone-cold and hard. Cooper just continues to pace the length of my office, mumbling something to himself.

"I promise I won't let anything happen to her," I assure Caine. He must see the sincerity in my eyes because, after a few moments, he nods in agreement.

"I will come back here at the end of the day. Do not let her leave without Cooper or myself," he says, deadly serious.

"You got it," I nod. I just want them to leave so I can help Kail as best I can.

Caine opens the door and warns, "Don't let anything happen to her."

I don't answer him. He either trusts me or he doesn't, I don't give a shit. Cooper gives a lingering look and then softly closes the door behind them.

"They're gone," I whisper to her. "You can open your eyes."

I watch as those gorgeous hazel eyes open and focus on my face. "How'd you know I was awake?"

"Your breathing changed just a few minutes ago," I shrug. "Tell me what happened."

"Insinuated threesomes are a major trigger," she groans and covers her eyes with her hand.

Please, I beg my dick. Don't react.

"Caine said something offhand, and it just reminded me of them and what they did to me together."

"Why would Caine say something like that? Are you ... ah ... dating them both?" Why am I getting so involved with this girl? I can already feel my career slipping through my fingertips because of it.

"Yeah, I guess I'm dating them both. I know it's not normal, but it is what it is." Her voice is small, and she sounds uneasy.

"Is this a forced situation, Kail?" I ask. It's not really making much sense to me after what she's been through. She wouldn't want to casually date a few different guys. Nothing about Caine screams casual either.

She closes her eyes and shudders through a breath. Her chest rises and falls rapidly as she tries to control her emotions. I kneel on the floor beside the couch and gently brush some of her hair out of her face.

"Why are you being so nice to me?" she asks in a hushed whisper.

"I'm not too sure," I whisper back as I watch her pouty mouth move. She is the most exquisite thing I have ever seen.

She leans up and brings her mouth closer to mine. I can feel her breath on my lips, see the flecks of gold in her eyes, and smell a lingering scent of men's cologne on her skin. Jealousy, raw and debilitating, courses through me, just in time for me to pull back from her and stand.

I hear her exhale and look back as she falls back to the couch. I sit at my desk and pick up the phone to call her out of her classes. This will be a long afternoon while she's in here, and I'm tempted to risk everything.

She sleeps soundly on my couch as I lean back in my chair and watch her like a fucking perv. Knowing what Lance and Justin did to her only makes me want to find them and make them bleed. There were many rumors in high school about them double teaming girls, but when it morphed into rape accusations, I knew something more was happening behind the scenes.

It's frustrating, seeing them get off every time because they come from money. The rest of us feel helpless to do anything because our bank accounts are missing half the zeroes they have.

There was this one case, I was going into senior year, and they were headed into sophomore. Justin Landry was throwing his epic end of the summer party, and most of the school was invited. Jeanine Fontenot, who was in my grade, crazy smart, and drop dead gorgeous, attended. She wasn't a regular at the high school party scene, and she was a sure shoo-in for valedictorian. She's also Cooper's older sister. This party had a shit ton of alcohol, and the drugs were scattered in bowls all over the place.

That night was a shit-show, and I left early because I knew I was on the brink of passing out. After that night, none of us saw Jeanine Fontenot again. She didn't return to JFK, and from what I heard, was homeschooled. No one could figure out what happened, but there were rumors. She was seen dancing between Lance and Justin most of the night, and her cup was constantly being refilled.

When she disappeared, some thought maybe she was pregnant and hid out at home. Then there were rumors she was ashamed of her actions, but I always wondered if she became a victim of the rape duo. Over time, though, I will admit she was forgotten, and my life carried on … until now.

She stirs just as the last bell of the day goes off. It's easy to see she's exhausted, and the sleep was something she needed desperately.

"Thank you, Oliver." Her voice is groggy with sleep. "I needed this."

"You did." I agree with her and stand at my desk. "Are you not sleeping well at home?"

"I'm alone a lot," she admits with her eyes downcast. "Papa works late hours, and I don't enjoy being in that house alone."

"Because you fear they will return?"

"Yes," she nods.

"Can't you ask your father to be home more?" I can feel the

anger inside me rise. How dare her father neglect his only daughter?

"I don't want to bother him. Next year I will be out of here anyway." She shrugs as she stands. "Thanks again."

I nod and watch as she leaves my office, then I quickly google the Richards. The first page of results concentrates on her mother's death, the hit-and-run, and the tragedy it left behind. Then a few links come up for a used car dealership, Charles Richard Used Car Lot.

Maybe I need to speak to the man himself directly.

I pull up to the dealership, which looks dark and empty. Not one customer in sight, and the lights on the inside are off. It's five in the evening. Maybe he went home. But something inside me says he didn't or else his daughter could sleep better with a man in the house to protect her.

I pull on the front door, and I'm surprised to find it's open even though no one's inside. There's a desk, but the computer is off, and the seat is empty. I walk the perimeter of the front room until I see a narrow corridor. There are two doors, one is open, showing a toilet and sink, and I shut the other. I grasp the knob on the shut door and let it swing open. Sitting at a desk with his head bent over and sniffing a white substance into his right nostril is who I'm assuming is none other than Charles Richard.

"Oh!" He jumps to his feet, his nose still coated in a white powder. "Sir, we are closed for the day."

"Maybe you should lock your front door? But I can see how that could slip your mind." I point to the lines on his desk.

"How can I help you?" he grits out with a fake smile.

"I am obviously looking to purchase a car." I hold my arms out. "Unless you are not open for business. There are other car lots around here."

"No, no," he rushes from behind his desk and ushers me back

out into the front room. "We are always open for business. What type of car?"

I follow him around the lot as he tries to find me the perfect 'family' car for my wife and three kids. Yeah, I lied my ass off, but I found exactly what I was looking for when I came here. Kail has no proper family anymore, and the thought makes me feel heartbroken. I don't know what it is about her, but I feel like everything that's happened has led me to this point in my life and to her.

I pull up her address on my GPS and head in that direction before I can talk myself out of it. It's going to be a long night, but I need to see when her father finally makes an appearance—if he does at all.

DESECRATED FLESH

Kailey-Himari

TWENTY-TWO

After a mostly silent ride with Caine, I come home to an empty house, and it looks like Papa hasn't been home for days. I start to feel terrible that I haven't checked in with him until I realize the role is reversed. Why hasn't he checked in with me?

When he hasn't come home by eleven, I head to bed and try to sleep, but I'm restless and can't seem to turn off my brain. Some of it is because I'm alone again, but mostly it's about what happened during the day. The incident with Caine in the bathroom and then my episode at lunch. Will I ever be normal again?

I get out of bed and sit in my window seat. Mama would read me bedtime stories from here while letting in the light of the stars. She believed our ancestors were out there, shining on us and helping to guide us. I look up at the sky, and I feel her. I know she's out there.

Our street looks deserted. All the houses are dark, and the streetlamps are dim and yellow, barely illuminating the road. I live on a cul-de-sac, so we don't get much traffic this far down the street. It's quiet and exactly what my mama was looking for when she found out she was pregnant.

A car is parked on the other side of our street, but right in front of our house. It's a black sedan, and from here, I think I can see someone sitting inside. There are two other houses in this semi-circle, but it's parked across from mine. I quickly jump back from my window, and my heart gallops through my chest as I imagine who it could be. Lance? Justin? Both of them?

I rush to grab my phone on my side table and punch out a text message to the first person I think of. It's a strange relationship we have going on, but I trust him.

Me: Someone is parked on my street. I'm scared.

He doesn't answer right away, and I curse myself because maybe he's asleep. He has school in the morning too. I pace my room and try to calm down. I lock every door and window since that summer. It's become somewhat of a ritual every night. I'm safe. No one can get in. I repeat it over and over again until I hear the chime on my phone.

Oliver: Open the front door.

What? He's here? He came here to check on me. I rush down the stairs and through my dark house to the front door. I unlock it and fling it open quickly. He's leaning against the house, his clothes slightly rumpled and his silver eyes shining bright. His eyes slowly roam over me, and I look down. Fuck, I'm standing here in an oversized t-shirt and panties. I feel my cheeks heat, and when his eyes meet mine, there's a twinkle of amusement there.

"Sorry…" he starts.

"Sorry…" I say at the same time, and we both chuckle. "Go ahead." I wave him on to speak first.

"Uh…" he rubs a hand along his neck. "The car parked there," he points to the sedan. "Is mine."

At first, I'm speechless, surprised he's the one camped outside of my house. Next, I'm so overcome with appreciation, I don't realize what I'm doing until I feel my arms thrown around his neck and my face buried deep into his chest. He smells like a safe place, my very own haven, and I tighten my hold. His arms encircle my waist as he slowly walks us back into my house and shuts the door behind him. I haven't moved, my face still pressed against his chest.

"I don't think it's a good idea for the neighbors to see you hugging a teacher in the middle of the night," he says, his voice low. "I didn't mean to scare you with my car. I just didn't want you to be left alone after the day you had."

His hands slowly drop from my waist, his fingers skimming past the t-shirt's hemline that's ridden up to reveal the bottom half of my ass. I gasp as his fingers meet my skin there and instinctively press myself into him. His low groan sends a shock of arousal through me, and I can feel the flood of wetness inside my panties. Unfortunately, his hands drop back to his sides with a willpower I only wish I possessed right now. But I want his arms around me, I want to be comforted by him, and I don't want to be alone.

"Please," I pull away from him slightly. "Hold me, Oliver."

"I'm your teacher…" he sounds pained and unsure.

"You're my guidance counselor," I correct him and press in closer again. His quick intake of breath tells me he's feeling everything I am. "Please."

His fingers tentatively touch my outer thighs and lightly trace along my skin. The touch is teasing and sensual, my skin lighting up with goose bumps. My face is pressed into the curve between his pecs as I unclasp my hands from around his neck and slowly run them over his shoulders and onto his chest. His heart is beating just as quickly as mine, and now I know for sure Oliver wants me too.

His fingers stop on the skin where my thighs and ass meet. I can feel his hesitation. I curl my body, pushing my ass against his hands. His groan is the only warning I get as he pushes me to the wall and grabs my ass in handfuls. I'm pulled up close to his body, his chest brushing mine, and his face in the crook of my neck. His hot breath fans my throat, and I curve into him, our pelvises brushing, eliciting moans from us both.

His hands continue to knead my ass, and his fingertips slide under my panties, bringing them closer to my core. His mouth glides over the sensitive skin just under my ear, and I rub myself along the obvious swell in his pants.

His hands suddenly stop moving, and his body tenses. "Kail…" his voice is guttural. "We can't do this."

"Don't stop." I'm not above begging. My body feels like it's been dipped in gasoline and ignited.

He squeezes my flesh once more then drops his hands and takes a step back. The space he creates between our bodies effectively cools my heated core, and I rest my head back against the wall.

"I'm sorry. I shouldn't have done that," he whispers harshly as he runs a hand over his head.

"I want you," I admit to him. "I'm not ashamed of that."

"It's obvious how I feel, but it doesn't make it right."

"I'm eighteen, Oliver. I can make my own decisions," I retort.

"You're still a student at the school I'm employed at," he shrugs and turns back towards the front door. "Get some sleep, Kail. I'll be right outside."

Before I can tell him to go home and get some sleep himself, he's out my door as if the house is on fire. I lean back against the wall and try to collect my thoughts. I am now entangled with three vastly different guys, and I want them all equally. Not one of them stands out above the rest, so how the hell do I choose? I know Oliver will make it easier by refusing to take this any further, but I can't help how I feel. I want to touch him, I want to feel him, and I want to kiss him so badly to see if he tastes as good as I imagine he does.

I drag myself to bed with thoughts of Caine's forceful attitude, Cooper's sweet nature, and Oliver's quiet intensity.

The first thing I did this morning was check to see if the car was still parked across the street. It wasn't, but it was comforting to know he had been there, watching over me as I slept alone in this big, quiet house.

I throw on a pair of skinny jeans and a long-sleeved Henley. I leave my hair in massive waves down my back and my face clear of makeup. This look reminds me of the old Kailey-Himari, the one who dressed for comfort and not to impress. She didn't care about how many boys liked her or which boy she liked. She loved to dance and be surrounded by genuine friends.

The horn blares from my driveway. I roll my eyes, but a smile stretches along my face. Cooper is becoming predictable like he once was, and the thought warms my heart. I grab my bag and step outside. He's leaning against the Wrangler, his arms crossed over his wide chest. His hair flops and moves in the breeze, and his sunglasses cover his eyes, but his mouth is turned up in a grin. I feel the tug in my chest as I take him in. Cooper has wormed his way back into my heart.

I walk towards him, my hair blowing across my face and my stomach twisting with nerves. Once I'm standing in front of him, he drops his arms, and I reach up to pull his face to mine. His mouth is soft, and he tastes like a mixture of coffee and mint. The kiss is a lingering sweet one, and when I pull away, grinning at the look of shock on his face.

"Good morning." My voice is husky and low.

"Nuh uh…" he shakes his head. "Get back here. I want more of that sweetness."

I giggle as he pulls me back in and kisses me again. This time, the press of his lips is more demanding, and his tongue slips between mine to have a proper taste. He flips us around so my back rests against the Jeep, and he draws himself closer. I moan into his mouth, and his hands tighten on my waist, dragging me against the growing bulge in his pants. Our teeth clash, his hands wind into my hair, and there's zero space between us. His groan is swallowed up by my mouth as I dig my fingers into his sides.

His hands leave my hair, then he places them on the Jeep at either side of my head. He pulls away from my mouth, and I whimper at the loss. My panties are soaked, and I just want to give my body what it's searching for, Cooper as deep as he can go inside me.

"Sha," his voice is raspy and low. "I have to stop. I want you so bad."

"I want you too, Coop."

"I feel like I have been waiting forever to hear you say that," he whispers. "What happened yesterday?"

"I want to tell you—"

"But you don't trust me yet," he finishes my sentence.

"I want to trust you."

"I understand why you don't." He looks so sad, but he's right. Trust is earned, and I'm not ready to completely fall for Cooper, or anyone else. I have been wronged too many times in the past.

He steps back and opens the passenger door for me. His eyes

give me a final once-over before he closes the door and jogs around to his side. I watch him as he pulls himself up, his arm muscles flexing and those delicious veins popping out of his skin. He turns his head to me and grins. I return one back and relax into my seat as we head to school.

Thinking of school reminds me of Oliver, and I can't help but feel nervous but also disappointed. I understand the consequences of his involvement with me, but I can't help it. I want him too.

The parking lot is filled when we pull in. I see the other three standing beside Caine's truck, and as per usual, Brody looks irritated. I know he and I were the closest at one point, but now it's like I don't even know him. I wish I could go back and change how things went down with us, but I know I can't.

I jump out of the Wrangler, and Cooper scoops me up in his arms to plant a quick, sloppy kiss on my mouth. When we pull apart, I laugh and shove his shoulder. That's when I feel him, dark and demanding at my back.

"My turn, ma petite." His rasp sends a shiver through my body. I turn and look at Caine through my lashes. After what he forced on me yesterday, I should hate him, but I'm feeling anything but.

"Then take it. That's your way, right?" There's no anger in my tone. I sound eager and willing.

Cooper chuckles behind me, and Caine flashes me a rare, genuine smile as he pulls me in, our bodies completely flush.

"It is," he answers me just before he plunges into my mouth. Caine tastes of sin and bad intentions. I'm frigging hooked.

Just like everything he does, he dominates my mouth, forcing my body to bend to his will. I don't fight it because I want it. I want him so bad. His teeth rake over my bottom lip, his hands grab onto my ass, and he rubs himself into my stomach. He's hard and so goddamn delicious.

"Ahem." I hear someone clear their throat behind us. But that doesn't stop Caine. No, if anything, it spurs him on more.

He deepens the kiss further—I didn't think it was possible—and the sounds coming from me are almost embarrassing. I want to slide to my knees and beg him to violate my mouth again. I want him to wrap his fist into my hair and drag me to the nearest bathroom. Jesus, I'm depraved.

He pulls back until our lips are just a hair's breadth apart, both of us panting and both of us grinning. "Good morning." His voice is gravel, rough and hard.

"Morning," I whisper back.

"If you two are done," Brody's voice sneers. "We should get inside now."

Caine presses a soft kiss to my lips and pulls away. "I'm not near done," he states.

I search out Cooper. I don't want to hurt him, and what Caine and I just did was intense. He's standing off to the side, his sunglasses still covering his eyes but that familiar grin still in place. I walk towards him and watch as he adjusts himself in his pants. His fingers reach out, and he interlinks our hands.

"I was trying to figure out how the hell to work myself into that equation," he murmurs to me. "You look completely ravished."

"I'm not sure if I'm doing this thing right," I confess. "How am I supposed to act when I'm with one, and the other is watching?"

"You act how you're feeling. I promise you, both Caine and I love to watch."

I feel my cheeks heat, and he chuckles at my reaction. The thought of one of them watching doesn't scare me as much as it should. Maybe these boys are slowly replacing all the bad things that have happened to me with good, fresh memories. Ones filled with pleasure and not pain.

"Kailey-Himari Richard!" Kimmy's voice booms through the parking lot, and I cringe like a child being scolded. "Where the hell were you yesterday?"

I turn and face a very pissed off best friend, and rightfully so. "Sorry, I wasn't feeling well…"

"Girl," she stands in front of me with her arms crossed. "I'm gonna need more than that. These episodes have been happening since I met you. I thought you were getting better until yesterday."

"I—"

"She doesn't owe you an explanation, Kimmy." Brody comes to stand beside me, cutting me off. "You may be her best friend, but if you knew about these 'episodes', why didn't you try to help?"

"What?" She looks shocked and hurt at his words.

"Brody, stop." I put my hand on his arm. He stiffens immediately and shrugs me off.

"We need to get to class," he retorts and walks away.

"Kimmy, I'm sorry, I just have some stress at home with my pa, and sometimes it all gets to be too much."

"Sorry," her voice breaks. "I was just worried about you."

"Don't worry," I smile at her. "I still have this." I lift my wrist and show her the Gris-Gris.

We link arms and follow the Golden Four into the school. If you told me this would be my reality a month ago, I would've laughed my ass off.

"Kailey Richard?" I hear a voice at the front of the class.

I look up and raise my hand. "Here."

"You're wanted in guidance." The secretary exits the class as my heart feels like it's dropped into my stomach.

I get up and pack up my bag, feeling everyone's eyes on me. I walk by the teacher, who gives me a small smile then I exit the classroom. The walk to his office is long. My nerves are skyrocketing, and my steps are slow. I don't want him to stop seeing me. I feel like what happened between us is scaring him, and he'll back off.

I stand in front of his door and try to collect myself. The door opens, and the first thing I see are steel-gray eyes. He grabs my arm, pulling me inside and shutting the door. His breathing seems erratic as he slowly walks me backward. My thighs hit his desk, and I have nowhere else to go. He stands in front of me, both of our chests heaving and brushing together.

"I can't get you out of my head," he says quietly. "It's wrong, but I can't do it."

"Don't," I plead, unsure of what I'm asking for.

He bends down, his hands resting on top of the desk on either side of me. "Don't what, Kail?"

Oh god, having him this close, his breath hitting my cheeks, his eyes dark with lust, and his body heat seeping into mine is like the most pleasurable torture.

I step into him, our lips brushing. "Don't get me out of your head."

His tongue comes out to wet his bottom lip, brushing against my lip too, and we both gasp at the contact. I want his kiss so badly. I crave it.

Neither of us moves. "You're dating Caine and Cooper." His voice is low, and his lips moving over mine.

"They like to share," I whisper back to him.

He moves his face to the side of my mouth. His tongue comes out, and he lightly runs it up my cheek, stopping at my ear. I'm trembling with want. First Cooper, then Caine, and now Oliver is giving me a serious case of orgasmic deprivation.

"I wouldn't mind sharing either, if it means I get to have you." His words are so soft, but I feel the impact in my chest.

"Oliver…" my voice cracks, and I almost lose my footing when he presses his extremely hard and very impressive erection into me.

"Am I making you uncomfortable?" he asks as his mouth runs up and down my throat.

"No." I tip my head to give him more access.

His left hand moves and wraps around the outside of my thigh. He squeezes briefly and then moves it behind my leg, tugging lightly. I relax and let him guide my leg up and around his waist, leaving my center wide open for him to settle into. He presses in tight, and we both groan at the contact. My hands end up under his polo shirt, and I was correct in my previous assumption … my guidance counselor is stacked.

He lifts his head from my neck and looks down at me. His gray eyes are stormy and dark. I feel like his prey, but at that moment, I want nothing more.

"Kiss me." I moan and push my wet, aching pussy onto his cock.

"Fuck," he hisses and leans down as he licks his lips.

The ring of his phone makes him jump back and slam his back against the office door. I'm more frustrated than I am startled, and I'm realizing this is the female version of blue balls. I am this close to pulling a Caine and forcing Oliver's face between my legs. He is rushing around the desk to pick up his phone as I groan.

"Ballon," he grits out with frustration. I turn and run my eyes over his features. His black brows are tugged together in the center and his eyes look as hard as their color. "Yes, I will have that for you this afternoon. Thank you."

He slams down the receiver and places both hands on his desk, his head hanging low.

"Is this where you say something like, 'Kailey this was wrong?'" I ask, my voice laced with sarcasm.

"I've got to get to work on this report for the principal. Text me later." He's not looking me in the eye, and his dismissive attitude pisses me off.

I decide right here and now not to be Oliver's chew toy any longer. His back-and-forth indecisiveness is giving me whiplash. I turn on my heel and grab my bag. Fuck him. I feel the weight of his eyes as I leave his office and let the door bang behind me. I'm proud of myself because I didn't spare him another glance.

The rest of the day is quiet, and I have been dodging Georgina and her pack of hounds. I heard from a few girls in PE that they were looking for me. I know when they catch up with me it's game over. I can't take on the four of them, and I don't want to have a constant bodyguard.

"Here," Caine grunts inside his truck as he hands me a credit card. "Buy a cocktail dress for this weekend."

"What?" I look at him in surprise. "I own dresses, Caine. Besides, I can buy my own if I want a new one."

"Take the fucking card, ma petite. This is me being nice, don't piss me off."

I snort and take the card out of his hand. "Maybe I like you pissed off." This is definitely my neglected vagina talking.

"I know." He flashes me a grin, and I gasp at how beautiful he really is. "I like the color red on you."

I guess that's his way of saying he wants a red dress. "Okay," I acquiesce because I know if I fight him, he might just go buy the most hideous dress he can find and force me to wear it. "Who am I going with?"

"Me and Coop." He looks at me like I'm going crazy, like our situation is typical.

"Okay."

He pulls into my driveway, and I look at the large empty home in front of me. I know Papa came home at some point in the early morning because his coffee mug was sitting in the sink when I left for school. Not that he attempted to check on me at all.

I'm lost in my thoughts until Caine slips his fingers into my hair at the base of my scalp and roughly tugs me over to him. His mouth slams into mine, and I open for him, needing this more than him. He growls deep in his chest and drags me over to straddle him in the driver's seat. My arms circle around his neck, and his steely hardness presses into my already aching core.

"Come inside." I know I sound like I'm begging, but I've had enough of the teasing touches. So far, Caine is the only one who has taken things beyond kissing, and I want more.

His head hits the headrest on his seat, and he groans long and deep. "I can't." His jaw looks tense, and he feels like he's vibrating with anger.

"Excuse me?" I ask. What the fuck does he mean he can't?

"I made a promise, ma petite," he says, his voice low and dangerous. "I said I would wait until you and Cooper…" he trails off, sounding regretful.

"Fuck you guys and all the fucking teasing," I grumble as I disentangle myself from his lap. "I'm buying a fucking vibrator."

His large hand wraps around my throat, and he forces me back into his space. "Watch it, Kailey," he says through his teeth. "If I'm the first to fuck you, I'll fucking break you." His mouth crushes into mine once more, and I melt into him. He pulls back and looks at me with angry eyes. "And I will fucking break you."

I tremble at his words, but not from fear, because what Caine doesn't know is I'm already broken, and I won't let anything else break me again. He must see the emotions flit across my eyes, because his mouth turns up into a sinister grin.

"Ma petite, I know something happened to you, and like I've told you before, I will find out what. But understand this, I don't intend to break your body." He leans in, his mouth against my ear. "I will rip your very soul out of your body, covet it, destroy it, and then wait patiently for you to pick up the pieces … only to do it all over again."

I believe him, but my mouth never could stand down from a challenge. "Pretty words, Caine, but I'm waiting for action." I slap his hand off my throat and lean in to press a sweet kiss to his cheek. "I'll see you tomorrow."

The silence confirms the shock he feels at my words, even if his face betrays nothing. I get out of the truck and turn to watch him leave. Caine will be my catalyst on the road to finding myself, and I know I will pick up pieces of my soul when he's through, but fuck it… I'm enjoying the ride.

DESECRATED FLESH

Kailey-Himari

TWENTY-THREE

The rest of the week goes by, and I have effectively ignored Oliver's texts. My papa has been making more of an effort and started coming home in time for dinner. I took Caine's credit card, and with little effort, convinced Kimmy to come dress shopping with me.

Kimmy has a romantic weekend planned with Henry and can't come to the party, which means I am left to trust that the boys are really on my side. I still doubt it every day, and this will be the biggest step in building trust with them.

The bell rings for the end of class and the start of lunch. I have been enjoying my lunch periods with Caine and Cooper, even though I have to endure Brody and Georgina. She's been persistent in trying to get my invitation revoked, to which Brody vehemently refuses—this should worry me—and Cooper refuses to go otherwise.

"Boo!" Kimmy's voice rings out through the crowded hallway. I wait for her to catch up to me. "I'm taking off early. I need to drive all the way to Tulane."

"Okay." I hug her close. "Drive safe, and have a great time."

"I will!" she squeals and runs off in the opposite direction.

I walk to the cafeteria and find Cooper waiting for me outside the doors. He's becoming sweeter by the day, and I know my heart is on the verge of falling.

"Sha," he holds out his arm for me. "Today is crawfish Friday. Did you bring your bib?"

"No," I giggle and let him lead me to the lunch line.

We stand in the line, and he hands me a gift card. I look at him in question when I see it's for one of the most expensive salons in town.

"For your hair and makeup." He looks a little embarrassed. "Girls like that sort of thing, right? I made you an appointment for right after school."

"Thank you, Cooper." Relief flows through my body as I smile widely at him. I was panicking about hair and makeup, especially because I won't have Kimmy's help.

"I'll pick you up at eight, then we'll take the scenic route to the yacht." He leans in and kisses my temple.

My phone pings a few times through lunch, and I know who it is because Kimmy wouldn't dare touch her phone while she was driving. So I ignore it like I have been all week and continue eating while sitting between Caine and Cooper.

"Miss Kailey Richard. Please report to guidance," The overhead speaker system blares out the secretary's voice.

"Wow, called to guidance during lunch." Georgina taunts. "You must be a fucking basket case."

The other hounds chuckle, and I don't give two fucks about their feelings when I lean over and plant a sweet kiss on Cooper's mouth then the same on Caine's—who lets it be sweet.

"I am." I look at Georgina as I stand. "So I'd watch your fucking mouth."

The four of them look at each other nervously as Caine snorts into his crawfish. "I'll be waiting out front," he says to me.

"Okay," I nod.

I'm fucking pissed. How dare Oliver pull rank and announce my name over the school intercom? Like I'm not already enough of a freak. I walk straight inside his office without knocking and slam his door shut. He startles and stands up.

"What the fuck do you want?" I sneer at him.

"Kail—"

"Don't call me that, Mr. Ballon," I cut him off.

"You're not answering your texts. I needed to make sure you were okay." He keeps his voice level, but I can see he's nervous.

"Is that what you do with all your students?" I retort, trying to hit him where it hurts. "Seems pretty unprofessional, don't you think?"

"You know how I feel about you." His hands slam down on his desk as his eyes flash with anger. Finally, something.

"Do I?" I mirror him and slam my hands on his desk too. Now we're eye to eye.

He runs his hand over his head and lets out a breath. "Please, sit down." He motions to the chair behind me.

I do as he asks and wait for him to speak with my brow raised. There's nothing I can say to him.

"I heard you and Cooper in the cafeteria. You're going to Georgina's yacht party? Don't you think that's a terrible choice? What if those girls do something to you? Or what if Lance shows up?"

I don't say anything. I have thought of all these things, and I've decided to trust that Caine and Cooper will take care of me.

"Nothing?" His jaw flexes, and I know my silence is getting to him. "I can't help you if you won't help yourself," he huffs.

"Is that all?" I stand up and grab my bag. "I can't keep missing all these classes for guidance."

"You have my number." His hand scrapes along the five o'clock shadow at his jaw. "Use it if you need me."

I don't answer as I storm out of his office. I've been doing that a lot lately. My anger drains quickly, and I see his situation for what it is. Having an affair with a student wouldn't only ruin his career but his reputation as well. Nobody would care that I'm eighteen, only that I'm a student, and he'd be looked at as some pedo.

I turn around and face his closed door. I want to go in there and apologize. I want to hug him and say I understand, but I shouldn't. This space I've created between us because of my anger is probably what will save him from me.

When the last bell sounds, my nerves take over, and I doubt my decision to go to this party. Why did I think it was a good idea to lock myself on a boat with at least five people who hate my guts? What if Lance shows up? My hands shake as I stroll down the hallway and exit the school.

Caine is waiting for me inside his truck, as usual. Our routine has become solid, so I barely drive my car now. I get in and try to buckle my seat belt, but my hands are shaking, and my breathing speeds up.

Caine notices because nothing gets past him. "What's up?"

"I don't think I should go tonight." I finally get the fucking seat belt clipped.

"Why not?" he asks as he drives us out of the parking lot.

"Because the person throwing this shit actually hates my guts." I look at him like he's crazy.

"Georgina won't be thinking about you tonight. She's too busy trying to get back into Brody's good graces. Besides, when are you going to knock them down and claim your rightful place?"

"Rightful place?" What the fuck is he talking about?

"Where you were four years ago, with all of us eating out of the palm of your hand."

"You're delusional," I snort.

"Delusional?" he growls at me. "I would've done anything for you back then. Anything, Kailey. And I only knew you a few fucking months. How do you think the rest of them felt? How they probably still feel?"

"Zeke is happy with Faith, and Brody fucking hates me."

"Zeke feels obligated to Faith, and Brody hates himself more," he counters.

"Hates himself more?"

"We know something happened to you, and he blames himself for letting you push him away. He didn't fight hard enough."

"He's told you this?" I ask, sounding skeptical.

"We're brothers. We don't have to say shit. We already know

how the other is feeling."

I laugh at that, a full belly laugh. "I think your radar is broken. Brody hates me, and trust me, I know when he truly hates someone." Like how he hates his parents. I know all about that, and even with that knowledge, I can see he hates me even more than them.

"Whatever," Caine shrugs it off. "Cooper has set up a car to pick you up for the appointment and bring you back after."

"Okay." I lean over and kiss his cheek. "I'll see you later."

He grabs my chin and pulls me in again. "I'm not Cooper. I don't want your sweet little kisses. Kiss me like you fucking mean it, or just get the fuck out."

Why are my panties soaked at his words? Oh, right... I'm being tortured with orgasm deprivation. My hands come up, and I grab his face, pulling him in and closing the space between us. I have his bottom lip between my teeth, and I clamp down until my mouth is flooded with the copper taste of his blood. I release it and swipe my tongue over its plumpness, then plunging into his mouth. I kiss him thoroughly, my tongue swiping every surface, and then I pull away, planting a few soft kisses.

His face would be comical if I wasn't so irritated. His shock is evidence enough. He never expected me to do that, and to be honest, I'm slightly shocked too.

"See you later," I breathe and jump down from his truck. He doesn't say anything to me, and I stand in the driveway watching him drive away.

The salon is decadent.

They have long velour drapes hanging along the windows, crystal vases filled with plush roses, and champagne by the bottle. The ladies themselves look decadent, with perfectly styled hair and flawless makeup.

I let them have their way with my hair and makeup because I don't have the slightest clue what I want. I only make one stipulation: do not make me blonde. So now I am under a heater with foils sticking out of my head, 'caramel highlights' one girl insisted on, and shrugged my shoulders. I have a lady rubbing lotion on my feet and legs while I bake, and another is painting my nails a bright red to match my dress.

I have never had this experience before. When I got to the age of wanting to look good, my mama died, and they raped me, stripping me of the desire to care about my appearance. It's just now dawning on me how much I do like looking put together and pretty, especially when it's impressing a few boys I like.

"You have gorgeous skin," the lady doing my nails coos. "What's your routine?"

"Routine?" I ask her with my brow raised.

"Oh, hell, sweetheart," she chuckles. "You're so lucky."

Okay, I guess. I have no idea what half the shit these girls are saying means. I have something called toner going onto my head right now, and the shellac polish on my fingers and toes will last weeks. Great. Whatever.

The finished product is breathtaking. I look like a completely different person. I'm not so sure I like not looking like myself, but I can admit I look good. They straightened out my unruly waves, and my stick straight hair hangs to mid-back. The caramel highlights make my hair look lighter without being too obvious, and the makeup is loud but tactfully done. My smokey eyes bring out the green, and my bright red lip accentuates their plumped size.

"You look amazing," the owner of the spa gushes. I can only imagine the amount that was on the gift card to make them this attentive to me. "Mr. Fontenot will be drooling."

"He better be," I retort. "This was hard work."

The ladies laugh and usher me out to the waiting black sedan. I have barely enough time to get into the dress and shoes when I get home. Kimmy picked out the lingerie underneath just in case I want to make a special guy lucky, her words.

The ride back to my house has the driver giving me odd but appreciative looks. Maybe he thinks they switched me out for a whole new person. Fuck, I'd totally think that too. I try to tip him when I'm safely back home, but he refuses and says Cooper has more than looked after everything.

I'm dressing in a hurry because I literally have fifteen minutes before Cooper arrives. Somehow, I am tangled in the corset, and the garter hooks are stuck inside the ridiculously small g-string. I finally get myself together and thank whoever designed this front closure corset. I've never been huge in the boob department, but this corset makes me look at least a full cup bigger. I spend a few precious minutes admiring what I wish I had without the struggle.

The dress is a rich red satin, strapless with a sweetheart neckline. The skirt falls to my feet, but the slit on my left leg hits me on the upper thigh, showing off the red garter and nude stockings. Kimmy promised me they would pair, and she was right. I look older and sophisticated with a touch of seduction. I undo the Gris-Gris at my wrist and clasp it in my hand. I can't wear it tonight, and I can only pray I will be okay until I get home and put it back on.

The doorbell rings just as I'm smoothing down the front and brushing out my hair. The ladies gave me the tube of lipstick they used for touch-ups, and I drop it into my matching, drawstring purse. I step into my peep-toe red shoes then slowly make my way downstairs.

I open the front door and Cooper is standing there in a slate gray suit, black shirt, and a red tie. His hair is gelled back, and his face has been freshly shaven. He looks so fucking gorgeous, it hurts.

His eyes are roaming over my face, hair, and dress with a wide-eyed expression on his face. His mouth hangs open, and his hand is frozen in front of him as he holds out a corsage for me.

"Sha," his voice is a faint whisper, his lips barely moving. "I … you're … holy shit."

"You too, Coop," I giggle a bit and step into him.

His hand finally drops, and he drags me in against his body. "You're stunning." His voice still holds an awed tone.

"Thank you," I whisper as I look up at him through my lashes. "You look very handsome too."

I finger his red tie, a very close match to my dress. "Kimmy bought two and gave them to us."

"She is thoughtful that way." I smile.

"You are going to steal the show tonight, you realize?" His mouth presses to my cheek.

"I doubt it. Georgina will probably show in a princess wedding gown."

He chuckles and runs his fingers through my hair. "Stunning," he whispers again as he leads me to the Wrangler.

He holds my hand the whole way to the wharf, and when we get there, he runs around so he can open the door for me.

"I thought we would wait here until Caine arrives," he says, looking around. "He said another minute. That way, you can walk in with the most handsome guys here on your arms," he grins and straightens his tie.

"Sounds good to me," I giggle at his arrogance.

"Wow," I hear from behind me and turn.

Caine is in an all-black suit—of course—with a matching black shirt and the bright red tie. He looks like he went to the barber after dropping me off because his lineup is fresh. The scruff of his chin and cheeks has been tamed and lined as well. He looks gorgeous.

"Yeah," I nod as I look him up and down. "Wow."

He steps up to me, still looking me over from head to toe, and pulls me in for a hug. "I like this, but the homeless look will always be my favorite," he whispers in my ear.

I snort loud enough to cause Cooper to laugh, and I feel Caine's chest vibrate against mine. He leans down and kisses my forehead. Something so rare and sweet from Caine.

"Maybe I will convince Cooper to give you a quick fuck in the bathroom so I can be the one to strip this dress off you later," he murmurs to me while we're out of earshot of Cooper.

"Tsk," I tease him. "That doesn't seem too fair to Coop."

"I don't care," he shrugs, making me laugh because I know he's being totally honest; he really doesn't fucking care. His hand finds the slit on my thigh, and I stifle a moan at the contact. "Garters?"

"Yes," I whisper and smile when he groans under his breath.

"C'mon kids," Cooper holds his arm out for me. "Let's jam!"

"I'm not dancing with you," Caine grumbles to Cooper.

"Don't start, Caine," he chastises. "Think about us dancing together but with sha in the middle."

Caine looks me over and exhales a breath. "Tight in the middle."

I'm suddenly hot, thinking about having both of their bodies pressed into me. This time, I feel myself become slick with arousal at the thought. Finally, my heart beats faster with a feeling other than fear when I think of a sexual situation involving all three of us.

"Bebelle," Zeke calls out from the line ahead of us. "You look beautiful."

"Thanks, Z." I smile at him and try hard to ignore the glower Faith is throwing at me.

She looks stunning as well in a short black dress and her hair curled around her shoulders. I wouldn't admit it to her face, though, and if she doesn't stop looking at me like that, we're all going to find out if she can swim in that attire.

"Watch those eyes, Faithie," Cooper singsongs. "Before you catch some hands."

I hold in a laugh, and Caine chuckles. Faith quickly turns forward, and Zeke throws me a wink. He looks handsome in a dress shirt rolled to the elbows, showcasing his tattooed sleeves on each arm. His hair is perfectly tousled, and his green eyes hold a glint of mischief.

I don't see Georgina or Brody anywhere, and I exhale a sigh of relief. The yacht is a huge, three floored vessel. Thank goodness it's docked and not going out on the water because I would have more anxiety feeling trapped and unable to get off.

Inside the yacht it's luxuriant. There's a flowing fountain of pink champagne and wait staff in uniform offering flutes of it. There's a string band playing soft music, and twinkling golden lights cast a warm glow.

"Did your father see you in that dress?" Caine asks, his eye meeting mine over the flute of his glass.

"No, Papa works late tonight."

"Again?" Cooper inquires.

"I guess the dealership is busy," I shrug as I try to look unaffected. The truth is, I'm worried, but I still don't trust these boys with any information about my papa.

He's been coming home, but he looks a mess, with his clothes always disheveled and his face lined in exhaustion. His eyes have been noticeably glassy, and I can't figure out if it's due to lack of sleep or if he's taken up the bottle again.

They accept my answer, and we find our table. I'm seated between Cooper and Caine. Coop has his arm around the back of my chair, and Caine's hand sits possessively on my upper thigh. They both smell uniquely amazing. Cooper smells like a blend of sandalwood and citrus, and Caine has a warm, leather scent mixed with a woodsy musk. Both are alluring and so sexy, I just want to lean in and breathe them both in.

Georgina enters the room to a vibrant tune by the band. I was right in my prediction: she shopped or had that bright white dress made at a wedding boutique. The skirt for sure has to have a hoop underneath to make it balloon that wide. Her overly orange skin is fluorescent, and her makeup is loud and kind of clownish, but what the hell do I know about these things?

"She looks like an Oompa Loompa on crack," Caine says under his breath, causing me to choke on my champagne.

"Like Donald Trump's stunt double, just more hair," Coop adds. I can't hold it in. I cover my mouth with my hand and laugh. I can feel the tears gathering in my eyes as Cooper chuckles, and Caine's mouth turns up into a rare smile.

The look in her eyes is pure hatred, and I swear, she senses me because her eyes meet mine. The hatred doesn't surprise me. She's been happy enough to make my life a living hell for four years, but it's the flash of jealousy when she sees me sitting between my boys that has me pausing. She's with Brody, and I am nowhere near him. I haven't even seen him tonight. So what the fuck is her problem?

"Hey, everyone. Thank you for coming to my party tonight!" The mic screeches a bit, and I snort because it sounds exactly like her voice. "I'm so glad to see most of you." Her eyes land on mine, and I try my best to keep my face blank. "Have fun tonight. Let's enjoy the music, and I expect to see you all lined up for pictures later."

The crowd claps and whistles while I continue to drink the never-ending flow of pink champagne. It means a lot if I can drink and feel safe with them, ending my years of no drinking rule.

Georgina has always had it out for me, even before I ended my friendship with the guys. She was always trying to worm her way into the circle, and the night after Mama's death, she succeeded. That's why her vile attitude makes no sense at this point, because she's exactly where she's always wanted to be, at Brody's side.

Speaking of, the man himself walks into the room, and I feel like he has sucked the air out. He's in a black suit with a gray shirt underneath and an untied bowtie sitting around his collar. His hair is on the longer side but brushed back off his face and curling around his neck. His eyes shine so bright out of his face, the pale blue reflecting light as he walks towards us. I can't deny Brody has always owned a spot in my heart, and it's still there now, after all these years.

Georgina spots him and watches as he makes his way to us and bypasses her. She has to know that's not for me. I just happen to be at a table with his close friends. The looks she's throwing me say otherwise, and I groan as I tip back my third glass of pink shit.

"Take it easy on that stuff," Caine says into my ear. "You will be drunk off your ass in no time."

"Good, it'll make this thing livable."

Cooper chuckles and rubs the skin on my shoulder. Goose bumps explode along my arms, and I hold in the moan that threatens to escape.

"The happy … threesome … is here I see," Brody sneers at us, and I roll my eyes. "At least you look like you bathed, Kailey."

"She looks fucking ravishing, and you know it," Caine snarls at him. "Too bad you will never know how she smells or … what she tastes like. Bothers you, huh?"

I snort at that and shake my head. "You really are delusional," I say to Caine.

Brody is looking at me like shit stuck to his shoe as Caine buries his face in my hair. "That's not a face that doesn't care," He whispers in my ear.

"What's up?" Cooper asks Brody.

"Georgina wants pictures with us eight." He's still staring at me with disgust.

"No," Caine answers firmly. "Tell her to fuck off."

"I'll second that," Cooper nods.

"Remember what this is," Brody points between the three of us. "Don't lose your heads over a new pussy."

He turns on his heel as I'm reminded of how all this came about. I'm just a means to an end to them, and I feel stupid for forgetting that.

"I need the bathroom." I go to stand, but Caine's hand holds me firmly in my seat.

"Don't let his words affect what we have here. Yes, I was never on board for this, and I was against this situation. But Cooper has always been a firm Kailey protector, and over the years, we've accused him of being too softhearted for you. So if you want to be pissed, be pissed with me. It's only recently I began to see I want you too."

"Sha," Cooper interjects. "Brody may have his motives for this relationship, but you have to remember he's not in it. It's us three."

"I know," I say, even though I'm not sure I know. I just need to get away from them for a few minutes to collect myself. "I just need to pee out all the champagne."

I can see the skepticism in Caine's eyes, but he lets me go, and I follow the signs to the restroom. Once inside, I lock myself in a small stall and lean against the wall. I don't know why I give Brody this power to destroy me, but he does so easily with his words, and like the sharp edge of a knife, they pull back my skin in layers. Soon I will bleed out at his feet, and I will be front row for his celebratory show.

I hear the restroom door open and the swish of tulle and satin. I know who it is. There's only one person on this yacht whose dress is that ostentatious.

"Did my boyfriend say something mean to you?" Georgina jeers.

I take a deep breath and open the stall door. May as well face her head-on. "No, I had to piss out all that champagne," I retort.

"You're pathetic." Her voice is filled with venom. "Everything about you screams fucking loser. You think just because you're some kind of victim, you can just suck them all back in?"

What does she mean by victim? A loud buzzing fills my ears as I begin to hyperventilate. What does she know?

"Oh, you're scared?" Her face comes into mine. "Little miss slut who acts like she didn't enjoy it."

My heart beats forcefully in my chest as blood hurries to my head. I feel like I'm about to faint.

"I remember that night because it changed everything. Poor little Kailey catches the boy she's in love with, in bed with another girl. So she runs into the arms of his big brother and his best friend," her taunts continue. "You really are a slut, and Brody knows all about it."

Brody knows what happened to me? Did he see it? I was too intoxicated and forced to keep my head down, so I never knew how many were actually there. I only know Lance and Justin were the ones to defile me.

"I heard you begging them to fuck you." Her words are bullets with the perfect trajectory to my heart and stomach. I feel like I'm dying. "'Please' you begged, I heard you."

"You witnessed my rape and did nothing? How evil are you?" I say, barely above a whisper.

"Rape?" She laughs a loud cackle. "Can I tell you a secret?" She gets closer to me, like we are lifelong best friends sharing gossip. "I told Justin that night before you got there how much you wanted him, how often you stared at him, and he was just all too eager to believe me."

"Why?" I ask her, my voice filled with shock.

"Because I needed you out of the way, and I knew what they liked to do … how much they loved to share. Cooper's sister cried about it to mine. She tried to say they raped her too, but she was another slut. Now look at you," she giggles. "Back to being in the middle of two dicks, being shared by another couple of best friends. Is that your preference?"

"Needed me out of the way for what?" I ask, my eyesight

becoming distorted with tears and my stomach turning.

"Brody. He was always meant to be mine. It's all about who you marry in this town."

The room spins, and I dart back into the stall to relieve my stomach of the sour champagne. I hear Georgina laugh as she listens to me vomit.

"Get the fuck off my yacht, slut," she calls out as she leaves the restroom.

Once I feel like the heaving has stopped, I stand to my feet and place my forehead against the cool metal stall. If Georgina knew, then did Brody know? And if he knew, then the others must know too, right? Maybe they thought I was some kind of slut who enjoys having threesomes. Maybe that's why Brody stuck both Cooper and Caine on the Seduce Kailey Mission. My stomach flips again at the thought, and I have to suck in a few breaths to calm the turbulent feeling.

I stumble to the sink and rinse my mouth out with water. I look at my reflection and startle at how distraught I look. I need to get off this yacht. I don't know what I was thinking coming here, and Oliver's words ring true in my ears. I didn't heed his advice, and now I'm in hotter water than I can handle.

I decide to sneak off this thing, and I know I have only one person who can come to get me. I just hope he didn't block my number. I wouldn't blame him because I was such a fucking bitch to him. His phone goes straight to voice mail when I try to call him, and I curse my luck. I fire him a text and refocus my attention on getting out of here. Once I'm off, I'll decide what to do from there.

I open the restroom door, and a hand clamps down over my mouth. "Hello, pretty Kailey-Himari. Nice to see you again." Justin's deep, gravel voice hits my ear, and I am literally frozen in fear as I take in the scene in front of me.

"I did my part. Now get the slut off my yacht," Georgina huffs as she turns and walks away in a cloud of tulle and poison.

Lance is leaning against the wall across from the restroom door with a wide grin on his face. "Hello again, pretty."

I struggle, my instinct kicking in as I claw and try to fight my way out of Justin's grip.

"Bring her in here," Lance calls from an open doorway. It looks like it leads to the back of the Yacht.

Justin drags me over to him then they both pull me outside and shut the door. I'm pushed up against the side of the yacht, and both of their faces loom in front of mine.

"Look how scared she looks," Lance snickers.

"She really looks like her mother, right?" Justin rasps. "Just how she looked the day we ran her down."

TWENTY-FOUR

"She's been in there a while." Caine says as he looks towards the narrow corridor that leads to the restrooms. He's been watching it for the last ten minutes.

"She's probably powdering her nose or something," I shrug. I know Brody shook her up a bit, but KH is tough.

"Hi guys." I hear Faith's soft voice to the left of the table. "Picture time."

"I already said I'm not taking any fucking pictures with you bitches." Caine, ever the gentleman.

"No, silly." She waves him off, used to his attitude. "Georgie also wants pictures of just you four guys. C'mon, please?"

"Fine," I huff as I get up out of my chair.

Caine remains seated, and I look at him with my brow raised.

"Get your mugshot," he sneers. "I'm not leaving until Kailey gets back."

I shrug and follow Faith to where a cameraman is set up, taking pictures of everyone. I find Brody and Zeke standing off to the side and head over to them. Brody looks irritated, but fuck, that's his usual look, and Zeke looks bored.

"What you said to KH was fucking wrong," I say to Brody as I stand next to them.

"I don't give a shit. She needs to stop looking comfortable at our functions. She has a purpose, and once it's done, she's out." His voice takes on a dangerous edge.

"I don't know what you thought this situation was exactly, but for me it's real. I'm in love with Kailey." Honesty is always best.

"Then you're a fucking idiot," he chuckles sarcastically. "Once she finds out how much we know, you can pretty much kiss her ass goodbye."

"It's not just me," I shake my head. "Caine's in pretty deep too."

"Nah, Caine is in until he gets balls deep in her, then he'll back out," Brody argues.

"Guys," Zeke interjects. "Not here." He looks at our surroundings, and I agree with him. This isn't the place to discuss such matters. Too many listening ears.

"Where's Caine?" Brody asks.

"He doesn't want his picture taken," I shrug. "I really don't either."

"It's to shut Georgina up," Brody growls. "I can't hear her complain anymore."

"It's time you dumped her," I tell him.

He doesn't respond because it's the same run around we always get into. He complains about Georgina, and I tell him to dump her only for him to be cozied up to her again the next day. His family sees Georgina as the perfect fit for Brody's future, and he's inclined to agree. Her wealth and family's social standing are exactly what he'll need when he pulls away from his father.

"Hi Cooper." I hear a small voice beside me. I turn my head and see a sad looking Casey. She looks beautiful, though in a yellow gown and her hair twisted up into some intricate bun.

"Hey Case." I smile at her. I want to keep things civil, but I don't want her to get the wrong idea.

"Where's your date?" She has no malice in her voice, just curiosity. Hopefully, she's resigned to the fact I am serious about KH.

"Freshening up."

"She looks beautiful." Sadness bleeds into her tone, and I want to soothe her.

"So do you, Case." I place my hand on her shoulder.

"I didn't want things to be like this." She sniffles and I hold back a cringe. "I don't hate Kailey, but when Georgina said we had to make her life hell at school, I just obeyed. I don't want to be that girl anymore."

"Then don't. You are your own person, and a great one at that," I nod. "Georgina can do her own bidding."

"You're right," she says with a determined look.

I wrap my arm around her shoulders and bring her in for a quick hug. A flash goes off, and a photographer lowers his camera. "You guys are a great looking couple."

"Wait…" I hold out my hand, but he's already gone.

"Don't worry," Casey says to me. "I will get Georgina to delete that one." Then she disappears into the crowd.

I decide to fuck the photoshoot when I see Zeke and Brody with fake ass smiles on their faces but boredom in their eyes and go to find Caine and KH. They are who I really want to be hanging out with right now. The table we're assigned to is empty and I want to curse Caine if he's off trying to coax KH out of those garters. He better have the decency to at least wait so I can join.

I look around the crowded dining area, but there are too many people, and I can't see that blood red dress anywhere. I do spot Georgina's hideous wedding gown, though coming from the corridor where the restrooms are. I head after her and tap her shoulder. She turns quickly, her face looks frightened, and her body is tense.

"Whoa," I hold up my hands. "You good?"

"What do you want?" she snaps, her face a mask of fury.

"Chill out, I'm looking for KH."

"KH, KH, KH!" she mocks and turns her back as she stalks away.

Fuck, that girl is all kinds of fucked-up, and her attitude gives me a bad feeling. Georgina has always been out to get KH, and I can't help being afraid she's done something to her. The only thing keeping me from freaking out is the fact that Caine is missing too, and I know he would rip apart anyone who dared hurt her, even Georgie.

CAINE

I've been sitting here listening to this shit band playing some stupid fucking shit you'd hear in an elevator while waiting for Kailey to get back. I know she's upset by what Brody said and it took everything in me not to smash his smug, lying face into the table. He misses her … he's been missing her since the summer she dropped us. This is his way of acting out like the child he is. I'm about to beat him for it like the fucking daddy he needs.

I noisily scrape back my chair and decide to go wait for Kailey by the restrooms. I don't want her fleeing because some cum smear decided to be an extra prick today. I round the table and almost get bowled over by a pile of fishing nets stinking like my grandmother's perfume.

"Fuck!" Georgina spits out, and my hand itches to squeeze her throat.

"Maybe wearing a dress that's bigger than the room is a fashion faux pas."

"Whatever, Caine." She goes to move around me, but I grab her upper arm and pull her back.

"Where are you off to in such a hurry?"

"I have pictures to take." Her mouth curves down into a frown. Georgina may be beautiful to most people, but all I see is the rot of an evil girl.

"You came from the restrooms?"

"No." Her eyes skate to the side. Little bitch liar.

"You see Kailey?"

"No!" She tries to yank her arm out of my grip, but I hold tight.

"You know what happens to little girls who lie to me?" I revel in the way her eyes widen as I lean into her ear. "I tie them up with fancy little knots and watch them swing from the ceiling."

Her squeak of fear makes me grin, and I wait with my brow raised for her to tell me the truth.

"I was in the restroom. Kailey wasn't in there, okay?" She still looks sketchy, but I don't have time for her antics or the stench of too much Chanel No. 5.

I release her arm and watch as she stumbles away from me and disappears into a crowd of fucking losers in puffy skirts. My girl has that understated, sexy look, hinting at how sensual she really is. Yeah, I need to find her and sink a few fingers into her pussy.

I start towards the corridor when I hear a female sniffing and crying. I follow the noise to a little alcove and find Connie. Her mascara is running down her cheeks, and her face is red and splotchy. She has on a pink bubblegum dress—kind of hideous—and her hair is a mass of messy curls.

"Fuck," she hisses and stands. I push her back into her seat and stand in front of her.

"Why the waterworks?"

"You know why, okay?!" She raises her voice, seeming to forget how much I hate that.

I bend down until my face is level with hers. "Use your words, Connie."

"You know how I feel about you and seeing you with her. It's so cruel."

"I told you the deal with us from the beginning. It was fucking and that's it. You agreed."

"I know! Is that what it is with her, too?" She hiccups through a sob.

"What it is with her is no one's fucking business. Now pull yourself together. This shit is embarrassing."

She gets up quickly and pushes past me. I know I'm harsh, but if I'm not completely honest with her, she will find a shred of hope in there when there isn't any. She knew from the jump what this was. I made myself explicitly clear, exactly what I wanted her for. She was fun, though, I will admit that, but I can teach Kailey the things I like too. The thought of having her tied to my bed causes my dick to twitch.

Yeah, she's going to be a lot of fun.

The corridor is empty when I enter, and the dimmed lighting gives it an ominous feeling. I see the women's restroom up ahead and knock on the door. When there's no answer, I open the door and step inside. There are two stalls, and both doors are open. I notice two things right away. One: the far-left stall has a faint makeup print on the wall, like maybe a girl wasn't feeling well and pressed her head to it. I head inside and look around some more but can't find anything else. Two: the smell of Georgina's atrocious perfume lingers in here, but there's also an undernote of the citrus perfume Kailey was wearing.

Either Georgina came in just after Kailey or the bitch lied about being in here with her, and if I had to put money on it, I would go with the latter. What did she say to her to set her off? I can only imagine it had to do with us four and our nefarious plans to take down Kailey and her dad. I will admit she was just a prop in the beginning, but after my party, I realized my feelings for her never really went away.

A few girls in Barbie looking dresses rush into the restroom, giggling and whispering behind their hands. When they spot me, they stop short and give me a weird look.

"What the fuck are you looking at?" I snarl and push around them.

"Is that Caine?" one whispers.

"He's so freaking hot," another answers.

Mindless drones. I leave the restroom and the giggling hyenas. I look down both sides of the corridor and see a door on the opposite end. It would lead outside, but why would she go out there? Unless a vicious Georgina confronted her, and she decided she didn't want to stay. It's a good possibility.

I head to the exterior door, but when I try to open it, it doesn't budge. Like maybe something is blocking it from the outside. She couldn't have gone this way because if I can't open it, there's no way she could. I turn around and see the restrooms, no other doors. Would she be in the men's room? I open the restroom door and find it empty, lacking even the slightest hint of her perfume. This doesn't make sense. She could've only exited the way I was watching. I wouldn't have missed her and that bright red dress. Unless it happened at the precise moment I was talking to Connie. Maybe she saw us together and dipped out.

I get back out to the main room and scan it quickly. I see no Kailey-Himari. There are another two levels, but I have a feeling she somehow got off this yacht. I see Cooper sitting at our table and make my way over to him. He sees me and looks around me expectantly, but his face falls when he sees I'm alone.

"She's gone," I tell him.

"Gone? How?" His confusion is plain on his face. "How would she get home?"

"If I were to guess, Ballon," I ground out and clench my teeth until my jaw cracks.

"Why him?"

"Because she trusted him with sensitive information, Cooper. He knows what happened to her." I speak to him as if he's a toddler. He's fucking acting like one.

"Let's get Zeke and get this guy's information."

Finally, he's looking pissed.

DESECRATED FLESH

Kailey-Himari

TWENTY-FIVE

The wind is blowing hard as we stand on the yacht's deck. Justin's words are still ringing in my ear, and his hand is still wrapped around my mouth. They killed Mama? But why? I'm shocked and rendered immobile as I watch their eyes eagerly scan my face. They want tears, hysterics, and for me to fight. It's how they get off, I should know. I refuse to give it to them. I need to somehow outsmart them and get as far away as I can.

"Let's get her off this fucking boat." Lance looks around nervously.

"Pull that bar down. It'll stop anyone from coming out here." Justin nods his head towards a bar that swings down to secure the door.

I want to kick Justin in the balls and jump the fuck off this yacht, but his legs and pelvis are pressed firmly against mine. I can't take them both on, and I can't see a way out of this. I refuse to be their victim again, though, so they can do what they want, but I won't make it easy this time, and then I will kill them.

Justin's hand snakes up and into the slit in my dress to stroke my thigh. I keep my face neutral and not let myself react. It's what they want … what they need.

"Not going to fight this, Kailey?" Justin taunts, and his fingers skim over my g-string.

"Bro, she's with Caine now. That fucker is into some freaky shit. She's primed for us now. Probably fucks both him and Cooper at the same time," Lance snickers.

"Is that true?" Justin's fingers press harder into my tender flesh. "Do you get fucked by both at the same time? Did we prepare that ass for them?"

A whimper escapes as he pinches me hard down there. I feel his length harden as he grinds himself into my stomach. He just needed to hear me in pain.

"Let's get off this thing and bring her somewhere we can enjoy her. Last time wasn't long enough," Lance whines.

"I agree," Justin growls into my ear. "Last time wasn't long enough to do all the things I wanted to."

I concentrate on not letting their words affect me and try to picture my mama's face in my head. I can't believe they killed her, and I can't figure out a single reason they would want to. I need to get out of this so I can get home and tell my pa.

Justin hauls me off the wall and pushes me in front of him, his hand still firmly around my mouth. Lance takes up the lead, and they take me down the makeshift steps then across the dock. Once my feet hit dirt, I try to twist out of Justin's grip, but it only causes him to pull me back and press his hardness into my ass.

"Keep it up and I'll fuck you right here on the road," he snarls into my ear.

Lance runs ahead and stops at a red Corvette. I recognize this car—it's Justin's. When Brody turned thirteen, he snuck it out of the garage and took me joyriding with him. Lance opens the driver's side door, and I freak out. There's no way I'm getting in that two-seater car.

I struggle again and end up firmly slamming my elbow into Justin's side. His grunt of pain is followed by him picking me up and jamming me facedown onto the back of the car.

"Let's see what you got on under this skirt." He sounds angry as his fingers bite into my cheek.

My muffled screams and frantic movements do nothing to help me. Lance leans against the car, watching as he strokes his dick through his pants while Justin is working on lifting my skirt over my ass with one hand. My logic escapes me, and I no longer try to stay calm. I need to fight them off of me no matter how much more they enjoy it.

"A red, lacy g-string." Justin groans long and deep as his fingers slide down my ass crack and push against my pussy. "Who is this for?"

"Pull them off. I want to keep them," Lance says, his voice catching as he continues to rub himself.

Justin's hand lifts from my pussy and lands with a loud crack on my ass cheek. "That's for letting someone else fuck what's mine."

"And mine…" Lance trails off, sounding like a petulant child.

Justin doesn't bother to correct himself. He really feels like I belong to him. "I took your virginity; your blood was all over my cock." He pushes his cock into me again. "I didn't wash it off until the next day. I enjoyed having it there and smelling your scent on me. I want it again."

My stomach heaves at the assault of his words and the memories they produce. Pain floods my body as if I'm right back on that forest floor. My muffled screams become desperate, and my struggling becomes frenzied. I can't break again. I won't survive it.

"Hold her hands down," Justin demands Lance. "I'm not waiting any longer. Let's see if this pussy is still tight. I want to watch it bleed."

Lance immediately does as he asks, like a good little dog. He grabs my hands from the other side of the car and pulls my arms out straight, effectively halting my upper body movements. I feel the tears come then, coursing down my face at the realization I am completely helpless.

They rip my panties off my body, and a stinging pain rips through my hip from the force. His hand tightens around my mouth, and he shoves two fingers deep inside me. The pain skates up my spine as I scream into his hand. He doesn't let up as he roughly thrusts in and out of me.

"How does she feel?" Lance is panting.

"Tight, still like a virgin."

Lance groans, "I want to fe—"

His words are cut short as I watch his body jar, and a bright red spot appears on his chest, then he slowly sinks to the ground. Justin stops his assault on me and slowly lifts us both to standing, his hand still around my mouth.

"Let her go, Landry." When I hear his voice, my body sags with relief.

Justin turns us both to face Oliver, and I'm surprised at what I see. He's not a teacher standing in front of us. He's dressed in dark clothing, his hair obscured by a backwards hat, and a gun sits in his outstretched hand with a silencer attached. He looks lethal and dangerous.

"Ballon," Justin says, low and menacingly. "Don't get in the middle of this. Our families work well together."

"I don't give a fuck about either family. Hand her over." Oliver sounds dangerous, not anything like the man I've come to know.

"So you can shoot me too?" Justin taunts.

"Right now, I only care about her. Let her go, or you'll have bigger problems. What's one pussy when you can force as many as you want?" His words are harsh and degrading.

"Now I know you haven't had this particular pussy." Justin laughs as he shoves me forward.

I land on my hands and knees, the gravel digging into my skin painfully. My purse that's been secured around my wrist the whole time finally snaps, and everything skates across the road. I stay where I am on my hands and knees and let the shame of everything that's happened wash over me. I don't know how much Oliver saw, and I can't help but feel dirtied and damaged.

I hear Justin getting Lance into his car, and then the gravel kicks up as he takes off, the stones hitting my shoulders and face. I feel Oliver's hand touch my cheek as he lifts my face up to look at him.

"Come on, baby. Let me get you out of here."

I break apart at his words. My sobs wrack my body, and moving from this spot becomes impossible. He bends down and scoops me up into his arms like I weigh nothing. He takes me around to the passenger side of his sedan, gingerly puts me in the seat and does up my seat belt. I'm still overcome with raw, debilitating emotion as he goes back out and picks up all my belongings. Once he's inside the vehicle, he reaches over and brushes my hair back from my face. His touch is sweet and filled with sincerity. It kicks up my crying to a manic level.

"Hang on," he says as he pulls away from the wharf. "I'll take you to my place."

"Ol-i-ver..." I try to form words around my break down.

"They... kil-led... Ma-ma..."

"What, baby?" He reaches over and grabs my hand. "Just relax. Tell me everything when we get there. Gather your strength."

His hand rubs soothingly against mine, and it works in helping me try to control myself. He doesn't let go of me all the way back to his modest bungalow. He pulls into the driveway then rushes around to my door to lift me out. I cling to him tightly, my face buried into his neck and my tears soaking his shirt.

He sets me on a plush couch and runs off quickly, returning with a shirt and track pants.

"I'll give you some privacy to change. Do you like tea?"

His kindness is making it difficult to speak, so I just nod and watch as he leaves the room to make me tea. My phone vibrates from my broken purse on the couch. I reach inside and see Caine's name across the screen. I throw the phone back down as another sob escapes my chest.

I've been so fucking stupid. What the fuck did I expect? When you play with fire, you get burned. But in my case, a fucking inferno scorched me. I should've seen this coming; I'm parading around with the Golden Four after being raped by a close relative to them in the past. Have I lost every brain cell in my head?

I practically rip the dress off my body and fling it as far away from me as I can. Then I pull on the sweatpants, rolling the waist and pulling the t-shirt on. Oliver's scent billows around me. He smells of crisp rain in the summer, and it soothes me further. I process and compartmentalize everything slowly. Even though it was terrible, I push away the physical abuse I suffered tonight. I need to focus on all the things that were said first.

"Here, drink some chamomile." Oliver comes back into the room.

"Justin knows you," I say to him, hoping it will prompt him to speak.

"The Landrys work with the Ballons occasionally." He's being obtuse.

"Spit it out, Oliver. I need to know everything."

"I can only tell you what I know, and it's not much." He sits beside me as I accept the tea. "My family is essentially like a mob. They have their grimy hands in all criminal activity here in Louisiana. The Landrys are similar but hide it behind a nice, polished, legit exterior. My family disowned me after I graduated from high school because I refused to join the ranks. I still have cousins, though, who will kill for me." He scrubs his hand down his face. "The Ballon name is connected to everything wrong here."

"I see." I take a sip of my tea. "Can you teach me how to use a gun? I need to kill Lance and Justin."

His jaw drops, and he's staring at me with a look of confusion.

"Oliver, I can't let this happen again. Look at what happened tonight. They will keep trying until they succeed." I place the mug on the coffee table and scoot closer to him. "Justin admitted to killing my mama tonight. He said he and Lance were the ones who ran her down."

His face morphs into anger, and his eyes flare. "Are you sure?"

"Yes," I nod. "Why would they do that? They practically grew up with her." My voice catches with emotion.

"They were most likely hired to do that," he says. "Did your mother owe them something? Borrow money from them? I know they can be brutal with their collections."

The recording of my papa comes to my mind, and I gasp. "Papa owed them money. I heard a recording from Brody where my papa was begging for them to give him more time to pay it back." My hands cover my mouth, and I shake.

"Are you sure that tape was legit? And why would Brody play that for you?" His eyes are still filled with anger.

"He was forcing me to date Cooper and Caine so they could extract more information about Papa."

"You're being forced to date those two?" His hands curl into fists.

"At first, yes," I nod. "But now I care about them. I just feel so stupid because I don't know if this is all one big scheme. They treat me like they care, but Brody likes to remind them in front of me that I'm nothing but a means to an end."

"I think we need to have a serious conversation with your father."

"I don't want to do it tonight. I just need to process and forget." He wraps his arm around my shoulders as I slide into him.

"Okay." I feel him nod into my hair. "Want to watch a movie?"

I nod and watch as he brings up Netflix on the TV. We settle on a comedy, but within the first fifteen minutes, it's clear neither of us is in the mood to laugh. Having him pressed in close to me, rubbing my back and kissing my head, puts me in a different type of mood. It's confusing after everything that's happened tonight, but I want him, and I just want to erase them from my body.

"Oliver," I whisper.

"Yeah, baby?" He sounds distracted, and my heart lurches at the endearment.

I run my hand up his thigh and stop at the very top, my fingertips dangerously close to his cock. I feel him stiffen up, and he moves away.

"Oliver." My voice is stronger, surer. "I want you."

"Kailey," his tone is pleading. "You've been through a lot tonight. It's not a good idea…"

I push myself up and crush my mouth to his, shutting up his concern and showing him how much I want him. Our moans mingle, and I slip my tongue between his open lips to tangle with his. He still hasn't touched me, his hands staying firmly at his sides. I need his touch so badly right now. I want to erase their hands from my body, from inside of me.

I crawl over and onto his lap, pulling my body in close to his.

"Kailey…" he says as his face burrows into my neck.

"Please, Oliver." I grind into his cock, eliciting a deep groan from us both.

He feels big, and a twinge of fear hits me. It's quickly wiped away when he growls and grabs my hips with both hands, guiding my movements. My core floods, and I feel the wetness seep through the borrowed sweatpants.

"Make me feel good," I beg him. "I want you inside me."

"Fuck," he hisses and runs his hands up under the borrowed shirt, feeling the corset. He pulls off my shirt and curses under his breath when he sees my blood red corset and the swell of my breasts.

I pull off his shirt next and salivate at the definition of his chest and abs. His muscles clench beneath my fingers, and I lean forward to lick and bite one of his nipples. The noises he's making guide me because this is my first consensual time being intimate.

His large hands wrap around both of my breasts as he massages them. It feels so good, but I want to feel his skin on mine. Thankfully, this corset is clasped at the front, and I slowly undo it, beginning at the bottom. With every inch of skin exposed, his forefinger glides following each clasp. When the last clasp opens, I pull the corset apart and let it drop to the floor. Oliver doesn't move or say anything. His finger is still firmly pressed to my chest, and I squirm, feeling self-conscious.

"Kailey," his voice cracks. "You are everything."

Then he leans forwards and licks one of my nipples while his hand glides up and over my other breast. The sensation of his rough tongue on my sensitive peak makes me rub myself shamelessly against his hard erection. He moves to lavish my other breast as my hands roam over his shoulders and down his chest, following the ridges and swells of his abs to find the drawstring on his pants. I pull the string and slip my hand down inside. I'm not completely sure of what to do, but I know I want to feel him in my hand.

He's wearing nothing underneath. My fingers brush along the tip of his cock, and I gasp at the silky-smooth texture. He lifts his head from my breasts and looks down at my hand inside his pants. His hips lift, and he pulls his pants down to get a better look. When his cock pops out, I gasp again at the sheer size of it.

He shifts under me and grabs the waistband of his pants. "Kailey … we don't have to do this. It's not why I brought you here."

"Stop." I grab his hands. "I want to, Oliver. I'm just inexperienced."

I wrap my hand around his cock, and even though I know it's silly. I compare him to Caine's. Oliver is just as thick, but he's longer, which would seem impossible. I slowly glide my hand up and down, feeling him jerk into my hand, watching with fascination as a bead of moisture gathers on top. I want to taste it.

I slowly ease off his lap and let my knees hit the floor in front of the couch. Both of my hands are on his knees, and I watch as he slowly strokes his large cock in his hand. With his cock close up to my face, it looks even bigger, and I try to swallow back some of the apprehension.

"Kailey," his hand touches my face. "Let me take care of you for tonight—"

"No," I cut him off. "I want this."

His isn't the first dick I've sucked—thank you, Caine—but this time I'm in charge because clearly Oliver is nothing like Caine. I wrap my hand around him and slowly glide down to the base and back up again to the tip. His groan is loud and deep, and a chuckle almost escapes my mouth. I hold it in and continue to watch his face as I slowly jack him off. He doesn't speed it up, doesn't insist I put him in my mouth. It's different from my experience with Caine, but I can say with all honesty, I enjoyed both.

With little thought, I lean forward and lick the bead of pre-cum off the tip. I'm not sure why a lot of romance novels I've read say the cum tastes great or they love it. I can only say it's not that bad. It's bitter with a tangy aftertaste, but it's not something I want to gorge on all the time. The sticky texture is gross too, but I like how much Oliver is enjoying me doing it. That's why I want to go further, and I wrap my lips around his tip then swirl my tongue to taste more of him.

"Fuck, Kailey," he groans. "That feels amazing."

The soft skin of his cock tastes like soap and something else uniquely Oliver. My tongue licks up his shaft and over the crease at the top. His moans get louder. I suck him deep into my mouth, his tip hitting the back of my throat, and I whimper at the feeling. I hollow out my cheeks and bob up and down, sucking and licking him thoroughly.

"Baby," he groans as his hands slip into my hair. "I need you to stop, or I will cum in your mouth."

I release him with a pop of my lips, and he picks me up and back onto his lap like I weigh next to nothing. Then he stands up, and I wrap my legs around his waist.

"I want you in my bed," he says, his mouth brushing mine.

"Okay," I whisper as my stomach swirls with excitement.

His mouth fuses to mine and we nip at each other's lips. His are so plush, warm, and I'm not able to stop sucking them into my mouth.

We enter a room, but I'm too focused on his mouth and how his hardness feels rubbing against my center with each step to look around. His hands hold me beneath my arms, and he tosses me onto a soft bed. Then he's on top of me, his hard body molding to mine and fitting perfectly between my spread legs.

We are both still dressed from the waist down, and Oliver is making no move to remedy that situation. He's kissing along my neck, licking up my collarbone, and ravishing my mouth like it's his last meal, but nothing else.

I bend my knees up and stick both of my feet into the waistband of his pants, then slowly push them down. His head comes up from my neck, and he stares into my eyes as I work his pants down to his knees. His cock rests on my lower belly, and I arch my back to rub against it.

"Are you sure?" he asks me again, and I hope this time he believes me.

"Yes, Oliver."

His gray eyes bore into mine for a few more seconds, and then he kisses his way over my breasts, paying close attention to them both. The feeling is amazing. Little zings of pleasure shoot straight to my core, and it clenches in anticipation. His tongue continues over my torso and dips into my belly button. Then he's at the waistline of my pants and pulling them down. Once they're off and thrown over his head to the floor, he pauses to stare down at my pussy. I squirm, feeling self-conscious as he runs two fingers through my slit. My ass lifts off the bed at the sensations, and I groan.

"You're so wet," he whispers. "I need to know what you taste like."

"Yes, Mr. Ballon." I don't know what makes me say it, but it sounds so fucking hot.

"Shit, that's hot," he agrees and spreads my thighs.

His tongue swipes through my folds and sucks onto my lips. I grab onto his head and pull his face in closer as he chuckles into me. Then his tongue is doing delicious things, and I feel the familiar pull of an orgasm. I don't want him to stop, so I lock my knees to the sides of his head as he thrusts his tongue inside me. Then he's swirling that talented piece of flesh around my clit, and I detonate into his mouth. I'm screaming his name as intense waves of pleasure move through me. He continues to lap at me until I whimper at the sensitivity.

He comes back up over me and kisses me, his tongue pushing its way into my mouth. He tastes like me, and it makes me clench hard, wanting something else altogether. I may have already come, but now I just want to feel him inside me, replacing all the painful memories with pleasure.

I reach between us and grab his hard, throbbing cock in my hand and try to position it at my center. As soon as the head of his cock touches my wetness, he sucks in a breath and pushes ahead. The head breaches my entrance, and I hold my breath waiting for pain. Instead, I feel stretched and immense pleasure. I push my hips farther into his, and we both moan as he sinks in a little deeper.

There's a slight burn from his size stretching me, but the feeling of us being connected like this, our bodies describing things our mouths have yet to say, is exquisite.

"I don't want to hurt you," he says into my ear as he trembles to keep himself together.

"You won't," I hold his face between my hands. "I want to feel all of you, Oliver."

His hand wraps around my thigh, and he brings it higher on his waist, spreading me open wider. Then he slowly sinks himself inside of me. Inch by inch, I begin to feel the fullness of him, and I hold my breath until he's fully seated inside me. His eyes are intent on my face, and he doesn't move again as he waits for my body to adjust.

His mouth meets mine in a sweet kiss that immediately turns frantic. I want—no need—him to move right now. I grind myself against him and gasp as my clit makes contact, sending spirals of pleasure through my core.

Oliver pulls out and then slowly sinks back in, the thrust hitting me deeper than before. His length surprisingly all fits, and I groan in frustration at how gentle he's being. I want urgency. I need to see him on the brink of losing control. I want to witness just how much he wants me.

My hands run down his ribs, over his sides, and around to his back. Then I slide them down and around to his ass, taking it by the handful as I force him to thrust into me harder. His eyebrows raise in surprise, but his face quickly morphs into one of fierce determination.

His hands slide under my hips, and he angles my pelvis up, then he really gives me what I'm looking for. His thrusts are harder, hitting me in places so deep, and his grip on me borders on pain, but mixed with the pure pleasure searing through me, it's euphoric.

The quiver starts in my lower belly, and soon enough, it intensifies, spreading throughout my body.

"Oliver, I'm going to…" My back arches, and I see stars as my orgasm explodes through me, making my pussy pulse around his cock.

"Oh, fuck," he groans, and he continues to pound into me.

His last thrust is hard and deep, and then I feel him pulsate inside me. The movement causes mini aftershocks to creep over my body. This is what sex is supposed to be like.

"Except I should've worn a condom," he groans as he withdraws out of me. Did I say that out loud? "I'm so sorry. I wasn't thinking."

"It's okay," I smile at him. "I've been on the pill since I was thirteen to regulate my periods."

"I'm clean," he says, still looking shameful.

"I think I am too. I mean, I only had that once…" I trail off. "Anyway, my OBGYN always gives me the tests when I get my pills renewed. I never heard back."

My stomach takes that moment to tell the fucking world how starving it is. The grumble is so loud it cuts through our slightly awkward silence, and we both burst out laughing.

"I know an awesome twenty-four-hour diner. I'm craving waffles," he laughs.

"Sounds amazing."

DESECRATED FLESH

TWENTY-SIX

I am in love with Kailey-Himari Richard.

She's my student, and I have broken the number one rule for any male teacher in my position. But as I sit here watching her laugh with the waitress, I can't muster up one ounce of regret. She's perfect, resilient, and so fucking brave. I can't even put into words how I feel. She chose me to be her first.

"Oliver?" Her voice sinks into my thoughts.

"Hmm?" I smile at her.

"The waitress is waiting for your order," she giggles, and the sound sends blood straight to my cock.

"Oh," I adjust myself in my seat. "Waffles, extra syrup, and some OJ, please."

"Coming right up."

The waitress leaves the table, and it's just me and the first girl my heart has ever skipped a beat for. Her hazel eyes shine with emotion as she looks at me and smiles. She's mine now, and I couldn't let her go for anything. My only refrain is finding out who else I will share her with. I know that sounds weird, and I know there should be some sort of jealousy, but there isn't. I want her to be completely happy. She deserves it after everything she's been through, and I find myself lucky just being in her sights.

I don't know where she stands with Caine and Cooper after

what happened tonight, but I can see how much they care for her too. I just don't like the proximity they bring to the Landry family. Putting her in harm's way is no longer an option I am comfortable with. We need to speak with her father. If a hit was put on her mother because he owed money, I would assume he knows more than he's let on, and after seeing him vacuuming up the white stuff with his nose, it's imperative that conversation starts ASAP.

"Caine and Cooper have been blowing up my phone for the past few hours," she whispers.

"You should text them at least, and let them know you're safe."

"Okay," she nods, and I watch her red painted nails fly over the face of her phone.

The diner is mostly empty save for a booth in the far back corner. Five people around my age are sitting quietly and drinking coffee. Not really drawing anyone's attention or standing out, except the one girl facing me. She has dark hair, golden skin, and bright blue eyes. She looks at ease in the booth, the man's arm next to her around her shoulders, but I know when someone is watching every little movement around them, because I used to be like her.

I draw my stare away from them and focus on Kailey. Her brows are pinched in the center as she reads her screen with annoyance.

"Everything okay?"

"Cooper is relieved I'm okay, but Caine is pissed I ghosted them," she huffs as she puts down her phone.

"Maybe you should tell them what happened?" I suggest.

"They'll tell Brody, and he'll never believe me," she shakes her head. "Then it would eventually get back to Papa, and I don't want him to feel guilty about it."

"I think if you're going to be in a relationship with us, you need to believe we all care for you, and trust would go hand in hand with that. Do you really think they wouldn't believe you?"

"Us?" Her eyes are wide.

"I thought after tonight … we … you and I…" Fuck, I sound like a stuttering kid with sweaty fucking pits.

"Do you want to be…?"

"Yeah," I nod. "I do."

"I don't want to hide our relationship." She toys with the napkin on the table.

I get it. While at school, we'd have to carry on as a student and teacher, but I like my job, so I don't want to lose it.

"I like my job," I say to her. "It beats being a mobster's son."

"I can understand that." She worries at her bottom lip, and it makes me want to lean over the table and suck it into my mouth. "I guess I can keep it a secret for the rest of the school year."

"We'll figure it out," I assure her.

Another group comes into the diner looking lit as fuck and in search of a greasy ass breakfast. Two of the four guys are staring at my girl appreciatively until they notice the other group. One guy shoulders the other, and they stare at the girl with the interesting eyes. They sit in the booth behind me, and I can hear them talking like the pieces of shit they are.

"See that hot ass chick over there? I haven't seen her here before."

"She's with a group, bro. One of those guys has got to be her man."

"Still smoking, though."

They sound high or drunk, maybe both. If one of them says anything about Kailey, I will hop into that booth and ground their faces onto the floor.

"Why do you look so angry?" Her sweet voice shakes away the disturbing thoughts.

"I want to keep you safe, and when you're seeing Cooper and Caine, I want them to keep you safe. We have to figure out a way to tell them, Kail."

Her head falls into her hands, and she exhales a long breath. "Okay, we'll figure it out. Caine already suspects something… I'll tell him first."

Caine is a fucking monster, so when she's with him, I know she's safe. I've watched the guy wrestle, and I've been to a few of his illegal fights. He's a fucking machine. Cooper is goofy and always has a smile on his face, but what people don't know is how dark his family is. I know he was also trained similarly to me—shoot first, ask questions later.

The girl with the eyes from the booth in the back gets up and makes her way to the counter. She leans there, waiting for the waitress to come back out from the kitchen.

"You shouldn't feel ashamed of what happened. It wasn't your fault. You're so brave and fucking strong for surviving that," I tell Kailey.

"I want Lance and Justin dead, Oliver. What they did to me tonight and …" she visibly swallows. "And four years ago… I wish I could do it myself. I know I'm not a killer, but I at least want to watch them bleed."

"I know, baby." I'm already thinking of the different ways to make that happen.

The girl pays her bill and heads back to the group in the corner. They have their heads close together and look to be discussing something of importance. The twats behind me are right… They don't look to be from around here.

"Caine wants to come pick me up when we're done." She bites into her lip, watching me closely.

"That's cool," I nod. "Do you want me to help you talk to him?"

"I can do it." I watch the brave determination seep into her eyes and feel a rush of pride hit my chest. My woman is amazing.

"Okay." I smile.

That'll give me time to make another surprise visit to her father.

Kailey-Himari

TWENTY-SEVEN

After ingesting about ten pounds of pancakes and sausage, my stomach feels uncomfortable, and sleep is screaming at me. I have fifteen minutes before Caine shows, and I can't help but feel nervous. He's intense and downright scary sometimes. Not to mention the fact that he says I'm in big trouble for ditching them tonight.

The diner has been fairly quiet except for the rowdy guys who showed up after we got here. Something about them sends warning vibes skittering throughout my body. They look slimy and completely inebriated. I watch as a girl from the booth behind me walks to the restroom, and the guys watch her like she's the meal they ordered. I don't like it … something feels wrong with them.

The waitress comes by with the bill, so Oliver is momentarily distracted, but I see it. Two of the guys get up and head in the same direction as that girl. I need to at least check it out and make sure she's okay, the way I wished someone had done for me.

"I need the restroom."

Oliver nods as I slide out of my seat. I feel the remaining two guys' eyes on me, but I'm not afraid. I can scream pretty loud when I need to. I stand outside the women's restroom, and sure enough, I hear them talking inside. They really followed her in here. I open the door forcibly, letting it bounce off the wall, then watch the two guys jump back away from the girl.

"Are you okay?" I ask her.

Her eyes are a deep chocolate and widened with fear. She

nods, and I look at the guys. "This bathroom is for chicks, unless there's something we don't know?" I pointedly look at their crotches.

"Our mistake." One of them smiles with a mouthful of yellowed, rotting teeth.

"Get moving." I point to the door and watch as they saunter by.

"Thank you," the girl says quietly. "I was about to scream my head off, and you saved us from having to explain a bunch of dead bodies."

"Huh?" I ask, raising my brow.

"Just kidding." She doesn't look like she's kidding. "My name is Adrianna." She holds out her hand.

"Kailey." I shake it. "Your accent is different. Where y'all from?"

"Canada." She laughs. "Just here for a mini vacay from work."

"Oh, nice!" I smile at her. "I'll let you use the restroom and keep an eye on the door for you."

"Thank you for what you did."

When I leave the restroom, I notice the booth with the seedy guys is empty and breathe a sigh of relief as I head back to Oliver. He's sipping a coffee and watching the group in the back corner of the diner … the one Adrianna was with.

Adrianna comes out of the restroom and places her hand on my shoulder as she passes, squeezing lightly. I smile at her and nod.

"What was that about?" Oliver asks as he watches her go back to her group with suspicion.

"Oh, nothing," I wave him off. "I just met her in the restroom. They're a group vacationing from Canada."

"I see."

A few minutes later, a hand appears to my left and places a business card face down on the table in front of me. I look up into the prettiest set of eyes I have ever seen. They look turquoise, like the brightest ocean.

"My friend told me what you did for her, and I can't express how grateful I am." Her voice is serene, but her body looks tense. "I couldn't help but overhear you earlier... Okay no," she shakes her head, and a mischievous grin comes across her face. "I totally meant to overhear what you were saying, and I heard your minor problem. I am a specialist in that field. I'm working on a resume if you need one."

I can't help it. A laugh bursts from my mouth, and she joins in, hers raspy and sincere. I flip her card over, and it has the picture of a decorated skull. The name says Black Slaughter.

"I mostly work out of Toronto or New York, but for you, I would make an exception. Believe your boyfriend here, you are a brave woman. Call me if you need my help." She pats my shoulder, and I watch as they all get up to leave. Each one smiles at us as they pass, and Adrianna stops at our table.

"Don't let her looks deceive you, she can be deadly. Thank you."

"Thank you," I nod at her. "I will keep this in mind." The card is in my hand. She nods, and I watch as they leave the diner.

"What was that?" Oliver looks completely lost.

"Those nasty guys tried to corner Adrianna in the restroom, and I chased them off."

He turns, and we watch as the group leaves in a black Mercedes. "I don't even know what to say," he shakes his head. "But that was great what you did."

"I knew if I screamed, you'd come save me ... again."

"I will always be there when you need me." His hand grips mine at the same time my phone pings with a message.

Caine: Get your ass out here.

"Caine's here," I tell Oliver, and we both look out the window at his black truck.

"Let's go." We say goodbye to the waitress, and Oliver grabs my hand as we exit the diner.

Caine steps out of the driver's side, and my stomach flips at the sight of him. My bad boy is dressed in a black t-shirt, gray pants, and a backward black hat. His eyes scan me over, looking for any sign of mistreatment, and when he sees I'm fine, anger flares in their depths. I've never been so excited for a punishment. What is wrong with me?

"I got her from here," he grits out as he stares at our interlocked hands.

"She's been through a lot tonight, Leblanc." Oliver's voice holds a warning. "She has quite a bit to tell you."

"She sure does." He nods at me to get in the truck.

Oliver pulls me into his arms and kisses my cheek. "He's rough around the edges, but I can see he cares about you."

I nod because I know he's right.

"Don't have all day, ma petite," Caine growls.

I release Oliver and get in the passenger side of Caine's truck. I hear them speaking, but I can't make out any of the words. Caine looks rigid as always, and Oliver just has a stern look on his face. Finally, Caine gets into the truck, and we pull away from Oliver. I watch him slowly grow smaller in the side view mirror.

"Caine…"

"Don't," his voice is rough. "You put me through hell tonight, Kailey. We'll talk when we get to my house."

"Fine," I mutter and rest my head against the seat.

"Ma petite," Caine's voice rouses me from my sleep. I slowly open my eyes and see his large house standing in front of us. The last time I was here was for that shit-show of a party where Lance showed back up in my life.

The black of night is fading as the sky lightens with morning. I turn and see Caine watching me intently.

"Let's get this over with," I huff as I open the truck door, and I hear him chuckle as he exits his side.

The house is quiet and eerily empty. No valets or security this time, and no butler waiting for us at the door. I know Caine's parents are rarely in the country, let alone at home, so I can assume it's just him and I here.

He grabs my hand a little too tight then leads me up the stairs and down the hall to a set of double doors. When he opens them, the inside is dark. Dark walls, heavy dark curtains on the windows, and even the bedding is a black satin. Caine tries his darnedest to intimidate anyone who attempts to get close to him; all of this is his way of warning people he's incapable of love. Maybe this is true. I can't say I know anything about him to be true, but what I do know is how he makes me feel, and it's an all-consuming intensity.

"Get on the bed. You have some explaining to do." His voice is low and gravelly.

I do as he says because it just makes things easier. My only reservation is telling him my deepest, darkest secret and worrying how much of it he'll believe.

His bed is firm—just as I imagined it would be—and his bed frame is made up of a thick reclaimed wood stained a dark brown. I sit crossed-legged and wait for him to join me, but he doesn't. Instead, he leans against the wall across from me with his arms crossed over his chest.

"Start," he demands.

"You were right from the very beginning," I start. "I had something terrible happen to me the summer I stopped talking to you four. It had nothing to do with Brody being in bed with Georgina—although that did upset me—it was what came after that."

My breath gets caught in my throat as pure fear causes my hands to shake. Am I really telling one of The Four what happened to me?

"And?" he cuts through my overwhelming fear.

"When I showed up to that party, I was extremely drunk. It was just after I found out about Mama, and I just needed to numb all the feelings inside me." His face softens a bit at that, and it encourages me to continue. "I ran out of the pool house to get away from Brody and a smug looking Georgina. I stumbled upon someone, and they took advantage of my state of mind—or lack thereof—and led me into the woods. I trusted him… I thought he was going to talk to me … help me with the pain that was seeping back into me slowly. I was wrong…" A sob escapes my chest, and I bury my face in my hands.

Caine doesn't speak, but I can feel the tension that has been radiating around him lessen a bit.

"Then his friend showed up, and they both … they…" I take a deep breath. "They raped me then left me in the woods, not caring if I could make it home or not. After that, I couldn't stand the thought of you guys because it would morph into what happened to me in those woods. Certain things trigger those memories, and I am once again laying on that forest floor, bloodied and unable to stand."

The silence in the room makes me fidget, and I refuse to look up and meet his eyes. "Who was it?" His voice is quiet but filled with fury.

I shake my head, still so afraid to say their names for fear he'll call me a liar.

I feel the bed dip at my feet, and I finally lift my tear soaked face to see him leaning forward with both hands on the bed. "Tell me now, Kailey. Who. Was. It?"

"Lance…" I whisper and gasp as I watch his eyes darken into something sinister looking.

"You said there were two of them." He doesn't even sound like himself.

"Lance came after," I swallow. "Justin… I followed Justin into the woods."

"That's why you left my house the night of the party because Lance was there."

"No," I shake my head. "He followed me out into the hall, and … tried to… He touched me." A shudder wracks my body, and I whimper at the look of pure murder on his face.

"What happened tonight?" he demands.

"Georgina called them to come get me." I look him in the eye for the next part because I want to see his reaction. "She told me she knew what they did to me that night. She said she told Justin I wanted him." Hatred coats my words. "She called them tonight and told them

I was on that boat. They came for me, Caine. Justin almost did it again, but Oliver saved me." I feel the tears drip off my cheeks as the heat of shame burns through me.

Caine leans forward and kisses my forehead. "Good girl." He praises and stands up. "I have to make a phone call. Do not move from that spot, understand?"

I nod. "Brody will never believe it," I whisper.

"I'm not calling him," he says as he leaves the bedroom, closing the door behind him with a soft click.

TWENTY-EIGHT

Murder, pure and potent, ignites through my veins like a flame to gasoline. I am ready to set everything on fire, even those I deem family. I dial his number, my hand shaking with barely controlled fury.

"You get her?" Cooper's voice sounds anxious.

"Yeah." My voice is low pitched and filled with promises of death.

"And?"

"She told me what happened to her, Bro. It's fucked-up," I growl.

"What happened?"

"I can't tell you over the phone. Come by in the morning, and hear it for yourself. Afterward, you and I are going hunting."

"Can't wait."

I hang up and lean my forehead against the wall. I knew Lance and Justin were into some fucked-up shit. Fuck, I'm into some fucked-up shit, but this is next level. She was just a child when they did that and then left her there. I can't begin to describe the fury I feel or fathom how I plan to dispel it, but what I do know is this: someone's blood will spill.

Now to deal with the girl who is currently sitting vulnerable on my bed. I understand she's been through a lot tonight, but it doesn't hide the fact she disappeared without telling Cooper or me why. She's been hiding this from us for so long, and I plan on reprimanding her.

She needs to start telling me everything.

I pull myself together and slip back inside the room. She's exactly where I left her, and I can't help but hum my approval. Her big hazel eyes are watching my every move as I close the door and come stand beside her.

"Four years." I run my fingers through her straightened hair—missing her mass of waves—and watch as she shivers. "You kept that from us … from me."

"I was scared and didn't think any of you would believe me."

"You trusted Ballon, though. Did he tell you who his family is by chance?" I grip her chin and force her to look at me.

"Yes, he told me," she whispers. Interesting, he must really care about her.

"Why him?" I ask, shocked I have a sudden twinge of jealousy.

"What do you mean?"

"Why did you call him tonight instead of coming and telling me or Cooper?" I ask her.

"Oliver and I…" she trails off.

"Oliver and you?"

"We're together."

"You are?" I squeeze her chin a little harder, and I smile as she winces.

"I care about all three of you."

"He knows that?" My knuckles are white with the effort of trying not to hurt her.

"Yes." She tries to nod but my grip on her chin doesn't let her.

"And he just accepts our girl will be passed around between the three of us?"

I watch as her face hardens, and defiance fills her eyes. "Is that what I am to you? A pass around?"

"Kailey." A warning.

"It's a legit question." She tries to shake my hand off her chin. "You said it, not me."

"Look around you, ma petite. You're in my room and sitting on my bed. No one has been in this room besides me and the maid."

"Stop." Her lip trembles. "I know you've had plenty of girls over here. Then there's Connie."

"Never in this room. I had a separate room for that." The tears pooling in her eyes makes my dick rock hard. "How important are you to Ballon? Does he see you as just a pass around?" I'll kill him.

"He shot Lance tonight, he came to get me just as Justin was going to replace his fingers with his dick, and he's been known to watch my house at night because Papa doesn't want to come home. I would assume I'm more than a pass around."

He shot Lance? Did he kill him? I hope not because I need to feel the sticky warmth of his blood on my hands before his life is expunged for good. I can't ignore Ballon has real feelings for Kailey, and that's all that really matters. If she wants him in our little circle of love, who am I to deny her? As long as she's just as much mine, I won't fight it.

"Has he told you he loves you?" I bend down so I'm face to face with her.

"No," she whispers.

"Has Cooper told you he loves you?"

"No." Her voice shakes with restrained emotion.

"Good," I grin. "Words are just that ... words. Make them show you before they say it." I lean in before I can stop myself and place a sweet kiss on her plump lips.

It's about all the sweetness I can give, though for now, so I hope she's ready to feel my love the only way I know how to show it. I slip my hand behind the headboard and grab a hold of the chain hanging down the back. I installed these here tonight, knowing I'd be bringing her here. The chain runs through my palm until the handcuff rests squarely in the center.

Kailey looks at the cuff then up to my face with questions in her eyes, "I need to teach you a lesson, ma petite. You deliberately hid information from me, ruined our friendship, and then tonight you called another person before me."

"Do what you gotta do," she says quietly as she holds out her wrist.

The submission in her demeanor has my cock pushing against my pants. No girl has had this effect on me, and I wrap the cuff around her wrist.

"Safeword?" I ask her.

She shakes her head as I walk to the other side of the bed and hold out the cuff. Her slim wrist comes out, and I press the cool metal against her skin.

"You need a safeword," I tell her as I walk to the bottom of the bed and look at her with her arms stretched wide.

"I trust you, Caine." She's looking me straight in the eye, and I can't help the groan that finds its way out of my mouth.

I shrug and grab both her ankles, dragging her down the bed until she's flat on her back. Then I reach up to pull off the oversized sweatpants she's wearing. Her legs squeeze together as she tries to hide the fact, she isn't wearing underwear.

"Open them wide," I demand and watch as she complies immediately. I can already see how addictive Kailey is going to be for me.

Her pussy is a darker olive than her skin, but the inside folds shine pink with her arousal. She's enjoying this too, and I plan on her enjoying it a lot more, after I punish her. I grab the silk scarfs from my dresser and tie her ankles to the bottom posts of the bed, making sure to keep her legs wide apart.

"Things can get intense," I tell her softly. "A safeword may be a good idea for what I have in mind."

"I've been through worse, Caine." Her voice is strong and unwavering.

Yes, you have, ma petite, and I will avenge that for you soon.

I open the top drawer of my dresser and look through my wide array of crops, floggers, and paddles. My fingers land on a supple, three tailed flogger, and I grip the handle tight as I pull it out of the drawer. I want her first experience to be a lesson but a pleasurable one. The tails are a soft lambskin, but when flicked onto sensitive skin, the feeling is a sharp sting followed by a tingling sensation.

Her head is up and watching my every move. When I hold out the flogger, her eyes widen, but I watch as her pussy grows wetter. I run the tails up her right leg, across her stomach, and then down her left leg, giving her a quick flick on the toes. She gasps at the slight pain and then moans as her head falls back. My cock pulses in my pants, and I have to grip it hard to hold back the overwhelming need to cum.

I run the tails back up her left leg and flick them out to snap against her lower belly, just above her pelvic bone. She whimpers, but her back arches into it, subconsciously seeking more. I let the tails run lightly over her folds, and she squirms on the bed, panting and anticipating the flick. I could punish her further for moving, for showing her pleasure and her eagerness, but I want her first time to be free of instruction. I want her to just feel.

I flick the tails out and watch as they catch on her folds, just below her clit. She hisses through the pain and tries to rub her thighs together to soothe the sting. Before she is fully recovered from the first contact, I flick the tails out two more times in quick succession and make sure the leather connects with her swollen clit.

"Caine!" she yells out as her body contorts on my bed.

My girl is flexible, so easing her into tied positions will be my favorite part. Her pants are loud, the sounds filling my large bedroom and filling my cock even more. I flick out the tails one more time against her clit and watch as the orgasm hits her, causing her pussy to leak its juices onto my bedsheets.

As her screams ring out around my room, I can't hold it in any longer and whip off my pants, throwing the flogger to the side. This staggering need be inside her can't be ignored any longer. My face is between her legs, and I run my tongue through her soaked folds in record time. She tastes of honey and my imminent downfall. There will be no coming back from Kailey-Himari.

She whimpers as my mouth and tongue devour her oversensitive clit. I kiss up her stomach, pushing her shirt up farther, baring her breasts. Kailey's body is lithe and long, toned and soft. Her skin is a beautiful olive color, and her perfect tits fit in my hand. She's always been my exact type, and no one else has ever come close.

I hover over her, and my cock jerks at the sight of her tear soaked cheeks from the intense orgasm she just had.

"Look at me, Kailey," I tell her and watch as her hazel eyes find mine.

I reach down and untie one ankle from the silk scarf, and pull it up and over my waist. I know she's primed and ready, so I thrust into her in one hard motion. I don't want anything between us, not even the thinnest piece of latex. Kailey is mine, and I will feel her wetness against my bare skin.

Her scream ignites something inside me, and I grin as her hands struggle against their bonds. I don't let up on her, this is for me now after all. I pound an unforgiving rhythm into her, and the sucking sounds her pussy makes has me almost teetering over the edge.

My fingers slip under her ass, and I skim the tips down her crack. She gasps and tries to match my thrusts with her own.

"Caine... I'm going to ... again."

Her pussy clamps down so hard onto my dick, I can hardly move. Her pulsating core sucks me in farther, and I breathe through the strong need to cum. I wait for her to relax slightly, her thighs falling apart, and then slam into her again. Her pussy clenches with aftershocks, and I thrust one final time, spilling my load deep inside her.

Her eyes are closed when I ease out of her and reach down to untie her other ankle. I massage both ankles, and her little moan of appreciation makes me smile. Next, I grab the key for the cuffs from my side table and release her bonds, then massage her shoulders and wrists. I know she's tired, but she needs to be washed, and then I'll let her sleep. Surprisingly I want her in my bed too.

After a soak in the bath, I let her curl up in my bed and wrap my body around hers, needing to feel her skin against mine and her even breaths entering and leaving her body. I bury my face into her hair and let myself drift off while her scent surrounds me.

"Caine." Her voice pulls me from my slumber, and I jerk upright in bed. "Sorry," she cringes and holds out my phone. "It's been ringing off the hook."

I unlock the screen and see ten missed calls from Cooper and one from Brody. Brody I ignore because him and I need to have a face to face before a chat on the phone. I dial Cooper and wait for the impatient fucker to answer. Kailey curls back against my side, her hand on my stomach and her leg wrapped around my thigh. I could get used to this.

"Fucker." Cooper picks up, and I grin.

"What the fuck is your problem? Why are you blowing up my phone?"

"Do you know what time it is?" he snickers, and I roll my eyes.

"Noon-ish?"

"Try four in the afternoon. You guys really knocked each other out, huh? I won't even hold it against you that you didn't wait for me."

"Four?!" I sit up again, and Kailey moans in protest. I haven't slept this long in ages, if ever.

"I'm bringing donuts," he chuckles.

"And coffee!" Kailey calls out.

"Tell mon sha I would bring her the moon if it was possible," Cooper coos, and I hang up on him.

Motherfucker better be bringing coffee, though.

TWENTY-NINE

Kailey is sitting on Caine's bed, completely at ease, and dressed in his oversized t-shirt. I watch as her pouty mouth blows air onto her hot coffee, and my dick decides now's the time to say what's up. Not you, Fucker.

Caine is perched on the edge of the bed, and I'm in the chair across from them both. I will admit, when I came in here this evening, I felt like I had been replaced. Seeing her mussed up hair and more than satisfied look on her face, I instantly felt like maybe my shot had passed. But when her hazel eyes found mine, the genuine smile that came across her face soothed some of those worries. Some. Now I'm hearing about Ballon being thrown into the mix, and I'm not sure how I'm feeling about it all.

"He's been there for me every time," Kailey whines as Caine rolls his eyes.

"Only because you never gave us a chance to be," he answers levelly.

"We can't dictate who you want to be with, sha." I try to hit a middle ground. "We just have experience with the Ballons."

"I know," she nods. "He has nothing to do with his family."

"You are never really free from a mobster family. They just let you be until they need you, and then you can't refuse," Caine explains.

"Getting back to the topic," I wave them both off. "What exactly did he save you from?"

I hate being the only one who doesn't know shit, and if I judge the way Kailey's squirming, then it's something huge.

"Do you remember the summer I stopped talking to you guys?" she asks, her voice small.

"Vividly," I retort. I do, it was painful and filled with rage.

"Something happened to me the night of Brody's party that summer." I watch as raw pain reflects in her eyes, and I can see as her memories battle to be set free. "I showed up to the pool house really drunk."

"Then you caught Brody in bed with Georgina and ran out," I add in, and she nods.

"Yeah, I ran out and found a few people I knew." Her hands shake as she puts the coffee cup down on a side table. "They led me into the forest … then proceeded to rape me and leave me there."

White hot, searing rage rushes through me, and I jump up to my feet. "What?"

"Sit down, Coop," Caine says, but his eyes tell me he understands.

"Who, KH?" I demand.

"Lance Kilmer and Justin Landry," she whispers as tears course down her cheeks.

I get it. I see why she didn't tell us. Brody would run her through the mud, laughing the whole time. Him and his brother are tight. I sit down and drop my head into my hands. I don't blame her for never trusting us. What we put her through for most of high school… I don't think I can forgive myself.

"Cooper?" She sounds scared.

I look up at her, and she gasps when she sees the tears run down my cheeks. I have no words, and I can't think of anything that would help anyways. Right now, the only thing I want to do is hunt down those fuckers.

"I'm sorry I didn't tell you," she whispers.

"Sha." I get up and sit next to her on the bed, taking her hand in mine. "I don't blame you. I would've done the same in your position. I can only promise you that nothing will happen to you ever again. Caine and I—fuck, even Ballon—won't let another motherfucker touch a single hair on your head."

Caine grunts his agreement, and Kailey leans forward to fling her arms around my neck. Her little frame is trembling, and I try my best to soothe her by rubbing circles onto her back.

"There's more," she says, and Caine's head snaps around to look at her.

"What do you mean more?" he grounds out.

"I just found out last night," she huffs and crosses her arms over her chest. "You can punish me later."

A grin crawls across Caine's face at the mention of punishment. Sadistic fuck.

"What else?" I ask her, breaking their heated stare off.

"Justin said something last night, and I need you guys to be completely honest with me." Caine and I both nod, and she continues, "He said he and Lance killed my mama." The last part comes out a hoarse whisper, wrenching my heart in two.

Caine looks just as confused as I do. "Are you sure?" he asks her.

"Did you know?" She looks from me to Caine.

"Of course not," I answer.

"No," Caine says at the same time.

"Do you think Brody knew?" she asks.

"Brody was tight with Mrs. Richard... I can't see him knowing that." I scrub my hand along my cheek. "Could they have been trying to upset you?"

"No," she shakes her head.

"Why the fuck would those two even show up to a Georgina party?" I ask. Nobody goes to her parties willingly because they are always over the top.

"Georgina called them," Caine answers. "She handed Kailey over to them, knowing what they did to her before."

"She witnessed it, or at the very least heard what was happening in those woods. She admitted as much," Kailey sniffs.

That vile, disgusting, evil bitch. She's always had it out for KH for as long as I can remember. When a girl is jealous like she was, there are clearly no limits to what she'll do. There's more to this puzzle than what KH knows, and I know I should be telling her everything, but my loyalty is strong for the four guys I count as my brothers. It doesn't mean I'll never tell her, just that everyone needs to be on board.

"I need to find out why they killed Mama. Was it because Papa wasn't paying back his money? Was it a hit to scare him into paying?" She's crying again, and I can't help but let the guilt of what I know weigh heavy in my heart.

"We'll figure it all out," Caine says quietly, and I know his black heart is feeling the same way as I am.

"I need to ask Brody," she nods. "He must know more than anyone, it's his family after all."

"He'd never tell you even if he did," Caine tells her honestly. "You ripped his heart out the day you turned your back on us, and he was never the same."

"I agree, sha." I reach out and twist a piece of her hair around my finger. "Brody was different after that."

"I should get home and try to get a hold of Papa. I need to ask him what he knows."

My heart skips a beat at her words, and I try to think of a way to talk her out of that. Talking to her father and bringing up all this speculation will cause hysteria, especially when he learns how much she knows. His loan from the Landrys is probably something he never intended for her to find out.

"I have to make a call." Caine holds up his phone and leaves the room.

"Cooper, can you take me home?"

"Yeah, get your stuff together, and meet me downstairs."

She nods, and I watch her get up and prod into Caine's large bathroom. Once she's closed the door, I leave the bedroom and search out Caine.

"Look, Ballon," I overhear him. "I don't want her talking to her father yet. I don't know how rational he'll be when he learns what his daughter knows. I don't want any harm to come to her."

I stand at the office door and watch as he berates Oliver Ballon, KH's newest boyfriend.

"All right, cool," he nods. "Text me when you find him." He hangs up and looks at me. "I have Ballon searching for Richard. He's already been by Kailey's house and the dealership, and the guy is nowhere to be found."

"Odd."

"Yeah," he agrees.

"Kailey asked me to take her home, so I'll chill there with her."

"All right, man, sounds good." He stands up. "Call me the second her father shows up."

I nod and wait for KH to come out of the room. When she emerges, her face is washed of tear tracks, and her hair is piled up on top of her head in an unruly bun. She's gorgeous.

"Let's go, Coop," she exhales. "I want my own bed."

"Don't make me spank you." Caine's voice filters out from the office. "You enjoyed my bed."

"For everything other than sleep." The secret smile on her face has me wishing I was here last night.

"I will be checking in with you later, ma petite," Caine calls out as we descend the stairs.

"Of course," KH mutters with a small smile.

We may be a rag tag group of varying degrees of fucked-up, but I know we'd do anything for Kailey-Himari.

Kailey-Himari

THIRTY

The exhaustion I'm feeling is bone deep. Every time I close my eyes, I hear Justin mocking my mama's death, or I feel his fingers ripping into my flesh. Oliver helped to tear down my fears of intimacy and replaced them with something loving and pure, then Caine began the process of ripping down all my walls and forcing me to truly trust him. This was the therapy I always needed. It's unconventional and hard to understand, but it works for me. There's one person I left out, and not purposely, but because his role in all of this is the biggest.

Cooper made all of this possible. He forced himself into my life, created chaos, and then stood back and let me put myself back together. He looks at me like I'm his whole world, and the fierce protectiveness in his eyes makes me feel invincible. I will never have to be alone again, he made sure of that.

"You need to stop squirming and try to get some sleep," Cooper says as he lies beside me in my bed.

"I'm worried about Papa. I can't get a hold of him, and I haven't seen him in a few days."

"Does he do this often? Disappear for days?" he asks me quietly.

"Lately, yes."

"Have you tried asking him what's going on?"

"Honestly? No. I just figured he was busy with the dealership, but then all these things started coming out," I shake my head. "His supposed money problems, taking a loan from the Landrys, and then Mama's death and its connection to that. I'm scared to know the truth, Coop."

"We'll be with you every step of the way, sha." This is what I'm talking about. Cooper is quick to stand by me, protect me, and show me his true feelings. He's been trying to convince me from the very beginning his intentions and feelings were true, but I am only just now seeing it.

I turn and curl my body around his. My arm wraps around his waist, and my leg envelops his thigh. I squeeze him to me, his warmth soaking into me, and his even breathing calms my beating heart. I look up and meet his dark brown eyes, eyes I've come to recognize as belonging to me... Cooper belongs to me.

I reach up and pull his face down to mine and kiss his lips. It's a sweet peck, but before he can pull away, my tongue runs along his plush bottom lip, and he opens with a groan. His mouth is warm, and his tongue runs along mine, sending shivers up my spine. Kissing Cooper feels like home. He was my first kiss—both as children and again as adults—and he'll be the first one I profess my feelings to.

"I love you, Coop. I think I always have, even when I hated you," I say against his mouth. "Since we were kids, you were always the first to play with me, the first to offer me a bike ride home, and the first to show our friendship might eventually be more. For all those things and more, I love you."

"Sha," his voice cracks. "I've loved you since before I even knew what that meant."

I push myself up and move to straddle his midsection. I know how this seems, three guys in less than twenty-four hours, but I don't care because it's only for me and them to understand. I want them all, I love them all, and I will have each of them. Fuck society and fuck what people see as normal because these three guys are my fucking normal.

His hands run down my back and rest lightly against the curve of my ass. He's not pushing for anything and leaving the ball in my court. That's Cooper, he'll never do anything he fears I don't want. I grind myself down onto him, and his hands tighten around my waist as I feel him harden between my legs. My hands snake up under his shirt, and I scrape my nails over his very toned stomach. I want to thank his coach for all the work he forces him to do to stay in shape. I can now fully understand Kimmy's obsession with Henry's new physique.

I pull his shirt up, and he leans up so I can lift it over his head, his cock pushing harder against my core. My pussy clenches in anticipation, completely insatiable, this bitch.

He has my shirt off next, and his mouth locks around a nipple while his hand toys with the other. I'm left with a pair of panties, and they do extraordinarily little to hide the state of arousal my pussy is in. I am soaked and just wanting to be filled with Cooper.

My fingers are tangled in his hair as I mercilessly rub myself against him, my arousal leaving a wet spot on his gray track pants.

"Take these off." I pull at the waistband of his pants.

I don't need to ask him twice. He lifts his hips with me still wrapped around them and pulls his pants and boxers off. His cock pops up between us, and I take it in my hand, giving it a firm stroke. He falls back again to the bed with a moan coming from between his lips. His stomach muscles flex as he leans back up on his elbows to watch me jerk him off.

It's not enough for me. I want him in my mouth, to taste him and run my tongue over the ridged velvet. I slide down over his body, and when he realizes what I'm about to do, a string of curses come from his lips. I chuckle and hold him steady in my hand as my tongue flicks out and tastes the tip. I moan as I take him fully inside my mouth and suck him softly. His hips lift up, and he forces himself inside a little more, his tip now hitting the back of my throat. I gag, and he groans around the constriction.

Suddenly, his hands are in my hair, and he's forcing me back up to face him. "I can't, sha." He's breathing hard. "I want to be inside you. Condom?"

"I'm on the pill." I pull my bottom lip between my teeth. "There are no condoms in this house... I never..."

He leans up and seals his lips to mine, and I relax back into his hold.

His hands move to my hips, and he drags my g-string to the side. Then he lines himself up and guides my hips to slowly impale me. I haven't experienced being on top yet, and the feeling is different. I feel fuller, it's deeper, and once I'm fully seated, my clit is pressing perfectly into his pelvic bone. The friction it makes against my clit combined with his cock deep inside me is amazing. I begin to slowly grind on him and watch his face as he watches where we are connected.

I can feel my juices pool around him, and the wet noises turn us both on further.

"I'm about to get rough here." His voice is deep with lust. "I've waited for this for so long."

I nod because forming words right now is impossible. He grabs my ass in his hands and arches his back. Then he's pumping up into me while forcing me down to meet his thrusts with his hands. Cooper is hitting all the right spots deep inside me, and this time when I feel the impending orgasm, it feels different. There's some pressure, and then I'm sailing over the edge as my body glides along an endless stream of pleasure.

"Fuck, yes," I hear him moan, and I look down between us.

What I see startles me, and I gasp. There's a puddle of fluid running over his stomach and down his hips to collect on my bed… Is that? Did I piss myself? Cooper is undeterred, though as he keeps plowing into me until finally, he's groaning and mumbling through his release.

I don't move and continue to watch as the moisture runs through the ridges of his abs. Heat flares in my face, and the embarrassment of what happened has me trying to get off him.

"What's wrong?" he asks with a worried expression.

"I … did that…" I point to what can only be urine.

"Well, I had a part in it." His grin is adorable, but I didn't think he'd be into this. "Why do you look grossed out? Girls squirt sometimes, and guys really like it."

"Squirt?"

"Babe, seriously?" he chuckles. "Did you think you pissed on me?"

"Yes." I crinkle my brow.

He starts to laugh out loud while still inside me. I can't help it and begin to chuckle along with him. There's still a lot I have to learn when it comes to sex.

"Come here," he growls as his hands lift me off his cock and drags my pussy up to his face. "I want to taste all that cum."

I squeal and grip the headboard to keep from falling over. Then his mouth is sealed to my pussy, lapping up both his cum and mine. The embarrassment quickly turns to pleasure as I greedily grind myself into his face. I'm so lost in the sensations, I don't even stop to think if he can breathe. In no time, I'm coming again all over his mouth and chin, but Cooper just licks it all clean.

I fall over and onto the bed beside him, feeling completely boneless. These last few days have been filled with intense sex, and all three of them know exactly what they're doing in that department. I'm fucking blessed.

THIRTY-ONE

I look in on Kailey sleeping soundly in her bed. She's had it rough these past few days, and I know she needs the refueling only sleep can bring. I quietly close her door and head back down to the kitchen where Cooper and Ballon are talking.

Ballon being the newest addition to this love square is something I'm trying to get used to. Right now, I do see the benefit of having him around. He has resources to track down Kailey's father and to find out where Lance and Justin are. The first one needs to be questioned, but the latter have to die.

"Richard's credit card was used at a gas station in the bayou two days ago," Ballon says as he taps his finger over his laptop. There's not one bit of legal activity going on in this house right now.

"What the fuck is in the bayou?" Cooper scratches his chin.

"Besides great food and parties?" I grin wide. I love living on the bayou border.

"Maybe a dealer?" Ballon throws out. "I paid him a visit last week and caught the guy doing blow in his office."

"Same shit that put him in money problems the first time." Cooper shakes his head.

"You think the Landrys sent their own son out to kill Mrs. Richard?" Ballon questions.

"It's not far-fetched," I reply. "But it feels like we're missing a large chunk of this."

"When do we talk to Brody?" Cooper asks.

"When we have enough proof that he can't deny," I tell him.

"If he comes after Kail for this, I will kill Brody Landry," Ballon vows.

I respect him that much more for saying it to Brody's closest friends. "I'll help you," I say with a nod because I will. From this moment on, no one is more important than Kailey. "I think it's time we hit up Brody and tell him how this shit is going to go down," I tell Cooper.

"We're telling him what happened to KH?" Cooper asks.

"Nah, that's going to have to be Kailey when she's ready, but we do need to find out why Justin and Lance ran down her mother," I reply.

"I'll stay here with her and continue to try and find her father. Traffic cams must have picked him up somewhere," Oliver states, his nose still in his laptop.

The drive to Brody's house is less than five minutes, this is why he and Kailey were best friends. I pull up to his gate, and when the guard sees who it is, he just waves us through. I see Brody's Charger, Zeke's motorcycle, and Justin's 'Vette sitting in the driveway.

"Don't act irrational, we have to be smart," Cooper tries to reason with me when he notices Justin's car. "Let's talk to Brody first and go from there."

We get out of my truck, and the front door opens. Brody is standing there with his arms crossed over his chest, watching us as we get closer.

"Where have you guys been?" he snarls. "You left the party early last night."

"Wasn't feeling it," I shrug and brush by him, entering the house.

"What? You guys spend the night double teaming the slut?"

"Watch the shit that's coming out of your mouth, Bro." I turn back around and get in his face.

He throws his hands up, walks around me, and into the den. "Touchy," he sing-songs.

"Stop giving him ammunition," Cooper growls at me and walks by to follow Brody.

I take a few seconds to pull myself under control. I don't need Brody seeing Kailey as a way to control us because she's our weakness.

When I join them, I find Zeke lounging on the couch watching TV, Brody is pouring himself bourbon in a glass, and Cooper is leaning against the wall. My eyes zoom in on the blood stain soaked into Brody's white carpet, and I walk up to it to get a closer look.

"Someone piss you off?" I ask Brody.

"Lance and Justin had a run-in with a rival pusher. Lance got shot in the shoulder," he says with a shrug.

"Is he all right?" I don't give a shit if the motherfucker is dead.

"Yeah, he's upstairs now. The bullet went straight through. He just needed some stitches."

"That's going to be a bitch to get out," Cooper says, nodding at the carpet.

"What have you guys found out about Kails?" Brody interjects. "You seem nice and cozy now, so you must have something."

"Her father has been missing for a few days now, and Kailey seems to think her mother was a targeted hit," I tell him with my brow raised.

"She was," Justin says as he strolls into the room. "This isn't news to us."

This piece of shit has my blood instantly boiling. Just seeing him and knowing what he was doing to Kailey less than twenty-four hours ago makes me see red. Cooper's hand lands on my shoulder, and he squeezes hard.

"We know, man." Cooper is a better actor than I am. "But it's news to her. I'm still trying to work out how she figured it out."

"Maybe your girlfriends have big mouths." Justin grins as he sips his own glass of bourbon.

"Casey and Connie don't know shit," I growl. "We never cared enough to fill them in."

"Faith is blissfully ignorant of anything we do," Zeke pipes up.

"Georgina's mouth is as big as her pussy," Justin says with a dark chuckle. "I bet she'd love handing Kailey information that could ruin her life."

"I spoke to her," Brody says coolly from the bar. "The two brain cells she owns don't know shit."

This is how I know Brody only sees Georgina as a girl to fuck when he needs a release. He's downright disrespectful to her, and she knows it. Her hatred for Kailey stems from him and what we all can see. He still has feelings for Kailey, we see it whenever his eyes land on her and how they watch her closely.

"Looks like you two have to make your new girlfriend talk," Justin sneers. "I find a good spanking does the trick."

Breathe, don't kill everyone in this room. I have to keep repeating this mantra in my head to stop myself from ripping Justin's head off.

"We need a fucking chill night. How about we throw a small, intimate gathering, get drunk or stoned, and watch some females dance," Zeke throws out, and Cooper looks at me.

We came here with a similar idea to lure Justin and Lance away. It's even better, though someone else came up with the idea.

"That actually sounds good, brah," Cooper nods. "It's been awhile since we had a small party."

"My house tonight," Zeke throws out. "I already have the alcohol stocked."

"Sounds good," Justin says as he rubs his hands together.

"Bring Lance," Zeke nods at him. "I'm sure my mother has enough painkillers to knock out a horse."

"I think that's just what the doctor ordered, getting lit and fucking bitches." Justin leaves the room.

"You guys coming?" Zeke asks me and Coop.

"Yeah," I nod.

"Bring Kails," Brody cuts in. "She needs to see what this life is about, if you two plan on keeping her."

"She's been feeling a bit under the weather…" Cooper starts.

"Bring her," Brody cuts in with a demand.

Cooper nods and grabs my arm. "We'll go let her know."

"Ten tonight," Zeke calls out as we leave the room.

"I'm going to kill Brody right after I've finished off Justin," I growl as soon as we are back outside.

"Try to keep it together a little longer." Cooper claps his hands. "This worked out better than we ever imagined."

"Almost too good, huh?"

"Do you think they're on to us? Would Zeke really do that?" Cooper asks as we get in my truck.

"They've always been tight," I answer as I pull past the gate. "And Zeke is a fucking tech genius. I don't know, it was just too convenient."

We don't have much of a choice at this point. Whatever Brody and Zeke have planned or not planned, this will be our one chance to take out Justin and Lance.

Kailey-Himari

THIRTY-TWO

"I'm not going," I shake my head. "I would be insane to agree to this."

"Sha, we need you there," Cooper pleads.

"Go upstairs, and get ready," Caine demands. "You'll be with us, nothing will happen."

"I was with you both on that boat!"

"And we didn't know shit about what was happening to you!" Caine yells back, his voice booming around the room. Then he calmly continues, "Now we do. You won't be taking a piss without one of us wiping your ass."

"Classy," Oliver snorts from the kitchen.

I know there's no point in arguing. Caine will literally carry me up the stairs and force dress me. I'll get turned on, and we'll end up fucking like bunnies.

"I found a traffic cam that picked up your father's vehicle. It is indeed in the bayou." Oliver comes into the room. "I'll go check that out while you guys deal with those fuckers."

"Sounds good," Cooper nods.

I go to Oliver and wrap my arms around his waist, burying my face into his chest. "Thank you."

"Stay with the guys," he kisses the top of my head. "And be

safe."

"I will, I promise." I look up into his face, and he leans down to kiss me. It's not a sweet kiss, it's possessive and hard. Like he's letting Cooper and Caine know he has just as much stake in this as they do.

When he pulls away from me, I'm slightly wobbly on my feet, and my mouth feels bruised from the force of his kiss.

"Go get ready," he grins at me.

I turn with a nod and make my way up the stairs.

"Do I get one of those too?" Cooper teases Oliver, and Caine chuckles.

"Only after you suck my dick," Oliver retorts.

"Did you think that was a deterrent?" Cooper continues.

I chuckle as I get to my bedroom. I'm happy the three of them are slowly coming around because I can't lose any of them.

Once I'm dressed in a black pair of skinny jeans with rips in the knees and an oversized black hoodie, I head back downstairs. There's no way in hell I'm dressing provocative for a party with my rapists. I even secured my Gris-Gris back on my wrist. I learned my lesson, and it's never coming off again.

Caine and Cooper are waiting for me, and Oliver is gone. I hope he's safe, and I hope he finds my papa. His phone has been going straight to voice mail now, and I can't help but think something happened to him.

"Let's get this over with," I huff.

They both nod with solemn looks on their faces.

"What exactly will happen tonight?" I ask them.

"What needs to happen. Like I said, you are not to leave our sides," Caine grunts as we follow him out of the house.

Zeke's house is just as opulent as the other houses. Perfectly manicured lawns, water fountains, and security at every corner. The grass is like the deepest emerald from in-ground irrigation systems, so plush you just want to roll in it.

"Why are you staring at the grass?" Cooper chuckles as he takes my hand.

"Because this isn't grass, it's pillows of green." I shake my head. "Does this grass ever turn slightly yellow? The Louisiana heat makes mine look like straw."

Caine chuckles from behind me and places a hand on my back. We get up to the front door with three security guys standing guard. They wave us through, and then we enter into what feels like a bass induced earthquake. The music is so loud, my eardrums feel like they're about to bleed, and wherever I look I see half naked females dancing on any flat surface.

The booze and drugs look to be in abundance, littering every table. I follow behind Cooper with Caine bringing up our rear into a room where the music is muffled, and the lighting is dimmed. My fear kicks in from years of mistrust, and I fight the urge to run from everyone. I feel sweat gather between our joined hands, but Cooper just squeezes me tighter.

"Look who made it," Brody says from behind the bar. "Kails, you want a bourbon? I remember how much you like it."

This fucking asshole. "Sure," I shrug. "Only if Caine or Cooper pour it."

"You think I'm going to drug you?" he smirks.

"I don't know you well enough to accept drinks, that's all," I answer smugly.

I watch as his face darkens with anger and feel a bit of regret at my callous remark. Brody and I were the closest for many years, but nothing I said was incorrect... I don't know him anymore.

"Caine strides forward and grabs a fresh bottle of bourbon off the shelf, pouring me some in a glass. Brody watches us the whole time, his demeanor and attitude growing darker by the minute.

"Where's everyone?" Cooper asks.

"Faith and Georgina are doing a bathroom break, you know how chicks are," Zeke says and then looks at me. "Most chicks," he corrects himself with a smile.

I return the gesture and sit on a couch between Cooper and Caine. I still haven't seen Justin or Lance, but according to the guys, Lance wasn't as injured as I'd hoped from Oliver's bullet. The bourbon burns as it runs down my throat and into my belly. This will be my one and only glass, I will not let my guard down while I am surrounded by snakes.

The door swings inward, and in walks Georgina with Faith. They are both giggling and whispering to each other until their eyes land on me. Georgina's widen slightly like maybe she wasn't expecting me, and I would be worried if I were her too, now that I know she set everything that happened to me into motion.

She recovers quickly and slowly walks across the room to wrap her long, tanned arms around Brody's neck. She's so obviously putting on a show, but Brody looks downright uninterested. After she unsuccessfully tries to get his attention, Georgina sits her ass down on a bar stool and begins to text away on her phone.

"Fifty dollars says she's texting Justin," Caine says.

"You think they're that close?" I whisper back to him.

"I think they communicate about similar interests."

"You mean me." I look him in the eye.

"You amongst other things."

Suddenly, there's a cheer that erupts outside the doors, and I can faintly hear people chanting Lance's name. My throat feels tight, and I begin to bounce my knee rapidly. Caine's hand comes out and grips it, stopping the movements just before the door opens, and in walks Justin with a very drugged up looking Lance.

"I hope we didn't miss anything exciting," Justin says, throwing his arms wide.

"Looks boring as fuck in here," Lance slurs and stumbles on his feet. His eyes find mine, and his smile grows wide. "I take that back... maybe tonight will be interesting."

A growl erupts from Caine's chest. I place my hand on his

shoulder and rub small circles to soothe him. I don't want him to cause a scene and whatever they have planned gets fucked-up.

"Sounds about right," Cooper drawls. "Everyone who's anyone is already here."

"Funny." Lance cuts him the side eye as he grabs himself a whole bottle of bourbon. "I'm guessing you all heard my boy Lance here was shot at last night."

"We heard," Cooper replies. Caine doesn't make a sound, but his jaw is clenched tight, and he hasn't stopped scrutinizing Lance.

"These drug pushers are becoming brave little pricks," Justin smirks. "Caine, I may be needing your services to make a few disappear."

I look at Caine with confusion, what services?

"No problem," he immediately replies. "It is my specialty after all, making people disappear."

I have so many fucking questions at this point, and it's frustrating as hell that I can't ask them here. I take another sip of my bourbon and snuggle tighter into Cooper's side. He may look calm and collected on the outside, but I can feel the tension making his body rigid.

"I think we should have another game of spin the bottle." Lance stumbles again, and Brody rights him.

"I think if anyone else's lips touch my girlfriend's, I get to carve out their tongues and shove it up their asses," Caine growls at him. I'm so fucking turned on by his aggressiveness right now.

"Except for all her other boyfriends, right?" Justin taunts him.

"Other boyfriends?" Brody questions, his eyebrows crashing together.

"Who gives a fuck how many guys she's spreading her legs for," Georgina whines. "We'll be here all night discussing it."

Brody grins, and Justin chuckles. I can feel heat flare across my cheeks, but I refuse to jump at the bait. They can judge all they want to. I don't have to explain a damn thing, and thankfully, both my guys agree because they just keep their mouths shut.

"Or we can discuss how many your mother has, and make this party a weeklong affair," I say sweetly while sipping my drink. Sorry, I jumped at the bait. Besides, this bitch deserves my wrath.

Cooper chokes on his sip, and Caine chuckles darkly beside me. Georgina's eyes widen, and now it's her turn for her cheeks to flame. That's right sweetie, your mother is an actual slut.

"Nothing to say to that, Georgie?" Brody turns and faces her.

"Yes, we know Georgina's mother is a whore," Justin waves it off. "It's a woman's nature to just want dick, multiple sometimes. Right, sugar?" He's looking right at me.

Lance bites down on his bottom lip and moans like the fucking idiot he is.

It takes one second, just one for the whole room to explode. Caine's glass flies across the room aimed at Justin's face, Cooper is on his feet with Lance's throat in his hand, and Zeke has Georgina by her hair, dragging her back from the doorway she tried to run out of. Caine is up and running at Justin while Brody stands transfixed by the commotion.

"What the fuck is going on?!" Brody screams, breaking out of his stupor.

"Your brother here and his pet were the ones who ran down Mrs. Richard. Did you know anything about that?" Caine asks while his hand is holding the front of Justin's shirt.

"Mrs. Richard?" Brody's face falls for a second, but then his mask of indifference slides back into place. "That's fucked. We know what happened to her."

What the fuck is he talking about? Of course, we all know what happened to her. She was run down in the supermarket parking lot by two little wannabe mobsters for the Landry's reputation. But does Brody know that? Is he playing stupid right now?

"We have a few questions," Cooper growls into Lance's face.

"Fuck the questions. I can find the answers without this piece of shit," Caine snarls, and I watch as he sinks a knife deep into Justin's chest.

Justin's eyes widen as Caine lets him go, and he stumbles forward. He looks shocked, like he never expected his brother's best friends to turn on him. I wasn't expecting this either, but I'm rooted to my seat, literally shaking with shock. Georgina is screaming as Brody rushes to his brother's side.

"Fuck yes!" Cooper yells, and I watch as he slips around behind Lance and breaks his neck with his bare hands.

Lance falls to the floor with a sickening thud, and I can't say I'm sad to see him dead. Georgina is still screaming until Zeke backhands her across the face. That I wasn't expecting, but it shuts her up.

"Justin!" Brody's screaming his brother's name while holding the wound over his chest. But Justin is still, and it looks like he's either dead or awfully close.

I feel for Brody, losing his brother, but I can't say I'm sad to see my rapists finally getting their just desserts. My mama's murderers were dealt karma's cards. It would only be more perfect if Brody understood, but I know that will never happen, and the events in this room tonight may have very well caused a war between The Four.

I stand up from the couch and begin to walk slowly towards Caine, but the movement catches Brody's attention, and he stands abruptly.

"You." His voice is rough and filled with hatred.

"Brody…" I put my hands up. I want him to see I'm not a threat.

His hands and forearms are covered in his brother's blood, and drops of it are dripping from his fingertips. The look on his face can only be described as deranged. His pale blue eyes are wide, and his pupils the size of pinpricks. His hands tighten into fists, and his teeth are bared.

"You," he repeats.

The security chooses this moment to bust into the room with guns up, screaming for everyone to get on their knees, but no one moves. They threaten to shoot, but I hear nothing except the pounding of my heart, and I see nothing but the emptiness in Brody's eyes.

Gunshots ring out as Caine flies forward to grab me, but Brody is quicker, and he has me by my throat and shoves me into an adjoining room. I'm slammed against the wall as his bourbon-soaked breath washes over my face.

I reach my hands up to wrap around the wrist holding me against the wall as he tightens his grip and leans in close.

"This is Zeke's father's office. It has a reinforced steel door. Nothing can penetrate it; no sound can escape it." He's basically saying I'm trapped in here and at his mercy.

"I'm not afraid of you Brody," I gasp. "I never have been."

"My brother is dead because of you!" His voice echoes around the room.

"He killed Mama," I choke out.

"No, he didn't! Your father killed your mother." So he does know Mama's death was a warning to my papa.

I let the tears gathering in my eyes run down my cheeks. Mama loved Brody like he was her own, and he betrayed her.

"He raped me," I say, my voice hoarse from his hand.

"Who did?" His body stills.

"Your brother," I sob, my throat working against his hand. "And Lance. Both of them raped me that night."

Recognition dawns on his face. He knows what night I'm talking about.

"Stop fucking lying," he sneers.

"I'm not, it's why Caine and Cooper did what they did. They left me in the forest behind your house, I barely made it home."

"No." His hand finally leaves my throat to grip into his hair.

"Yes," I nod. "I hated you after that. Every time I looked at you, I saw your brother."

His eyes search mine for any falsities. He knows me, all my tells when I'm lying, and what he sees in the depths of my eyes makes his face fall.

"Brody, I…"

His hand grabs my throat again, and my head is slammed against the wall. This time, his grip is more than a warning, squeezing enough to completely block my air supply. Then he leans in, and his mouth is less than an inch from mine.

"I'm going to kill you," he threatens, and then his lips crash against mine.

I feel the blood from his hands all over my face and throat. His body presses into mine, and I feel him harden against me. Brody is an enigma and impossible to figure out. But he's forgotten I already figured him out a long time ago.

I'm kissing him back as he wrenches his mouth from mine. He gives me one final look then releases me. I bend over, my hands on my knees, and try to catch my breath. I hear a door shut and look up to see I'm alone in here.

I always wondered what our first kiss would be like. I should've known it would be bloody and filled with anger.

I open the door to the office, and Cooper rushes in with a gun raised.

"He's gone," I tell him.

Caine is close behind and grabs my face with both hands. "Is any of this blood yours?"

"No," I shake my head.

"I'll kill him," Cooper roars.

"He's not our enemy," I tell him. "He's hurting."

"Let's get you home, ma petite," Caine whispers and kisses the top of my head.

"I love you," I tell him, and his body stills. "I love you, Caine."

"I love you too." His voice is low.

I know he does. I know all three of my guys love me because like Caine said, actions speak louder than words.

EPILOGUE

The room is dark and smells of human excretion. The concrete floors and walls have absorbed so much bodily fluids over the years, the smell will never fully go away.

"Where is she?"

"Chained to the chair," Zeke answers, nodding to a far corner.

This was the only part of the night I planned. I needed to have a one-on-one conversation with this girl to see how much she knew, but I never knew my brother's life would end as well.

I walk farther into the darkness and hear her muffled cries. The room stinks of piss, and I know she's scared. She's never been treated this poorly and never expected to be put in this situation at my demand.

"You're going to tell me everything," I say into the pitch black. "Or I will leave you here to rot."

Finally, my eyes adjust, and I see Georgina bound and gagged to a chair. This is the cost of betraying The Four.

This is the cost of betraying me.

For all book updates and social platforms, check out my website

ABOUT THE AUTHOR

C.A. Rene lives in Toronto, Canada with her family, where most of the year varies from chilly to frigid. Most days you'll find her wrapped in her many blankets in bed while reading or writing her next dark, twisted story.

Her stories boast of inclusivity and refusal to be conformed in any small box. Writing across genres is a hobby and drinking wine is a must… Or coffee … with a splash of Baileys.

Ingram Content Group UK Ltd.
Milton Keynes UK
UKHW012051190423
420461UK00003B/67